Goldberg, Gerald Jay
    The lynching of Orin Newfield [by] Gerald
J. Goldberg.   New York, Dial Press, 1970.
    247 p.

    I. Title.

the
lynching
of
Orin
Newfield

by Gerald Jay Goldberg

THE NATIONAL STANDARD

THE LYNCHING OF ORIN NEWFIELD

Gerald J. Goldberg

the
lynching
of
Orin
Newfield

The Dial Press 🦁 New York, 1970

For Henny, Frances, and Carl

the
lynching
of
Orin
Newfield

1

O my God! Bat blind and turning everything upside
down as usual with the truth staring her in the snoot.
Dewey's got a *mustache*. Short and each little hair
trimmed neat as a pin. And those manicured fingernails
like something in a museum. Gorgeous. Besides he never
gets rumpled or sweats even in the hottest weather. Now
who the hell is going to trust someone who never sweats?
It's not natural. Do you see what I'm driving at? Stands
to reason he didn't have any more chance of getting
elected than a bar of soap. Mind you, not that I think he
would have done much worse than the clown we've got.
One a dunce and the other a beauty parlor. Take your
pick, ladies.

"And don't tell me he's got a couple of years to shave
it off before the next election. Won't make a damn bit of
difference regardless. The way I see it that man's a loser
clean or hairy."

"But don't you think he's clever, Orin?"

"Ha!" Peeling the shell off my sixth egg and gulping it
down in a swallow. The yolk just like the others, hard
as a pit, causing a little congestion inside my overalls.

Washing it away with a quart of the best raw milk in the state of Vermont.

"I don't know . . ." Alma fingering the handle of her cup.

"Well cooked, missus," I said, diplomatically changing the subject. "I think you got most of the germs. But in case you forgot I take mine three minutes, no more no less. Those tasted nearer three years."

"He looks clever to me, Orin," she went right on. Making believe she didn't hear me. "But I don't know. Maybe you're right."

"If I was you I wouldn't strain my head about it. They're all the same. Bad news. All those politicians. A crooked bunch."

Picking up her napkin, Alma dabbed glumly at the corners of her mouth. Holding her tongue. Keeping her illusions to herself.

"You heard me. A crooked bunch. All cut from the same turd. Nobody in his right mind would trust a one of them."

She didn't like it but she never batted an eye. Awfully agreeable I'd say. Either she was apologizing for the eggs or she was after something. As if I didn't know it was both. I finished my lunch in silence. Opposite this thin, jittery, pussy-willow gray ruin that once was my Alma. Behind her on the mantelpiece of the dining room fireplace the memory of the young girl she was. By Jesus, what a difference! A lively, smiling, round-cheeked beauty cuddling playfully against my side. Slightly out of focus. Her brother learned to take pictures through the mail. The top of her head barely reaching my shoulder as she glanced up to my face. With that old trick of hers of raising her eyebrows in amusement and now only wrinkles left to show for it. And me towering over her, chest out

2

in bib overalls, wide shoulders, hand on hip, no nonsense.
The eyes squinting straight at the camera, shrewd and
sullen. Still the same old Newfield I'm happy to report.
Caught candidly on his own land shortly after purchase.

That's right, his *own* land. Which to be frank with
you came the only way anything worthwhile ever does.
Hard. Scrimping and saving to buy the run-down property
two miles southwest of Farnum with what I could lay
aside from sales commissions. Pushing cultivators and
tractors for the John Deere people under the nagging
lash of smartass Dimick. Now happily deceased. And in
less than five thrifty years of being my own man, I turned
the place into a well-run moneymaker. Not bad for a
poor local boy, eh? Doubly so when you stop to consider
that practically everyone else my age had run off to the
cities. Looking for the quick buck. Afraid to stick it out
in a town grimly marking time like a patient with some
incurable disease.

Made no difference to me. I love a challenge. Take this
house. It was obvious the place was too big for us when
Alma and I first moved in. Ten rooms with an attic and
basement. Was I worried? Cool as an ice bag. In time I
expected we'd grow into it, fill the empty spaces with
kids. But the kids never came. Not for any want of trying
on my part I assure you. Even after the second year I
kept telling myself, keep pumping, Newfield. And finally
I did it. Overall it happened three times just the same
way. Each time her arms and legs swelling up instead of
her belly. And then about her sixth month the fluttery
kicks that had seemed so full of promise would die away.

"She's a negative!" Dr. Whiting told me after the loss
of the first. "One in eight. Very interesting," he admitted,
"but nothing to write home about, you understand."

Whiting called it the RH factor. Something dangerous

in her blood that was killing our babies. I tried to get the better of it but it was no go. So I took his advice after the third miscarriage and gave up. Too much of a risk for Alma. It was bitter. The worst I ever experienced. And then on top of that discovering that she was paying secret visits to some old quack in Stratford. A miracle-worker smelling of garlic with a cataract in her eye. I soon put a stop to that. But I forgave her everything. And took it out on the property.

It's like this. Whether houses change men or men change houses depends on which has the stronger personality. Ours had been a tough old mustard-colored sonofabitch. The shutters were useless, so right off I stripped them from the windows. Painting the clapboards all over a smooth milk-of-magnesia white. Then there was the little problem of the main path leading from the road to the house. Who needed it? Inside of three months it was gone, disappeared under crabgrass and milkweeds. The front door sealed off with heavy strips of felt to keep out the wind. I never came in that way. Easier to walk up the driveway and go in through the dining room and I preferred it. The way any man might who wanted to get at the heart of things right away and didn't believe in prologues or putting on airs. And when at last I saw I couldn't handle the upstairs rooms, I closed up the entire top floor. Cut off the heat and saved money.

Oh that's Newfield all right, the spitting image. Captured forever in reliable black and white on the mantelpiece. With Alma at the beginning of it all standing before the old barn. You'd think that's out of focus too if you didn't know better. The original so warped it appeared to ripple as if under water. Deranged tin horse weathercock pointing straight down. Demolished the

4

whole shaky mess as soon as I could afford to build the large new one. My sixty-three giant Holsteins presently cavorting inside. Beautiful, healthy animals. Udders the size of washtubs! Plus all-new stainless-steel machinery. Everything changed for the better but Alma. How do you explain it?

Just one last sip of comforting milk. Wiping my mouth off, I belched fiercely and gave in.

"All right, goddamnit." Rising from the table and pulling on my muddy rubber boots. "I'll get you the rat trap."

Alma, who had known better than to say anything more about it throughout lunch, drank her black coffee and said nothing.

I banged my fist down on the shelf of her breakfront, knocking the dust off her company china. "Believe me, I've got better ways to fuck off than to go into town."

"I didn't mean this minute, Orin. It can wait till tomorrow. There's no need to go on Christmas."

"What the hell's that got to do with it!" Taking my plaid cap from the shelf, I slapped it on my head so hard that the earflaps fell down.

Alma looked away, continuing to drink her coffee in silence.

"Just quit carrying on," I said, and jammed the flaps back up under the brim. Throwing open the dining room door, I unlatched the glass storm door that led out into the side porch facing our driveway.

"Nobody's forcing you, Orin," she called softly after me.

I stopped, glanced back over my shoulder, and scrutinized her pale, lined face. Alma always did have a beautiful speaking voice. "Coffee stirs you up," I warned her. "You drink too much." And pushing open the storm door, I let it slam behind me, quivering all paper products and shaking her cup in its saucer.

The double garage joined to the big old house was filled on one side with Alma's rusty 1939 Plymouth. A no-springs, baby-blue relic, its fenders filigreed by salt. At speeds above eighteen miles per it leans around corners like a racing yawl. But Alma doesn't care much for driving anyway. The other side of the garage crammed to the roof with two-foot logs cut for winter. The over-flow, neatly stacked on the dining room porch, leaving only a narrow aisle to get in and out of the house. As I left I nearly tripped over Ben. Alma's dog, stretched out between the logs soaking up sunshine in his tight brown Airedale curls. Without hardly stopping I brought my good leg back and kicked him in the ribs, a wind-busting blow that sent him flying.

"Get the fuck out," I said kindly, as I like the animal. Ben scrambled slapdash, ducked beneath the porch, cowered in the mud.

A fine day. Unusually warm for so far along in the year. Christmas, but as far as I'm concerned it was just another good twenty-four-hour stretch, something to work on, to be done. Which would have to wait now until I got back from town. Across the way, sunbeams twinkling on the barn roof. The home of the stars. And adjacent to it the tenant house I put up for the handymen. Of which I've had my share and then some over the years. Coming and going like sightseers who didn't care for the view. Expecting to be paid for the crimes they didn't com-mit. Present incumbent included. Carter's the name. Finishing up his second year with me, an endurance record based on inertia and alcohol. It's drinking that's cost Roy Carter every job he ever had, and at sixty-four he's locally a well-known offender. Stranded by reputation, a prospective drug on the skimpy Farnum labor market. For my needs he's better than nothing I suppose, so I've kept him on. A frail whiner but occasionally of some small use. Working cheap. We get along. Just.

Four of his kids were playing out front of the house. Oh, of course he's got lots more too. Older and living with his first wife somewhere around East Corinth. A regular Johnny Appleseed this Carter. These were only the youngest. Bouncing up and down on a giant black inner tube stippled with orange patches. Mud-covered, shrieking, their flashy blond hair falling down their long, pinched, Carter faces, having the time of their lives.

Like rabbits. I climbed into the new Ford pickup parked alongside the two-rail fence. Backing it around hard, I rolled out the driveway and onto the Old Turnpike. It's all that drunken bastard is really good for. I rammed the shift into high gear and sped away, tires kicking up the mud.

Ben was barking. In the rear-view mirror I caught sight of him running wildly after me, his stubby tail shaking with excitement. Slowed down and kept a casual eye on him. A quarter of a mile and he flags, gives up the chase, and stands with his mouth gaping in the middle of the road watching the truck go off without him. Slobbering in his Chinese beard.

Any cluck can plug up a hole was what I decided. Leaning back to enjoy the smell of newness in the cab's rubber mats and upholstery.

But the Ford did more than smell good. I pressed hard on the juice and it leaped forward, sped up to the one-lane Mink Brook bridge that marked the eastern boundary of the Newfield acres, splashed across it through puddles of melting snow, and sailed on smoothly over the cordu-

7

roy road as if it was polished marble. The brook now on the left-hand side of the turnpike. Frozen only around the edges and higher than usual because of the heavy fall rains. Water whipping along beside me, Reynolds Wrap in the sunlight. On the right a stand of silver maples bare-boughed and twiggy against a seamless blue sky. "Bucolic Vermont" by the Valley National Bank and Trust Co. Their calendars always geography, never flesh, almost as if they're afraid that a solid thigh or a good nipple might undermine savings. Women never interfered with *my* bank account, and I've been looking for fifty-seven years.

Ahead was the Spooner place, a dented yellow school bus propped up on cinder blocks. Cylinder of propane hooked into its side like a kidney drain. Never make the calendar. Out in front sat old man Spooner himself in his rocking chair. The fattest man in the world. Bulging overalls, battered gray felt hat, black cane, white beard, and melon belly falling between his legs. A look-alike for the African chief we have in Alma's one volume of the *Encyclopedia Americana*. Only white. How she came by it is another story that I'll get around to later. As I drove by, he flashed such a big, warm smile and waved his cane so enthusiastically that it was as if he had been waiting there all day just to see me pass. I gave him a stiff nod right between the eyes. No sense in being unfair to the old man, though I didn't intend to put out too much. Not after last summer when his seventeen-year-old Elrod, who had been doing chores for me, walked off with my ball peen hammer, spare jack, a couple of ratchet wrenches, and God knows what else.

"Don't ever let me catch your thieving ass on my property again," I advised Elrod, while collecting what he had hidden under his mattress. Breaking the boy's

8

arm was an accident. Didn't intend to do that, but despite what he said don't believe to this day that I've got everything back.

I suppose Elrod's a tinkerer like his older brother Wayne. Nothing Wayne likes better than tinkering with a good engine, and after a few beers it doesn't make a shit of a difference whose engine it is. He's been in and out of jail all his life. Alma begged me to offer the boy a job to help keep him from screwing up like his brother. As far as I'm concerned it was an object lesson to her. Most people aren't worth a damn.

Hitting the brakes at the foot of Balch Hill I stopped the truck. A little skid, but quick and sure. Firestone tubeless. About a hundred yards up, a herd of deer was grazing on the hill, nibbling away at the black margin of the wood. There was only one buck among them, a big guy who seemed to be on guard duty. He stood apart, head high and the sun hopping around his huge antlers. It was hard without glasses to tell exactly how many points he was carrying but believe me he was loaded. Rolling down the window and leaning out to get a better look, I took him in. All of him. What a specimen! Rich cordovan brown and fixed to the earth like a statue. This one was a king. The rest of the herd munching around as if they didn't have a worry in the world. Why should they? He knew his business and, unlike human beings, wasn't about to fuck up by being less than himself, by picking fights and grudging favors. I began to feel mean and low. So down on myself about my behavior to Alma that it was some time before I paid any attention to the gas I was idling away dreaming out there in the middle of the empty road. Releasing the emergency brake, I swore that this time I really would do better. Then I heard it. Loud enough to be a cannon, and the big buck sags to the ground. Collapsed like a circus tent. The hunting season had been over for almost a month and here was some jerk on the loose turning nobility into dead meat. I blew up.

Flipped off the ignition, got out of the truck, jumped down the shallow embankment, leaped across the brook, stumbled, caught myself, and plunged upward through the underbrush climbing as fast as I could with my limp. It didn't seem to matter to me that deer, in general, are a pain in the ass. That two years ago they had gotten into Alma's herb garden and had it for breakfast. All I could think of was the waste. The sheer waste. I couldn't get over it. More than anything else I wanted to get my hands on that crumb and squeeze him until his buttons popped. He was somebody from the city, that was definite. From Rutland or Burlington, or maybe even as far away as Boston or New York, up here on vacation with his straps and buckles and his silver flask and his pale leather gun case. All that those people know is if it ain't paved it's the wilderness. Anything goes. My own property is posted thick with No Trespassing in letters so big you can see them through blinders. Do you think it ever made a difference? Scratch one ten-thousand-pound producer with high butter-fat content plugged in the rump by some weekend sharpshooter who mistook her for an elk. It was time to even the score.

But when I reached the clearing where the buck had been grounded, sweating and my fists knotted up into drubs, there wasn't a sign of anything with two legs. Or, for that matter, four legs either. The herd had flapped up their tails and vanished at the shot. I didn't expect to find any of them hanging around, but where the hell was the carcass? Taking my hat off, wiping my forehead on my flannel sleeve and looking around to see who's coming in search of a trophy. Not a soul. I went over the ground carefully and, higher up, found deer tracks in the thin blue patches of snow at the foot of the pine trees. But still no trace of the buck. No blood, no drag marks, no human prints around but my own size thirteens sunk deep into the soggy hill. It was almost as if the others had carted him off on their backs themselves, as if they refused to share him with outsiders, as if even dead he still belonged to the herd. But mysteries are for people who believe in God. Myself I don't care for them. Standing out there in the open as exposed as the buck had been, I sized up the situation. Motionless. Listening. My eyes studying the hillside.

"Come on, you sonofabitch!" I roared furiously. "I'm waiting." The air was crisp and clear and the sun beat down on my head and shoulders. It felt pretty good. Down below on the road the truck stood with its door open, as deserted as the moon.

2

I'm human. Anything I can't work out depresses me. So all the rest of the way into town I crawled and juggled this buck business looking for a handle. But every time it kept slipping away from me, squirmy as a ball bearing, and finally with a monster headache and no credible prospects I decided to call it quits. Forget about the whole thing. I wasn't about to tell Alma. It would only give her cramps. And anyone else . . . they'd lay out fancy explanations and under the counter put me down for the loony bin. Screwem!

Rolling down Main Street with a poker face to discourage idle curiosity. But there wasn't a soul on the narrow, frost-warped sidewalks and that cheered me up. Only sun-baked holiday silence and, on the corner of Wheelock and Main, Eppy's red-white barber pole as still as a stump. Everything looked closed down, pulled in, shut up. Out in front of the Farnum House, the flag was up but the porch was deserted, wooden rockers nodding lazily to one another in the afternoon breeze. No snow, no skiers. Tough. I could do without it.

The parking lot in front of Dan's Magic Dollar was

empty but that didn't worry me because Dan and his wife, Penny, were workers. Full-time, squeezing every drop out of their store like a stripped tit. They were OK. A little high on lime and barbed wire maybe and too eager to please, but OK. In the middle of the lot was an old gas pump, hand crank dangling, with the initials of a couple of generations of Farnum high school kids carved into its skin and, pulling up to it, I got out. From down by the river on Route Five the high-speed whine of through traffic hung thin in the air. Beyond the post office on the courthouse green, a Christmas tree and dead leaves and hard-edged shadows and Jacob Farnum paddling grimly up the Connecticut in quest of Indian snatch, his hooked nose gleaming like a zipper.

"Fill it up *this time*, Mr. Newfield?" asked Roger, popping up all innocent smiles and insinuation. Fat, brilliantined Roger, with pudgy hands and plaid shoelaces and a white apron he puts on after school and weekends and never gets dirty. Plus chronic smirk to tell you he's got you pegged. Believe me, this is one snotty kid.

"Three gallons. And clean the windows."

"Yes, *sir*," snapped Roger, saluting. No matter what the last word is, this little prick's got to have it.

On the curb in front of the door were bags of fertilizer and apples, rolls of chicken wire, coils of hose, rakes, sleds, shovels—the store's guts spilling out onto the sidewalk. Inside the clutter was unbelievable, but cozy and fragrant with the smell of coffee beans. As usual, the whole place reeked of the good life, palship and sentimentality. Though quieter that day than I had ever seen it.

In front of the magazine rack, Hatch and Plunket stood shoulder to shoulder in their Sunday-best soundlessly sharing a copy of *Girlie*. Their lusty eyeballs sunk

14

deep into their heads and looking mean and sullen. Two creeps. On the floor at their feet was some dressed-up kid I didn't know doubled over a comic book called *Pus* or something with this same mean look on his face. Probably just visiting for the holiday. Everybody hard at it. What concentration! As I stomped by, the men glanced up and nodded. That's better. But then we Newfields are a well-known family having lived in Farnum for generations. I admit mostly unemployed philosophers and penniless tenant farmers—all now departed. Quietly. Without fanfare. Lightweights to the end. But you see I happen to be something else. A wealthy Newfield, the first and only. And a town has to reckon with success. Envy it, respect it, brood over it until the flesh thickens and the mouth grows mealy. Can't leave you alone when you're living and, as for dying, no doubt they'll all want to have a hand in seeing me off. After making allowances for that tiny handful of questionable qualities I've been branded with behind my back: Newfield's niggardliness, his temper, his atheism, his silence, and yes, in the end even his contempt endearing him to the locals. For after all, says the reverend, who among us is without fault? And so the whole of Farnum pitching in, joining hands, coming together as one to send me packing. How touching. And in a small town with a voting turn-out of only fifty-eight percent for presidential elections. And all for me! Amazing.

At the back of the store, Dan was stooped behind the high, white meat counter consolidating hamburger—two trays into one—and spreading the pink meat over the top to keep up appearances.

"Be with you in a minute, Mr. Newfield," called Dan through the glass case. "Fine day, isn't it?"

The porcelain trays resembled hospital bedpans. On

top of the counter, a mythological wooden bird with the scroll neck of a flamingo and the beak of a hummingbird rocked gently back and forth. Every dip of its tiny pink head brought it closer to a thimbleful of water, but each time it came up short, frustration built into the mechanism. A Sisyphus with feathers. Now why in hell would anybody want to buy something like that?

Jabbing the meat with a double-pronged sign that read 59¢, Dan closed the case and rubbed his hands clean on his apron. "Well now," he said, leaning forward and giving himself to me like a present, "how can I help you, Mr. Newfield?"

"I've got rats in the house," I told him, laying it on the line.

Dan's eyes narrowed behind his rimless glasses and his face became dead serious. "We have just the thing for you," he said quietly, reassuringly. "Something new." As he sprang out from behind the counter, he reminded me of an undertaker, grieved to hear the bad news but pleased to be of service.

I followed him past the gun rack on the wall and the shelves crammed with canned beans and gallon jugs of New York State sauterne and port to the household pet counter.

"I've tried it myself," he confided, proudly handing over a toothpaste tube of anticoagulant rat-killer labeled $1.98. "You've never seen anything like this. One taste and you'll have them climbing the walls trying to get out of their own skins."

Couldn't get over it. Here was a guy who was almost as big as I was, but he looked so insignificant. It's what happens when your life is pushing other people's products instead of making something that can speak for itself.

16

"It's economical, clean, and does the job," he added, seeing that I wasn't convinced. "No fuss, no mess. All the bleeding is done on the inside. I guarantee it."

I handed back the tube and picked up a two-bit trap. "No thanks. I'll take one of these. That's good enough for—"

"Hold on," cried Dan excitedly, not wanting to see me spit in the face of progress for a measly buck seventy-three difference. "Wait a minute." He looked down to the magazine rack. "Virg," he called. "Virg!"

Summoned, Hatch tore himself away from his reading and came over. A wiry type moving slow and pompous like an authority. Oh just look at him, will you! Isn't that enough to make you retch? The school janitor, but the way he carries on you'd think he was the principal. He gave me a formal shake of his gray crew cut in passing and went up to Dan.

"What seems to be the problem?" he asked, dropping his head to study the cigar he was rolling between his bony fingers.

"Mr. Newfield here has a rat in the house and I was just showing him this." He held out the tube. "You've tried it. What's your impartial opinion?"

Hatch slowly weighed the pros and cons. "All things considered," he decided, shifting his weight and casting his eye up to the beams in the ceiling, "I'd advise Mr. Newfield to use arsenic."

"Arsenic!" squealed Dan.

Served him right for asking. Any jackass could see that the janitor couldn't stand anything about me—my six foot four and two hundred and thirty pounds against his five ten one hundred thirty, my local importance in the face of his self-importance, my overalls on his holiday.

Felt sorry for this Hatch, and if I wasn't so angry I would have peed in my pants.

"Arsenic," repeated the janitor, blandly. "As I see it, the danger lies in having them skulk off into some dark hole to die where you never know what's what. You see, when it comes to animals as shrewd as rats, it's not only doing them in that counts but knowing where you stand. Now with arsenic there's no question, because they drop in their tracks and you can take a body count at your leisure, so to speak. You see what I mean."

"But Virg," whined Dan, his face coloring up in blotches, "you don't use arsenic over at school."

"True," admitted Hatch. "Red squill is what we use, mixed in with a little Puss'n Boots. But Mr. Newfield doesn't have to worry about youngsters at his place."

"I'll take the trap," I said flatly, ignoring the son of a bitch.

"That's fine, Mr. Newfield," Dan conciliated, worried that he had pushed too hard and trying to smooth things over. "Will there be anything else? Some cheese for the trap perhaps?"

"Give me a small piece of salt pork."

Dan had a dumb look on his face, but he wasn't about to argue bait. Risk offending a good customer a second time. "Whatever you say, Mr. Newfield. Anything you say."

While I waited for the pork, I turned my back on Hatch and dared him to chitchat. Just one more word out of his stringy throat. One syllable . . .

"What's up?" It was Plunket's voice, drawling and hoarse and as thick as his head. In fact everything about Plunket is thick—his lips, his nose, his neck, his sideburns. And with meatloaves for hands, he spends forty hours a week sticking wires through round pieces of wood, the handles used in the city on department store boxes. After the textile mill went bankrupt and the furniture factory closed down, the only heavy industry left in Farnum, you might say, is Clark's Carriers. Four clucks in a Quonset hut. Plunket fits right in.

"Well then," wised off this Plunket as soon as he had heard Hatch outline the problem, "why don't he get a cat? They don't cost nothing."

I turned on him glaring like a furnace, and he gives me this stupid little grin. Alma's allergy was none of his damn business.

Plunket tried again. "How about cornmeal and plaster of paris?" he says to Hatch, as if I'm not there. Afraid to look me in the eye. "I hear that's good. Two parts cornmeal and one part plaster of paris. I guess it takes a bit for the plaster to harden, but they say it clogs them up real good."

Hatch didn't even bother not to glance at him. The matter was settled. "Arsenic," he insisted.

"Here you are, Mr. Newfield." Dan came up and handed over my pork. "Hope it does the trick."

"Well then, what about a five-gallon can half filled with water?" persisted Plunket, refusing to give up. "He could use a ramp and—"

Dan's wife Penny was up front at the check-out counter, a big woman with red cheeks and twinkly eyes in a home-knit gray cardigan buttoned up lumpy to the neck.

"And how are you today, Mr. Newfield?" she asked, winking and chuckling wildly at me as if she had just gotten off a good one.

I placed the pork and trap on the counter. Through the window I could see Roger outside with a paper towel in his hand lightly dabbing. Secretly admiring himself in the windshield.

"And will there be anything else? Cigarettes? Cigars? Pipe tobacco? Some mums for Mrs. Newfield?" She picked up a couple of big yellow ones and shoved them under my nose. "Aren't they beautiful?"

Unpinning two bills from my money clip, I told her, "The boy put in some gas. Three gallons."

As Penny rang up my bill on the register, Miss Ellsworth came through the door muffled up to her eyeballs against drafts. A little old lady in a big fur coat. For as long as I can remember, she's worn that coat regardless of the weather right around the calendar. After years of wear and tear, it looks like something that's been torn off the back of a flyblown, syphilitic buffalo. Pulling her khaki scarf down away from her mouth, she let out a tiny smile from between cracked, gray lips. "Merry Christmas, Mr. Newfield," she said sweetly. "Merry Christmas, Mrs. Hubbell."

"Merry Christmas to you, Miss Ellsworth," shot back Penny, loud and clear. "And your sister, too. Did she like the card?"

"Oh, *yes*." The old lady's eyes puckered up with pleasure. "*Ever* so much."

"I told you so."

"Do you think . . ." Miss Ellsworth hesitated shyly. "Do you think I might get another just like it for the New Year? I mean something that would accurately express my true sentiments. She's such a lovely person."

"I don't see why not," said Penny, laughing reassurance. "Why don't you go back to the card counter and look around and as soon as I'm finished here with Mr. Newfield I'll be along to help you."

Miss Ellsworth took a few steps and stopped to admire a tinseled SEASON'S GREETINGS hanging over the frozen

20

foods. She turned and looked back at me as if she had something on her mind. "Mr. Newfield . . ."

What now? She tried to get it out—wetting her lips and breathing hard.

"Isn't it nice . . ." she struggled, "isn't it nice that there are so many special programs on the TV?"

She seemed surprised at what she had hatched and then embarrassed because it was plain that I didn't know what the hell she was driving at.

"That's a fact," agreed Penny, bagging my purchase.

Miss Ellsworth smiled in relief. "This is my favorite time of the year," she said wistfully, as she went off. "It's so exciting."

Living alone with a queer sister who hadn't been outside their house in the last three years wasn't exactly the best thing for an old lady. Miss Ellsworth was going downhill pretty fast these days.

Taking my change and green stamps from Penny, I snatched up the package and was nearly out the door when I heard the Carter belch.

"And a Merry Christmas to you, Mr. Carter," came Miss Ellsworth's voice from the rear of the store. I stopped dead in my tracks.

"Regards to Mrs. Newfield," called Penny, flustered and bent on farewelling me out the door.

As I returned, she tried to laugh but it stuck in her throat. I walked past her, down the aisle to the back, and there propped drunkenly against the side of the walk-in freezer with his legs dangling out the rear door was Carter, a bottle of beer in his hand and a don't-give-a-damn smirk on his face. Clenching my jaw shut to keep from saying something I'd be sorry for, I stared down at him with murder in my eyes.

Carter raised his head. Pursed his lips as he took me in, nodded and held out the bottle unsteadily. "Care for a sip, Orin?"

"Did you clean out the gutters?" I asked him, trying to stay calm.

Carter gazed at the bottle in his hand, shrugged his shoulders, and sighed. "Suit yourself," he said. Turning away without a care in the world, he casually took another swig.

I lost my temper. Grabbing a green fistful of his old Army surplus jacket, I yanked him up like a bundle of twigs and held him in the air. "DID YOU CLEAN OUT THE GUTTERS?" I was shouting and rattling the sonofabitch around furiously.

Fear sobered him up. "Now hold on, Orin," he whined. "Damnit, wait a minute."

"You didn't, did you?" I growled, and disgustedly dropped him to his feet.

With an insulted expression on his kisser, Carter pulled down his jacket, making a big production out of straightening himself out, and felt for his tooth. It was a gold one, stamped 14K. He had bought it at an auction across the river in Brampton to plug up one of his gaps, but the damn thing was always dropping out of his head. At least once a day, I'd catch him down on his hands and knees moaning as he scoured the ground. Saturday nights he'd come hot pants into town and flash it around at the little high school girls trying to put them under. Satisfied that goldie was still in place, he stroked it affectionately, and then turned his watery eyes in my direction.

"That shit in the barn can wait," he says to me, bold as a pillow. "It ain't going nowhere. What's the big rush? Just lay off me, understand? Lay off."

I stared at him as he waved his beer bottle wildly

about and snorted defiance through his nose. Carter, I judged, had gone clean out of his mind. Then I saw his audience, Dan and Hatch and Plunket, who, having heard the commotion, had come over to gawk and spread rumors. They stood around sucking up the details.

"Come on," I hissed under my breath. "I'll drive you back."

Brushing past me, Carter appealed to the bystanders. "You saw him hit me, didn't you?" he cried, inflamed by their attention and raving with injustice. "You saw it. He's a bully. Treats me like garbage. Thinks I'm a slave. But he didn't count on my friends being around. You won't let him get away with it, will you, boys?"

Hatch took one step back. "Damnit, Carter, look out," he warned. "You're going to spill that stuff on my good suit."

"Don't you worry about that. What I get paid I can't afford to lose a drop."

Plunket, the comedian, slapped his fat hams in amazement. "You mean you get *paid* for what you do, Roy! I'll be damned! Did you hear that, Virg?"

"I heard it."

"Why that's stealing, Roy!" Plunket kept up his needling. "And at your age, too. Shame on you."

Carter polished off his beer in a gulp and with exaggerated care set the bottle down on the floor. His scrawny Adam's apple twitched, he belched, and tears filled his eyes. "My God!" he cried helplessly, drowned in self-pity. "He even makes me work on Christmas."

"Since when is boozing work, Roy? I always thought it came sort of natural to you, like ass pinching."

"Christmas!" moaned Carter, a tear dribbling down through his stubble like a pinball. "He even hits me on *Christmas*. The Lord's birthday! Our God! Why it's . . .

23

it's a *sin!*" He could hardly believe it, the phony. Wrapping himself around Hatch's shoulders, he pleaded with him. "Aren't you going to help me, Virg? *Aren't* you?"

The janitor winced in disgust and even his new suit seemed to shrink away. "Get the hell off me, you old fart!" he shouted, jamming the drunk in the ribs with his thumbs.

Carter reeled backward, tripped over the bottle on the floor, and skittering on his heels spun around like a flywheel.

"I warned you, Carter. Stop slobbering on the suit."

"All right, that's enough," I broke in, not caring for the way these bastards were treating my man. Unfair odds always rub me the wrong way. If I shook up Carter, it was for not doing his job, but what reason did they have to hassle him? Entertainment? Maybe for Dan, but as far as Hatch and Plunket were concerned I figured they were out for me, only being cowards they probably hadn't yet faced up to the fact. It was easier to run down my drunken property. "Let's go home," I said, and bent over to help Carter up from the floor.

"Leave me be!" he cried, scuttling away. "I can take care of myself. I hitched here and I'll get back the same way. I don't need help from nobody. None of you."

Serves you right, Newfield. Stick out a helping hand and you'll get it chopped off at the wrist every time. I spit on the floor to get the taste out of my mouth.

"Don't dally," was my final piece of advice.

"I'm really sorry about this, Mr. Newfield," Dan apologized, sniveling after me as I made for the door. "I didn't want to sell him anything today. But . . . well . . . you know how it is. We're all old friends here in town and—"

"Look," I turned on him, the scar over my eyebrow a double feature in his glasses. "You've got trouble. The law says you don't sell beer on a holiday in this state. Keep it away from him or next time you'll find yourself without a license. Understand?"

Dan's mouth fell open like a grain chute. "You wouldn't do that, would you, Mr. Newfield?" he whispered.

Throwing him a dead pan, I let him draw his own conclusions.

3

Thinking on my way out that now there'd be a new horror story. Featuring The Villain vs. Carter. Like the others they told about me among themselves. Black and bloody tales of crime and passion muddling history with spite. Ah the Farnum imagination! It must have something to do with the long winters. That time of year when they first dreamed their dream of Newfield murdering his own father and turning state's evidence.

Ladies and gents of the jury, I swear it was always the same. Whenever my old man lost a job, kicked off another farm for laughing too much and farming too little, he'd catch me staring at him, shrug his shoulders, and say, "You've got to make allowances, Orin. If the boss don't want you, it's not his fault. Hell, nobody's perfect. It's just that men can't bear what they see of themselves in others. The trouble is that humanity is a mixed bag of marbles and everybody thinks of himself as a purey. Do you see what I mean?"

I saw all right. He meant bad news and hard times and nothing I could count on but that goddamn shrug of his. As a kid there was a time I used to still believe in miracles. Hoping for a sign. Praying that he'd work out, make it, do the job so well that no one would ever call him names again or push us around. He caught me at it and, laughing, made fun of me until he had wormed out my secret. For a while he didn't say anything. Then he smiled, shrugged his shoulders, and walked off. He had no faith in magic. He was right of course. I never forgave him for that.

I suppose he loved his wife, but he was so resigned to losing her that it was hard to tell. Used up and ailing, she slipped out of his life one day between shrugs. When she died his biggest worry was another barber, so at thirteen I was shaving him regularly and cutting his kink. I did it for two years. For two years I stropped that goddamn razor until it glowed and was so sharp it could peel a mirror. For two years I held his chin up and rested the blade on his grizzled windpipe. Covering him over with the old coffee-stained tablecloth, I finally realized what I must have known all along, furious at myself, tightening the ends of the cloth as hard as I could around his neck and jabbing home the safety pin. He gagged, tugged at the cloth and, struggling, tore it off. I waited, but he didn't even bother to turn around. Leaning back in his chair as if he was exhausted, he said sadly, "You're getting pretty strong, Orin." That's all. No blows, no threats, no rage. Only, "You're getting pretty strong, Orin," and closed his eyes.

Shaking, I picked up the tablecloth from the floor and wrapped it loosely around his neck without bothering to pin it this time.

"Is that better?" I asked him, feeling guilty, trying to please.

"That's better," he agreed and, slumping forward, died.

"Dead," confirmed Dr. Whiting, when he arrived on

the scene. "A bad case of fright. Not the first and not the last. Nothing to write home about, you understand."

Off Main Street on Park in the back room of Ollie Howland's funeral parlor the wallpaper and the carpet had the same striped pattern, flowing into one another so smoothly that it threw you off balance. Potted plants of different sizes were all over the floor, jammed into the corners and sucking up the air. A coffin with the lid off was propped up on two kitchen chairs in the middle of the room.

"Come on. Take a look," invited Ollie, tickled pink. "You won't know him."

I hung back, steadying myself, and then slowly approached the box. Inside, his heavy work shoes had flopped clown-toed, pointing east-west, uncertain, immobilized. That seemed fair enough. He had always seen both sides of everything. I figured the shoes were safe, so I stayed with them for a while, hating the damn things for all I was worth. That helped. Feeling somewhat easier, I let my eyes crawl up his body, expecting the worst and sorry that I didn't own a pair of dark glasses to smooth things out. Never having seen a dead man before I had the silly idea that they were stuffed like any other carcass meant to last, puffing them up all out of shape. But there was no stuffing. Instead, his body looked as if it had been scooped out, fallen in on itself, collapsed. Someone had hung a bright red woolen tie around his neck. As far as I could remember it was the first time he had ever worn a tie. Above his shirt collar was a thin purple welt. It ran from ear to ear and though they had tried to hide it, I could still see the scar.

"Only a few little bruises," Ollie apologized. Bending over the corpse, he examined it and dismissed the evidence. "But with cosmetics and powder you'd hardly know they were there. Why he looks as good as new. Better."

I started to laugh. Ollie looked hurt, but I couldn't stop myself. Laughter spurted out of me uncontrollably, growing louder, coming so fast and hard that tears filled my eyes. Ollie became worried and shouted for his wife to come in.

"The Lord giveth and the Lord taketh away," soothed Mrs. Howland. "Look how nice his shirt looks. I washed it out myself. Sewed the collar button on, too." Her eyes lingered over the red tie for a moment with pleasure. "Won't nothing satisfy you, Orin Newfield?" she demanded angrily.

Because I was laughing and she didn't understand. Didn't see that it was the mouth. The right corner of his upper lip had been tucked back for a smile, but his crooked teeth were bared in a sneer. Honestly, a sneer! My old man who had lapped up shit with a grin, who had bent over backward all his life until it broke his ass, was in death finally taking sides, objecting to something, unwilling to eat it any longer. A weird, funny joke. Even if I could catch my breath, how could I explain it to her?

Behind me I could hear the Howlands' fury gathering like a wave.

"The lout . . . unnatural . . . I've never seen anything like it. That's no way to behave at a viewing . . . WHAT THE HELL'S WRONG WITH YOU, BOY? . . . he's crazy . . . no respect for . . . GODDAMNIT, YOU'RE A PERVERT! . . . mocking his own . . . Newfield's lucky he didn't live to see . . . That boy is glad his father's dead. You hear me, Ollie. *Glad*. He probably wanted to kill . . . YOU CRAZY MURDERER!"

They were out of their minds and that was funny, too. I leaned on the edge of the coffin, weak with laughter, and the weight of my heaving body set it rocking wildly. Opening his eyes, my old man gave me a long hard look, stone-steady and without emotion.

"Don't think I'll forget," he said, measuring his words carefully. "I'll never forget."

All of the laughter was drained out of me in a flash. But curiosity overcoming fear, I drew nearer, wide-eyed, to learn what else was on his mind. Slowly, his lips—an agonizing effort—his lips began to move again, to draw up, to part, and as I bent still closer not to miss a word, he spit in my face and, sneering up at me, contentedly closed his eyes.

I grabbed him by the shirt front. "You old bastard," I whispered privately in his ear to avoid scandal. "Come clean. What did you do with my father?"

From behind, the Howlands snuck up and, each taking an arm, jerked me off the corpse.

"No! Not another word," screamed Ollie in disgust. His face red as a balloon. "I've heard enough. Get out of here. Out. OUT!"

Her arms folded across her chest, Mrs. Howland smugly said nothing, satisfied to let God damn me at His convenience.

Because I had laughed. Didn't believe in their body. They swore I had done it. But I didn't kill him, your Honor. For crissake, he was all I had left. Not much, but you don't cross out your whole family with a single stroke the way you'd cancel a bad check. And note this, ladies and gents, they had only the skimpiest of evidence to go on. All they knew for sure was that once, day-dreaming, he had mashed up my leg with a cultivator. Put me in the Brampton hospital for two months of traction. That doesn't add up to murder in my book. Despite the rumors, I swear there wasn't a mark on him. I loved

31

the old bastard too much for that. Loved him despite the fact that I never could count on him. It's true, Judge. He wouldn't even live for me.

Hold on. I can explain that other business, too. Everything. Just one more nasty case of libel. Guilt by association. You see the Bromhowers owned the only house past ours at the dead end of the Old Turnpike. A young couple with a small farm. We didn't have much to do with them. But when Bromhower died, his car turning over three or four times and pinning him underneath like a bug, his wife was in a bad way, so I did what I could for her. Chickens I didn't need and their cows weren't worth a damn, but I took her corn and picked up a good disk harrow at a sensible price as part of the deal.

Mrs. Bromhower was a good-looking girl—tall, with straight blond hair that she wore tied back with a ribbon and a way of jiggling her ass when she walked that hadn't escaped my attention. She thanked me for the white pudding Alma had baked and invited me into the living room. We sat opposite one another in silence, waiting like two clenched fists. Edgy in mourning black, she didn't know what to do with her hands—fiddling with her collar, pulling down her skirt, reaching back to fix her ribbon, her breasts rearing up and tugging at the pearl buttons of her blouse. She picked up her pocketbook from the floor and rummaged through it without success.

"You can use mine," I offered, holding out my handkerchief. It was dirty, but what the hell.

She zipped up her bag. "Do you have a cigarette?"

Sunlight streamed in through the windows in straight lines and the glassy stockings on her long legs sparkled green and gold. On her ears, small gold rings shimmered. Hugging her pocketbook, she squirmed about on the beat-up couch as if *she* was the visitor and it was *my* house.

"Two days ago," she said, "two days ago he was alive." Her glance fluttered about the room and came to rest on her lap. "Now I'm all alone." She looked up at me, tears in her eyes.

"He kept a clean barn," I lied, trying to cheer her up, but it only seemed to make matters worse.

She turned away and hid her face in the pillow, letting me into the secret of her garters. Shoulders heaving, she cried without making a sound. Damndest thing I'd ever seen.

Getting up, I went over and dropped down beside her on the couch. "Here." Stuffing the handkerchief into her limp hand. "Take it."

For some reason that set her off worse than ever and she began to shake, roll, and thrash about as if she was going down for the third time. Since she was busy, I didn't see any harm in running my hand up her legs to pass the time. They were smoothies all right, as good as they looked, and I was just beginning to get comfortable when Mrs. Bromhower jerks herself up ramrod-stiff and, eyeing my paw on her property, gives me the cold squint of suspicion. Whoops! Tried to get rid of the damn limb but it was like a hot wire. I couldn't drop it.

"And what do you think *you're* doing?" she demanded to know, all brass.

Not being much good at explanations, I did the first thing that came into my head. Tickled her. Hoping maybe she'd take it as a joke, but she didn't laugh. She didn't cry either. She just sat there and stared at me as if I was out of my mind. I didn't care for that, so I figured I might as well be damned for a tit as a tickle. Yanking out her blouse, I reached up under her brassiere and grabbed on

33

to them. Hers were young and springy and they snapped right up to attention at the touch. A thoroughly satisfying experience. I tried to make the most of it because I could tell from the expression on her face that it wasn't going to last forever.

"Are you crazy?" she shouted. Pushing me off, she jumped to her feet and ran to the windows. "Can't you see the shades are up?"

By the time she was back, my overalls were down around my knees and my prick out, horn-hard and steaming.

She took the business-end in her hand and, examining it professionally, shook her head. "It looks like a toothless old woman."

Throwing her down on the couch. Hard. Hiking up her black skirt. "Don't fret, Mrs. Bromhower," I growled, furious at the time I had wasted beating around the bush with this whore. "I suspect it's got enough bite left in it for you."

The widow's face in the shadows was a death mask. "There's nothing . . ." she breathed into the darkness, "nothing worse than being alone."

"Depends," I said, ramming it home and watching the sparks fly. "I'll let you know when I'm finished."

Shortly thereafter Alma took a turn for the worse. Rarely left the farm anymore. Half the day she'd mope about the house drinking coffee, her hair matted and her clothes held together with safety pins. Cobwebs covered her Singer like vines. Oddly enough, about the only thing she kept up with was her presents to Mrs. Bromhower. Absolutely refused to let me go up there without a little something sweet to take the edge off the girl's grief. Whenever she got wind I was on my way, her oven would blaze up and out would come pies, cakes, brownies.

Whole bakeries! She baked in a kind of frenzy, almost as if she wanted to make sure I had plenty of reason for going. After a while it got to be embarrassing, so I just dumped the stuff in the brook on my way over. I'd be damned if I'd let my wife operate a catering service for some whore!

But, you understand, I couldn't say anything to her. Alma was nuts about widows. And orphans and stray dogs and failures and you name it. She's always had a soft heart. One of those troublemakers. Not having any kids does that to a woman. Normally, the first two or three toughens it up and makes them more natural. With her bad blood, poor Alma never had a chance.

To keep her company, I stopped visiting the widow and hung around our place for almost a month. Didn't see Mrs. Bromhower once in all that time. Alma perked up a bit, but what with one thing and another it got to be too much of a strain for me. I had boxed myself into a concentration camp of good deeds. It seemed as if any time I stopped smiling she was after me.

"It's all right, Orin," she'd say, the brave little soldier keeping her chin up. "I still love you. Regardless."

And to make matters worse there were the cars. Because of the dead end usually there was no traffic to speak of past our place. After Bromhower's death that changed. At first they crept out from town single scouts, but in no time they were parading down the middle of the road in whole squadrons and battalions. Standing by the window, I ticked off the names until my knees sagged. Even high school kids! Out-of-state licenses! Alma took one look and ran to her oven, but I beat her to the punch. Out the door in a flash and heading for a showdown with the widow.

I caught up with her on a hill out back wearing a man's

bathrobe and shoes, laces dangling and her fine hair loose and swirling in the breeze. Just coming out of the hen house, breakfast in hand. My fingers clamped down on her big-boned shoulders, anchoring her to the spot. "What's your goal?" I stormed into the wind. "Community service? The state? New England? It's got to stop somewhere."

Shaking her so hard that the eggs cracked and her shoes fell off. Mrs. Bromhower was in chicken shit up to her ankles and she knew it. Untying her robe, she held it wide open and flapping. Not a stitch, except for the triangular scrap of Persian lamb between her legs. First I realized she wasn't a natural blond.

"Feel this," she said, taking my hand and running it over her naked belly. There didn't seem to be anything to lose so I humored her. Feeling around when a tow truck drives up. Waves, whistles, beeps his horn, and zooms off. LaBombard, too!

"How's that?" inquired the widow, without batting an eye.

It was hot. "Don't try to change the subject. I want an answer."

She reached up and planted a kiss on my collar bone. "Congratulations, sweetheart! You're going to be a father."

"JUDAS!" I thundered, and blew her halfway down the hill. "IT'S A LIE!"

You did it, Newfield! There's life in that seed. Nothing wrong with the machinery after all. Sharks churning around on the inside just waiting to sink their teeth into something juicy. Hung like a hippopotamus. You old stud.

"As God is my witness. Let Him strike me dead this minute if it's not yours." She hugged herself inside her bathrobe as the sky clouded over, brazening it out.

I stepped down the hill and showed her the back of my

hand. "Whatever you got in there," I said, rapping on her belly, "it ain't mine." Another Newfield! Who else around here could produce anything larger than six feet that wasn't a cesspool or a tapeworm?

"It's yours all right and you'll pay for it. You've got the money. If you don't," she threatened, her lip twisted into a scabby hook, "I'm going to your wife with an earful. I'll tell everybody in Farnum how you raped me."

"Blackmail?" Laughing in her face and then stumbling merrily down the hill like a lunatic. Should have known better. No kid of mine would pick a slut for his mother.

"You'll pay, you big bastard," she screamed down at me. "Through the ass!"

It was from my handyman that I eventually got the pieces, your Honor, and I put the picture together myself just as I've described it. According to him, people in town were asking about Alma. You know how they love to keep up with the doings of the rich. Apparently they never saw her anymore. They were sorry she was feeling poorly. Or was something else the matter? None of their damn business. But the way I figure, it all stems from Alma making herself scarce. And Carter smirking as he told me. Hinting that the widow must run like a Model T once she's cranked up proper. A dirty mind. Stick to your high school kids, Carter.

You know me, folks. If there's one thing I can't stand it's slyness and beating around the bush. I admit right out that I've given Mrs. Bromhower a thought or two in the year since her husband's death. But as for the rest, not a word of truth in it. Not a single goddamn word. Local uncollected trash. You try to be kind to a young woman in distress, buy a few odds and ends from her, bring over some cookies, and before you know it they've got you inside her pants. And your wife pining away in secret suffering. There's a lesson to be learned there. Neighborliness is for eunuchs.

So you see it was all slander, your Honor. But I can live with rumors. Even though they're like diarrhea. Hard to stop and painful if prolonged. And on my way out thinking now there'd be a new one. Concerning how the sullen and brutish Newfield beat the hell out of his little handyman on Jesus Christ's birthday with malice aforethought and a foul and blasphemous mouth.

4

"Will there be anything else, Mr. Newfield? Air? Water?"

Fresh kid, this Roger. Stepped around the truck to make sure he didn't pocket the gas cap or drive a spike into the tires. Can't be too careful about the help. Aha! Pump meter just shy of the three. Goof-offs and con men, the whole pack of them.

"How do you like the windshield? Really sparkles now, don't it?"

What does he expect me to do, hug him? Pulled a paper towel from the dispenser, spat on the glass, and did the job right. The boy looking on with a pained expression that cheered me up considerably. Can't show kids anything these days. Wadding the dirty towel, I tossed it to him and got in. "It's paid for."

Roger hurled the wad into a barrel. "Call again, Mr. Newfield," he said, brushing his hands as he walked away. "Always a pleasure to serve you."

Gunned the engine and was about to run him down from behind when I hear someone shouting, "Stop! Stop!

Orin Newfield! Orin Newfield! Don't think you can get away. I see you."

Peaselee, D.D., at the gallop. Dragging behind him the madonna and child. Little bastard screeching inside his blanket like an accident. Knowing what I was in for, I turned off the motor.

"Orin Newfield," leaning in and hugging me around the shoulders. Clogging the cab with his wrinkled face and watery eyes. And looking me up and down, breathless. I'm a miracle. Lazarus fresh from cold storage.

"But it was only by chance that I decided to come this way. Only by the *merest* chance. And here you are. How wonderful!"

Blue veins twitching in his sunken cheeks, hair sprouting from his nose and ears. Who needs him? "Afternoon, Mr. Peaselee."

"It's been so long . . ."

Alma in a stiff white veil playing peek-a-boo with me from behind it. Won't come out until he had said his piece and his piece was a filibuster. But she was worth the effort. All cream underneath.

"Too long, Orin. I can hardly recall the last time."

"October. Front of my place. On your way to visit *her*." Exchanged friendly nods with my neighbor who was busy jiggling her baby.

"Of course! To be sure. To be sure. And how is Alma?"

"Will you shut up already?" screamed the widow.

Poor kid. He'll grow up quick. Already she was talking to him as if he was sixteen.

Peaselee beamed a blessing over the little bundle and gave it a pat. "Remarkable child. Were you aware," he whispered to me, "that Mrs. Bromhower was pregnant with him for almost a full year after her poor husband's

40

death? Eleven months and twelve days to be exact. Even Dr. Whiting, whom you know isn't given to exaggeration, called it unheard of. 'Very queer,' I believe were his exact words. A wonderful legacy from the dead to the living, don't you think? And who do you suppose is the god-father?"

Peaselee's fingers in the pale shit. Dumping diapers in the toilet and slopping out the mess, paste of chopped bananas and purée of chicken. Very adhesive. Baby oil splattering on his white collar and drool dribbling down his back. The Immaculate Conception. All rashes and heartache. Between the kid and his mother, they'll have the old sog sending messages up to his boss night and day, filling the sky with beggary.

"It's a responsibility I don't take lightly, I assure you."

"That's tough." So busy goo-gooing at the howler he can't hear the truth.

One-handing a falsy out of her shoulder bag the widow plugged up her kid with it, a rubber nipple on a green plastic ring. Colorful sucking but a dry run. It wouldn't fool me for a second. "Healthy pair of lungs," I congratulated her.

"He's hungry," she explained, cradling the bundle in her arms and shaking it down like a thermometer. "It's past his feeding time."

Checked my overalls to see where I was. Two fifteen on the big Elgin. Winding it up to show I'm a busy man and dropping it back into the pocket. "I've got to go. Nice to see you, Reverend."

"Healthy lungs, Orin, are the key, the bedrock and foundation for a healthy life. The good Lord blesses us with strong ones like this little fellow's and we pollute them with cigarettes and cigars and pipes. We've got to

41

stop smoking," he said urgently, wringing his hands. "I realize you don't care to hear me go on about your spiritual life, my boy, but this has nothing to do with it. It's your health I'm concerned with. Look at Mrs. Bromhower. I've succeeded in convincing her to give up the crutch of tobacco and see how much better she is for it."

Widow seemed pale and jittery. Not too reassuring. The best I could say for Peaselee was that he meant well. A lousy thing to say about anybody. "I don't smoke, Mr. Peaselee. Never have, never will. Don't have time for it." Started up the engine to give him a hint. "Can I give you a ride, missus?"

"My car's down the block."

"I'm so glad, Orin. So glad. You have no idea. And how is Alma?"

"Good-bye. I've got work to do." Peaselee frowning. Who the hell needs his permission?

"I'm worried about you, Orin. You drive yourself too hard. Surely today of all days you can take off some time. We're having our special Christmas service this evening. Why don't you and Alma come? We haven't seen her at the church in ages. It's our special Christmas service, you know, and this year we'll have Mrs. Russell back with us again at the piano. It will be lovely. Won't you come?"

"Shove it!" Grinning and lifting my cap to the widow, I showed them my tailpipe.

"Merry Christmas, Orin Newfield," cried Peaselee, waving after me. "Merry Christmas."

All forgiveness that Peaselee. He's in the right business. Let him tend to his and I'll tend to mine.

Barely an hour shy of milking and no sign of Carter as I passed the barn and turned up the driveway. About reaching the end of the line with that fuckoff. Drop him in a minute if it would cut down appreciably on the overhead. Department of Agriculture Bulletin No. 243. Do not fire Carter rashly. For maximum returns from herds larger than sixty use two able-bodied men or their equivalent one Newfield in the prime plus any drunken cripple will do. Only thing the government does worth a damn is print those bulletins. And maybe pay for free milk in the schools.

When I came in the house, Alma was waiting for me at the dining room table. Hadn't moved an inch. Guarding the dirty dishes to see that nobody walks off with them. Depressing. Doesn't even bother to pull out the gray hairs anymore. Shingles turning the backs of her hands into bloody rags. Sick nerves and aspirin shrinking her up. At least her eyelids looked good. Darker now in the white face and olive glossy. Very nice contrast. As they say, it's a bad wind that doesn't blow some good.

"It took you a long time, Orin."

"You seen Carter?"

"I was worried."

"Here's your trap. Cut off a small chunk of the pork and put it on tight or they'll pull it away in one bite. I've got to go clean the barn."

"I was so worried, Orin."

Hangs on like a leech, but why get upset? She missed me. Very thoughtful. Stepped behind her and tucked a few of the gray ones out of sight, kicking up a storm of dandruff. Show her I care about the way she looks. Keep up her pride.

"Did you run into anybody in town, Orin? Is that what took you so long?"

That woman has some intuition! A sixth sense! But in

43

her condition there was no point in mentioning Peaselee's invitation. Too weak to mingle with his collection plate. Might succumb to the hereafter. Can't have that.

"Carter's drunk. I've got to tend the barn. Aren't you going to clean up in here?" Stacking up the dishes by way of encouragement, eggshells flying, nothing to it.

"You don't have to, Orin. You're busy. I'll do it. I'm just trying to catch my breath."

Should have brought her that sampler in Brampton last year. A house is a machine for living. Damn right! Ours needs a new valve job. Might have set her on the right track.

"It's those two toes again. They're bothering me something awful, but they'll stop in a while. You know how the pain comes and goes."

"I know."

"Don't, Orin. There's no need. I'll take care of it in a minute."

"Sure you will." Scooping up a pile of dishes under each arm and clanking off to the kitchen. Decided I couldn't wait. She'd need a lifetime to recuperate. Comes up with new ailments quicker than Whiting can name them. Mortinson's toe, Salter's disease, Vincent's angina. Poor Alma! Always something with her.

"Let me," begged Alma, wobbling in with a tray of limp butter and a pitcher of warm milk. "You don't have time for that now."

I emptied her hands, led her gently back inside and sat her down. "Bait the trap. I'll handle this."

Alma reached up and squeezed my arm. "I don't know what I'd do without you, Orin. You're a good man."

Least I could do was help. Shipshape and snappy. First the milk and butter. Refrigerator squeezed in between two doors at the end of the long narrow kitchen, one to the

44

basement, the other to the back pantry. They both opened in until I fixed them, reversing the hinges and planing down the ends. This old house wasn't built for modern appliances, they took it by surprise.

Newfield, the ladies' home companion and helpmate. On the job, thrusting his hand fearlessly into the white vault. Eeeeow! Impaling his wrist on an icicle. Refrigerator shaken to its casters and floor covered with chunks of melting ice. Otherwise no damage. Peering in, he observes stalactites dangling from the freezing tray. Someone has failed to do her duty. Despite the pressure of other business, he remains tranquil, master of himself, equal to any emergency. He turns off the motor, he fills the shelves with pots of steaming water, he notes the printed warning that it is dangerous to use sharp instruments near coils and hacks away with a dull butter knife, freeing the ice trays. There's a right way to do everything. While waiting for the thaw to set in, he proceeds to polish off the dishes with a will. Letting the chips fall where they may. Wonderfully systematic! Every minute turned to advantage.

Slamming the dishes into the plastic drying rack and fuming. If Carter's not back by the time I'm through I'm going to break his ass. Definitely! No cooperation from anybody around here.

Turning to replace the ice trays I nearly went down, my bum leg skidding out from under me on the wet floor. Would have put quite a dent in the linoleum, which wasn't in great shape as it was. Mopped up the mess, switched on the refrigerator, and slammed the door. Silence. They don't make them that way anymore. Bashed the old wreck in the side and it started right up, humming its heart out. I've always said it, Newfield, you're better with things than people. A quick survey to see that everything was tucked in its niche and resting comfortably.

45

Out with the light. The satisfaction of a job well done. Plus sacrifice. Plus frustration and smoldering outrage. You can't beat cleaning up for a short-term emotional investment.

"Thank you, daddy," said Alma, swiveling around to clutch me as I passed through the dining room. "Thank you. But you shouldn't have done it."

All that gratitude made me suspicious. What now?

"I feel so ashamed of myself. I hate to make extra work for you. I don't know what's the matter with me lately."

She slumped over the table exposing more of her scrawny neck than I had ever seen before. Raw and rashy. Could be she's losing her hair. Surprised she never mentioned it along with everything else. Ah, the little vanities of women!

"If I could only get some rest."

"Set the trap and go inside and lie down. I'll be back in a couple of hours."

"I can't go down there, Orin. I can't. They make me feel so creepy. As if the house doesn't belong to us anymore. If I could only get some peace and quiet. That's all. A little peace and quiet."

I gave a listen. Except for the refrigerator inside and the ticking of my Elgin you couldn't hear a pin drop. Sharp ears. But then Alma had had a year at the State Teachers College at Lyndon Center. She could pick up the sound of perspiration dripping from an ant's crotch. Who needs so much formal education? Makes you overly sensitive.

"Honestly, daddy. I just can't."

"Course not." Wrapped the fingers of one hand around her neck to show her I understood and drew out the penknife from my back pocket. Those whining eyes of hers made me feel like a crumb. What the hell. How long will it take? Sliced off a hunk of pork, jammed it on the hook, and pulled the spring back into position. Easy does it. Trigger it now and lose a finger. The hard way. Not like a circular saw. When Meechum over the lumber yard lost his three they say it happened so fast he didn't know about it until he shut off the machine and tried to pick up the piece he was working on. Must have come as quite a surprise.

"Be careful, Orin."

Opened the door to the basement, turned on the light, banged down the wooden stairs. Head low to keep from cracking it against the hot-air ducts from the furnace. Head low to keep from stringing it up on the clothesline. The cement floor covered with coal dust from the empty bin. Oil saves time and trouble and we give you two and a half cents off on every dollar says Colburn, the lying bastard, but not one word about why they call it black gold. No noticeable difference in comfort between the two until the end of the month when the bill arrives. If Alma's lousy back hadn't gone out on her she might still be shoveling it in and saving us a little cash along with time and trouble. I can't do everything myself.

Hunched up in the corner and snickering was the three-hundred-gallon money-grabber. The washing machine was next to it, a horse of a different color. Secondhand but sturdy, with a fluorescent light to use it night and day. That machine doesn't owe me a cent. Took some pains to set it in just right. Short hose to prevent freeze-ups and two long metal pipes, connected by an elbow joint, extending to a drain hole in the middle of the floor. Be damned if I was going to trade in a sure thing for some undependable washer-dryer combination. The more parts the more chance for something to go wrong. But Alma all the time complaining about coal dust on the clothes in winter and bird shit in the spring. Scrape it off was my advice to her.

Above the washer on the wooden shelf a box of soap. The kind that does everything. Alma, the detective, had found it knocked over. The white powder spilled all around the floor dotted with tiny footprints. She was standing in a pile of dirty underwear screaming her head off when I rushed down.

"It's only Ben," I said, taking her round and trying to hug the quiver out of her body.

"No," she howled. "They're too small."

"Probably squirrels then."

"How could they get in here?" she scoffed, her eyes all the while fixed on the drain hole.

"How the hell should I know! They got in, that's all."

She clung to me and took a deep breath. "It's rats, Orin."

"You're imagining things. Come on."

"It's rats," she repeated hopelessly as I led her away, limp, shivering, her eyes squeezed shut against an army of rats.

The best place for the trap was by the drain, so I set it down there. Pork first to give them a good whiff. Cheese is for comic books, and between pork and bacon you can't beat pork. It's got more salt, and it's the salt that does it every time. They can't resist it. Shut off the light and gently close the door. That ought to get some action in a while.

"Did you do it, Orin?"

"Get some rest," I advised her as I hurried by. "You look terrible. I'll see you later."

"What's that!"

I stopped and listened. "What?"

"Didn't you hear it?" she whispered. "That bang? In the basement." She sat frozen in her chair, her ear cocked and her eyes white as fishbones.

"Goddamnit! It's no use. I'll never get any work done today." Stomped back into the kitchen and rushed down into the basement. So furious I forgot to duck and my head smashed into one of the pipes, denting it, and making a deep boom like a Chinese gong.

"Are you all right, Orin? Are you all right?"

"SHHHHIIIT!" I'll kill them all, all of them, and Carter, too. My good humor was ruined. But at least I hadn't come down for nothing. Alma was right. Caught by his tail and struggling to free himself from the trap was a scrawny-looking affair still chock full of mischief. Pleased to see it. Restored my faith in Alma's ears. Looked around for a weapon and spied the broom handle on top of the oil tank. My dip stick to keep tabs on Colburn's gauge. Just the ticket. Grabbing it up, I waded into the little bugger, hauling off with a whop, whop, whop. The rat squealing like a rusty pulley. Reared back for the finishing touch and brought it down hard on his jerking head. CRACK! Shoddy merchandise. Threw away the stump left in my hand and squashed the last squeal out of him with the heel of my boot. Crafty bastard. Tried to sink his teeth into it before leaving. Down the drain with all parasites and that's that. And pocketed the pork. Considering how fast it worked, I figured there was no sense in leaving it hanging around if I wanted to get out the front door. On the way up, scraping the gook off the bottom of my boot on the stairs. Protect Alma from the worst.

She was waiting for me in the kitchen, hanging over the sink with her back turned. I tiptoed past.

"Orin."

"It's all taken care of."

49

"Orin." She turned, clutching one of the plates I had chipped to her chest, face rigid, her eyes glazed and spellbound. "I've tried to help. God knows, I've tried. But you'd be better off without me. There's nothing I can do for you, Orin. You don't need any help from anyone. Never."

5

It didn't surprise me. Alma occasionally got things mixed up. For instance there was the night Ben came over and we got into one of our usual arguments. Started when he asked for something to munch on and I told him we didn't have a thing. Alma disappeared into the kitchen, returning with a tray full of cheese and crackers. Always looking for a free handout, that one. Let him eat his supper at home. Then he began picking at me why, as one of the biggest farm owners in the county, I wasn't a member of the Grange, the Farm Bureau, the Agricultural Conservation Program. I'm not a joiner, that's why. If other dairy men didn't know enough to run their own show, I wasn't about to do it for them. They were using Ben to get to me, but if they wanted anything from Orin Newfield they'd damn well have to come themselves. On their knees. Unconditional surrender. And I'd still say no.

We had been through all this before, so I judged Ben was warming up to something else and he was. Didn't appreciate the way I treated my handyman. Carter was saying I had sent him for a pitchfork and when he didn't move fast enough to suit me I had kicked him in the back of the leg to speed him along. Rolling his pants up all over town to share his black and blue with the citizens. People didn't like what they saw. He wasn't much, but, after all, he was a human being. And Alma siding with her brother saying I'm too hard on the old man. Mrs. Carter had told her of his arthritis, the stiff joints, his constant suffering. The only reason he drank was to make the pain bearable. Gullible Alma. She'd believe anything that tugged at the heartstrings. As I say, she sometimes got things confused. I was the one who was doing Carter a favor, not the other way round. Given what he did for me it was practically charity. The Red Cross wouldn't have done as much. Everybody else treated him like something they had coughed up. I was the only one who helped him. In all of Farnum, I was the only one willing to give him a job, a house. A chance for self-respect. The only one! But I didn't care what Ben thought, and to try to change Alma's mind was hopeless. She loved her brother so much she even named her dog after him. Ben the man and Ben the dog. That's immortality for you! I was saving myself for something bigger like a battleship, or a bridge, or, better yet, a whole town.

When I finally got to the barn, the goose egg that had popped out on my forehead throbbing, Carter was nowhere to be seen. Better not show his face around here now if he knows what's good for him. Couldn't bear to look at the gutters still crammed with the morning's slop. Like a smudge on a West Point cadet's dress uniform. Everything else gleaming the way it should, the whitewashed walls, the windows, the stanchions, the concrete mangers, and here was this stream of blemish stinking to high heaven. Put the gutter cleaner to work and set things to rights. Germ-free and blue ribbon. A showplace.

My pride and joy. But it took time and it was well after four before I was finished. Outside in the loafing pen the herd was beginning to fuss. Don't blame them, lugging around those full knapsacks between their legs. Hurry, Newfield, hurry! Even with all my machinery, tractors, hayloaders, lime spreaders, manure spreaders, milkers, balers, and blowers, and all new, I still hadn't been able to automate Carter out of existence. Not yet, but someday. Torn between self-sufficiency and big returns, Newfield bolted out of the barn in a sweat.

Cows swarmed and dithered as I entered the pen. Their flanks muddied because the bedding was too thin and the hayracks and silage bins near empty. Enough to make your heart ache. Goddamn that Carter, I'll hang his nuts from the weather vane for crows to peck at. Hauled the herd out two at a time, brushed off their bottoms, set them in the ties. Then up and down the alley reviewing the troops, hands clasped behind the back. You might say Eisenhower on D-Day. Lots of limp to let them know they've got the experience of an old campaigner behind them, hint of a smile because it's in the bag. Passed rump after rump instilling confidence, banishing unproductive thoughts, finishing up with Pia and Ursula and Co-co and Albertine and Samba and Buom-buom and Saltva, Rajas, Tamas and Camille. All present and accounted for. The names choice like the milk, adding a touch of class to the operation. Borrowed from Alma's *Naming Your Baby Around the World*. A cheap substitute for foreign travel and more rewarding. In all of Vermont who else had a cow called Woodip? Down at the other end of the barn Naughty Marietta rattling her stanchion impatiently. Get on with it, Newfield, and stop horsing around.

Flipped on the radio to ease their udders while waiting their next. WMTW from high atop Mount Washington, an isle of tranquility in a sea of noise. Coming up "Tales from the Vienna Woods." Good reception. Consuelo of the six teats chewing her cud in time to the music. Unusually talented even for a cow. Assembled two of the stainless-steel milking machines and settling down to business. Ordinarily it was three minutes per with hardly any hand stripping to speak of, but solo I didn't expect any records. Shook hands with Josette and Nicole as a warm-up and plugged them in. One liked her back scratched and the other her ears, so while the machines slurped it up I took care of the ladies' preferences. Jealousy unknown in the harem, all they asked for was satisfaction.

The heat poured out of the animals' bodies like huge radiators. Grade A performers on the mound, doing their stuff twice a day without fail. No mastitis, no Bang's disease, more sanitary than the nurses in the Brampton hospital. Pulled off the plugs and there was a hefty yield of some of the best whole milk in the county, the state. Lovely! Emptied the machines into the ten-gallon cans and took a quick breather.

Mopping up my armpits when Carter stumbles in, his nose shining like a warning light on top of some high peak. Appeared to have had a few more for the road before setting foot on it. Singing deck the halls with boughs of holly and slapped what looked to be a foreign beer bottle label on Babuchka's backside. Odd. Where's he getting the money for imported beer? Wanted to knock him down then and there and grind his wooden face into splinters but thought better of it and ignored him. Back to work I hooked up the next two, all business and total dedication, waiting for him to say his piece.

54

"Sorry I'm late, Orin. Held up by traffic."

Silence.

"Yes, sir. Detained by traffic. Did you hear me, Orin? Detained by traffic?"

"That so."

"That's right. None on the road. Had to leg it all the way."

He was hooting and snorting so hard I thought sure he was going to have a hemorrhage. Set the whole barn on edge with his carrying on, drowning out the music and short-circuiting production. Plugs pulling on air like four straws in an empty glass. Yanked them off and stood up. All the way. Carter takes one look at six feet four inches of snarl close up and changes his tune.

"Right you are, Orin," he says, dashing for the hand truck. "Don't say another word. I'll just hustle these cans straight into the milk house. We sure as hell don't want to have them souring out on us in here, do we? No-sireee!"

Relieved him of the truck and placed a restraining hand on his windpipe. Newfield wasn't going to be unfair to any man, his sense of justice was as strong as a judge's gavel. Maybe I have been too hard on him. Maybe he does have arthritis. Maybe he is in pain. Felt better for having swallowed my anger and allowed Carter to hear the voice of reason, subdued so as not to upset the herd any further.

"Are you sick?"

"Who's sick?"

"Get out of here and sleep it off. You're in no shape to work."

"Well, now that you mention it, Orin, I did take a bit of a chill in the liver on my way back from town. I'll just go home and get under the blankets and warm it out with hot tea and—"

"Get going. We'll subtract it from your pay."

Carter shriveled up like a used condom. Sobered he was about half his normal size. Handy for storage. The creases in his face deepened and his eyebrows were tents under which his eyes seemed to be hiding out, trying to keep dry. Carter was feeling sorry for himself again.

"You didn't think I was going to pay you for laying around in bed, did you?"

"Forget it," mumbled Carter, shuffling off. "I'll milk the other side." He put together the two machines that were left and dragged them out, talking to himself all the while. "Other people get bonuses for Christmas and Roy Carter gets subtractions. Someday there's going to be a squaring of accounts. Someday Satan is going to look up and say to his handymen, 'Ease off on that Carter. Can't you dopes see who he works for? That's hell enough for any man.'" Lugging the heavy equipment into place, Carter deliberately drops it to spite me. Rings on the concrete platforms like horseshoes.

"I'm warning you, Carter. I don't want any accidents around here. You ruin a cow and I'll take it out of your ass. Full value!"

He got the message. Aside from an occasional belch of defiance from the other side, things settled down after that. Peace restored to the strains of "The Merry Widow Waltz." Catchy tune. Newfield caught himself humming along with the music as he moved from stall to stall raking it in. Happy, happy, happy. Happy the dirt farmer, the lone ranger, the country free of entangling foreign alliances. He saw himself as a kind of hermitic super-nun living a Spartan life of self-discipline, order, and dedication. Most rewarding. Every act tuned to the bells. Behind schedule warned the Elgin and he tucked the bells back in his overalls. Carter an annoying but necessary inconvenience. Grunting, pissing, and moaning, loading a couple of ordinary eighty-five pound cans on the hand truck as if they were pianos and wheeling them off to the outside ramp that leads down to the milk house. Mumbling all the way. Someday, Carter, they're going to come up with that machine. Someday. With luck. And a little patience. Which is its own reward. O let it come soon!

Bunching up the hay in the trough for Carmen to munch on and when she's almost through whistled in her ear for a few more drops. Sexy Carmen, she loves that. Whistling away when something tells me to turn around. Mutiny! Carter lurking right behind me, breathing desperately and the color flicking on and off in his face like Morse code. I gathered he was working himself up to hit me but was somewhat afraid I might clout him back.

"I've got something to say," he blurted out shrilly, dancing up to me and then away. "I've worked hard for you for almost three years, Orin Newfield. Worked my fingers to the bone for peanuts, so I don't have to pussyfoot around with you or lie or—"

"What do you want?"

"I just spilled a can of your milk."

"You what?"

"I said I just spilled a can of your milk."

"That so."

"That's so. How do you like that?"

How would he like it if I forked him in the crupper? How would he like it if I put my fist through his face and it came out the other side? How would he like it if I ripped his ears out of his head and snapped off his toes one by one?

"You don't have to look at me that way, Orin. It wasn't

57

my fault. Don't think you can scare me. Where are you going?"

Marched out to the ramp to survey the damage. Below, the milk cupped in the muddy cowprints forming ten thousand muddy lakes. Pocket size. Minnesota must be like that. Tempted to go there one day and count for myself.

"Two cans, Carter. TWO. Don't you think I can count for myself?"

"Didn't I say two?" he whined, backing slowly away from me into the barn.

"Two cans shot to hell. Wasted. Down the drain. Wouldn't take my advice, would you? Well, then." Bearing down on him one step at a time. "I guess you'll just have to take the consequences."

"It was an accident, Orin. I couldn't help it. As God is my witness!" Whimpering now and almost tripping over the gutter and backed into an empty stall. No escape. His eyes rolled with fear. Screaming, "The truck just got away from me, that's all. Slipped right out of my hands. It could have happened to anybody. Accidents happen you know. You know that, Orin." He stopped suddenly, changed like the weather, and came toward me, a crazy smile on his lips. Came up so close I could feel his heart thumping wildly in my pocket. "You won't hurt me," he said. "You need me. I'm too valuable to you."

"NEED YOU! NEED YOU!" I roared, choking on the words. "You beer-breathed, knuckle-headed, butter-fingered sonofabitch. You're not worth a mosquito's fart. Need you." Howling at the thought. "I don't need anybody."

The herd kicking up a storm and carrying on at the top of their leather lungs. Nerves opened their cans like floodgates, the shit pouring out all down the line. They hate to see me upset. Sooner I get him out of here the better. Went to squeeze the pimple and Carter slips right between my fingers, collapsing at my feet. Heart attack. "Ha, ha!" Taunting me. "That's right, boss. You can't hit a man when he's down."

"Get up!"

"You see."

"No . . . men you don't . . ." Lifted Carter up and set him on his feet, pounding the dust off him. "But worms you pluck out of the ground by their tails."

"It was an accident, Orin. I swear to God. An accident! I'll make it up to you. I'll pay for everything."

"That's right." By the seat of his pants and the back of his collar. Taxied him down the whole length of the litter alley to the barn door, Carter screaming like a jet, and heaved him out with all my might. Airborne he flew for maybe as much as twenty feet before dropping back to earth. Now don't go puffing yourself up, Newfield. Probably only a favorable air current. Wiped the sweat from my face and there was the bump. But it felt much better now, much better.

Took notice of Mrs. Carter, surrounded by her entire brood, standing frozen up against the side of the barn. Out of harm's way. The kids staring at me dumbfounded, their mouths gaping and their eyes bulging out of their heads. Not so, Mrs. Carter. Fat and round-shouldered from the chronic drag of a loaded belly, some ten years younger than her old man but looking twenty older, Mrs. Carter took it all in her stride. Nothing could faze that woman. Always expecting the worst, disaster never surprised her. She glanced dully at the crumpled heap on the ground that was her husband and bided her time, waiting to mop up and begin again.

"Orin! Orin! What's happened?"

Damned if it wasn't Alma running across the road without anything on top. Quite a circus. Must have raised my voice.

"Can't you see the sun's down? Go back to the house. You'll catch something out here in that housedress."

"O my God!" she cried, her hands flying to her mouth at the sight of Carter's motionless body. Kneeling down in the mud beside him, she took his head in her arms. The neck seemed rubbery and his arms were twisted and pinned beneath him. "God! God!" she wailed, "what have you done? Orin . . . I think you've killed him."

The thought had occurred to me. Racked my brains but couldn't recall ever having seen Carter so quiet before. Unsettling. Went over and dragged Alma away from the body. She tried to say something to Carter's wife and kids but thought better of it and hid her face in my sleeve.

"What the hell are you mumbling about?"

She looked up at me, her cold face shaking like a blue tambourine.

"This time," she whispered, "you've done it for sure."

"Shut up!" Brushed her away and she bit on her fingers to hold back the tears. Ashamed of myself. Probably the first harsh words I've ever used to Alma, and all because of this goddamn evil lump of flesh and bones.

"Garbage!" I thundered, "we know your tricks. You won't get off so easy this time. Get up, you. Stop acting and get up."

Nothing doing. Frankly, I was worried. Toed him in the gut and out of his mouth gushed steaming bits and pieces full of life with not a trace of blood. That's a relief!

"Possum, handyman? Come here, missus." Motioned to the wife and she came forward without a word. Surprising how heavy Carter felt as I hoisted him up and loaded

60

him on her back. "Take him home and put him to bed. He'll be all right." Carrying the old clown piggyback, Mrs. Carter trundled off into the gathering darkness, her kids flying after her. Alma watched over them all like a godmother,

Wind shifted, coming from the northeast now. Didn't promise anything good. Leafless birches sticking up behind the Carter house, brittle against the evening sky, and the heavens turning as black as the inside of a cast-iron pot.

Be reasonable, Alma. What the hell have I done now? You'd think it was my fault. But Alma wasn't talking. Only shivering. "What's the matter with *you*?" Hanging around in the shadows was Carter's oldest, a scrawny ten-year-old who still had all the original hair he was born with. Just standing there staring at my feet. Expected to see cloven hooves, I imagine. "What are you looking at, boy?"

In the mud something twinkling. Picked it up and wiped it around. Gold! Carter wouldn't look the same without his tooth.

"That belongs to us. It's ours."

"I'm no thief, boy. Here, take it. Come on. Take it."

The kid hanging back, uncertain if he can trust me.

"Come on! I'm not going to eat you up."

Springing forward like a whirlwind, the boy snatched up his father's gold, sunk his teeth into my hand, and fled into the night.

"You tricky little bastard," I shouted, roaring with laughter. Spitting image of the old man. At least he doesn't waste his time praying for him. It was more than I could say for myself at that age.

6

That night. Wound up the Elgin and propped it up against the base of the lamp on my night table. Its silver case orange in the orange light. Sat down on the high four-poster, springs whining under me, and unlaced my work shoes. Feeling unusually tired with wild, tangled thoughts unraveling in my brain. Of Newfield growing old without a son and heir. Someone to collect his chipped and broken teeth regardless. Out of love. When the going got rough in the dust and swirl of that last busy moving day. To hang up on the wall over the fireplace and point to with pride and say *that's my father. Sat down to life like a feast. Poor bastard, bit off more than he could chew.* Boxers and travelers know. The legs go first. Can't bear them with fat legs and fat thighs and a fanny moving down Main Street that resembles two watermelons being rubbed together slow. For long last as well as looks give him the sleek greyhounds every time. And for Alma, tan oxfords. *No, I'm afraid they are not tan. They are bone. Your salesman is quite right, sir. Look tan to me. I'm sorry, sir. Bone is not straw and bone is not wheat and bone is not moth and bone is not sand*

and they are DEFINITELY bone. THESE are tan.
Grabbed both of them by the throat, one in each hand, and told them to quit horsing around. Police sirens! Struggling to tear a hole in the earth and escape when death sneaks up and pushes him out from behind. To Acapulco for a swim with Merle Oberon. To Malta for a peek at Napoleon's bedroom. To San Francisco for a look at a Chinatown the Chinese don't know about. With opium in the won ton and everything sub gum. The digestion not what it used to be but still good, thank God. Appetite of a rhinoceros, bowels like Old Faithful, and calluses on his hands and feet like the steel plates on a tank. Clanking along flat out up Balch Hill aching for the things you have as much as those you don't. A sure sign of the beginning. Of the end. As usual pulling off her clothes in the corner with her back turned. Shutting him out. Thirty-two years of marriage and still shy as a virgin. With many secrets of personal hygiene. Ashamed of her veins, her bones, her hair, her breasts and hiding old columns of Dr. Dalrymple in the bottom of her bureau drawer where his missing Eveready Clip-On Pencil Flashlight should have been. Who promises to blow them up as big as zeppelins with silicone, paraffin, beeswax, spun glass, shellac. What do you need him for, Alma? Has anyone ever complained? But she feeling nothing she had was good enough for him. Nothing she did. Nothing bore. Nothing. All of which wasn't the case. Married, you don't climb into bed with a microscope or T-square the corners for straight and square. Labored over until perfect, the cocker spaniels cut into the sides with a woodburner, and carried carefully to Mr. Morton at the front of the room. Who held up the bookcase for the whole class to see. And them barking and clapping and flopping over one another like seals. *I've had enough*

of your tomfoolery, Newfield. Don't let this happen again.
But of course it did. I forgive you, Alma.

Pulling her blue flannel nightie over her head and telling me something. A whole little speech with anxious eyes and quivering lips and the cheek resting lightly on her fingertips. Maybe my mind is up for renewal and I haven't been notified yet. A good night's sleep is all that's needed. My ears are yours, Alma, what's on your mind.

"No, I can't, Orin. I can't forgive you."

"Forgive me what?"

"What I said."

"OK." Emptied my pockets out on top of the bureau and discovered the pork. Didn't have the energy to fetch it into the kitchen over the cold floorboards. Husbanding my strength for Alma. Wouldn't be right to disappoint her tonight when she's feeling so down, might get the idea she's not wanted. Particularly dangerous during the holiday season when emotions run high, to judge by Miss Ellsworth. As a married man you have responsibilities, Newfield. Do your duty. Overalls neatly hung up, underwear in the laundry bag, and stark naked into bed. A frigid kiss on the rump from the sheet. Sniffed my armpits and they smelled of sour milk. Could be worse. Ready and waiting, Alma. "What did you say?"

"Why did you do it, Orin? He's so thin and small. You might have killed him."

"I should have."

"An old man. Less than half your size. With a wife and children to support."

"He spilled my milk."

"It's only milk."

"TWO CANS!"

"How many cans equal a life? Tell me that, Orin. How many?'

"I don't like the sound of your arithmetic."

"It's not as if we were poor and needed—"

"Enough of this crooked thinking! I've worked hard for everything I've got and no drunken sonofabitch is going to dribble it away."

"You've been rough, Orin, but never cruel. To beat up on that poor old man for only making a small mistake. And then to call him names right in front of his whole family. I don't see how I'll ever be able to look any of them in the face again."

"You won't have to. Soon as he's well enough to crawl out of bed I'm firing him."

"You can't."

"Watch me."

"But you can't. Not after what you've done to him. You have an obligation."

"Right. Wash up and come to bed. But no more about Carter. *No* more."

She took the hint, not another peep out of her. Only her sad eyes touching on everything in the room but me. A queer notion of punishment. And what had I done? Advised Carter not to work, warned him to be careful, and in the end administered justice. Fair and square, though it hadn't sounded that way. Nowadays bad packaging and even the truth looks dingy. I'm no salesman, Alma. Spying the pork, she picks it up and goes out in silence to the kitchen. Refrigerator door slams. Suddenly playing the tidy housekeeper, putting me in my place. Ho! Ho! On the other hand, could be afraid of rats in the night. I take it back, Alma. No offense.

"Well, aren't you coming to bed?"

"In a minute," she says, and disappears into the bathroom.

Rolled over on her side of the bed to warm up the

sheet before she got in. It's the little touches that win a woman's heart. Make her feel right at home, as welcome as a low bacteria count. And all nice and cozy. No need to leave a calling card, she'll know who to thank. Most grateful woman in the world. Wonderfully grateful. So what the hell's keeping her. Quiet as a cemetery in there. Called to check on her well-being, see that she didn't faint and fall into the crapper. In a minute, in a minute. Ten past my bedtime already. But at least now there were signs of life, action. Flushing. Splashing. Submarine gurgles. The clinking of bottles. Conspiring with her medicine chest. Putnam's annex. Heavy with capsules, tablets, syrups, and salves, secrets from the shrine of health. And all the showy colors of the medical rainbow. Only difference between ours and the main branch in town is that it's got canes and crutches hanging from the walls for the tourists. Catholics like that sort of thing.

Growing twitchy in the waiting room, a bit of light reading called for. Leaned across to Alma's night table and dusted off the little cockers. Lovely job of tracing despite academic slander. The bookcase filled with herbs, mushrooms, God, and volume one of the *Encyclopedia Americana*. Felt in the mood for volume one tonight, sample a few more pages. Nothing like a big book to help settle you down. Good for thumbing. And there's Archimedes with his lever and his laws and his screw. Nice likeness. A long enough pole and I could move the world too. Set it on its ear. Straighten things out once and for all and get honorable mention under the N's to boot. Newfield's lever. Very interesting but probably not for children. Sensed that I was a good deal calmer already. If I had known how useful A was going to turn out, I might have reconsidered and let Alma have the whole alphabet. But A seemed to keep her busy. Cost enough,

God knows. And since it's on my mind, I might as well put in here how she came by it. While I'm waiting, so to speak.

It was just around Christmas last year if I recall correctly. As I say, a dangerous time of waste and warpage. That this traveling gangster knocks on the door with a briefcase and manner, both uncommonly smooth. Are you the lady of this handsome piece of real estate, asks the smoothie. I am, says the lady of the house.

T.G.: And, of course, you're a reader. I can tell from those clear blue clever eyes of yours.

L.O.T.H.: They're hazel. What is it you want? I'm very busy just now.

T.G.: But you do enjoy reading, don't you?

L.O.T.H.: I know how, if that's what you mean.

T.G.: Congratulations, madam. I can't tell you how happy I am for you. I mean *really* happy, but how can you stand there so calmly? Don't you realize what you've just won? You lucky lady.

L.O.T.H.: What?

T.G.: Because of your position in the community and because we hope that you will tell others of our product, my company is prepared at this time to present you with an outright gift of a ten percent reduction in the price of a complete set of the *Encyclopedia Americana,* the foremost book of its kind in the world. More than one thousand pages in each volume and twice the

	number of illustrations of our nearest competitor. Now isn't that something?
L.O.T.H.:	Yes it is. Good-bye.
T.G.:	And with your order we intend to give you absolutely free and at no additional charge a set of our award-winning *Junior American Wonder Book* for the children.
L.O.T.H.:	We don't have any. Kindly remove your shoe from the door.
T.G.:	No kiddies! Surely a temporary condition. If you've read your Bible you know that even Abraham's wife was a trifle slow at first. And you're still decades away from ninety, madam. There's no reason to give up prematurely.
L.O.T.H.:	That's true what you say. About Sarah I mean.
T.G.:	Of course it is. And what are you going to do when the little ones, clustering around you and clutching at your apron, begin asking the questions that you can't answer? And slowly fall behind their classmates at school? And fail to win admittance to the college of their choice? And never realize the full potential of their God-given gifts? I ask you, what are you going to do?
L.O.T.H.:	Why that sounds awful.
T.G.:	But with the *Junior American Wonder Book* all that need never happen.
L.O.T.H.:	I really don't think—
T.G.:	It's never too early to plan. And believe

	me, I say this sincerely, your children will bless you for it.
L.O.T.H.:	They will?
T.G.:	Unfortunately, I don't have the *Wonder Book* with me to show you. But here. Take this copy of the *Americana*. Hold it in your hands. That's right, feel the genuine cloth binding. Run your fingers over the immaculate headband. Leaf through the thousand and one pages of quality paper. Quite an experience, isn't it?
L.O.T.H.:	How much is it?
T.G.:	We won't even talk about that. Your contract will arrive in the mail shortly. But I *will* need a little something right now in the way of a down payment. Say thirty dollars.
L.O.T.H.:	That's a lot of money.
T.G.:	Please. Do me a favor and keep my sample copy of volume one. I can see how attached you've grown to it already.
L.O.T.H.:	It does look interesting.
T.G.:	A check is perfectly acceptable.
L.O.T.H.:	My husband signs all the checks.
T.G.:	Cash will do nicely. And congratulations again, madam. You've made a wise decision.

Scoured the countryside for him, a hammer on the seat beside me. Planned to drive him into the ground like a stake. I wasn't about to let evil get the idea it was running the whole show. Financed by Newfield money. But it seemed he had moved on to a new territory and Alma's savings with him. You had to give him credit though. A slick operator, he knew his business. Someone was rapping at the window. Odd hour for callers. Put the lid down on Archimedes, pulled on my drawers, and went to investigate. YEEEOWWWW! Nothing serious. Never especially fond of that toe anyway. Nice ring to the instrument.

"Orin! What happened?"

"Nothing. Nothing. Are you planning to spend the night in there?"

"Almost finished."

The family heirloom still ringing. More music than it's produced in years. A present from my mother-in-law just before she kicked off. The old girl didn't have much but truly wanted to be remembered by her children. Very natural, I can understand that. She stripped off the ivory from the keys and gave Alma the black notes and Ben the white. Crazy about her daughter. All right, hold your horses, I'm coming.

Threw up the sash and peered into the night. Narrowly missed getting smacked in the kisser. The limbs from the apple tree in front of the window thrashing about like gypsies. Wrung the neck of three guilty parties, a bit of instant pruning, and thought that should do it. Besides it's good for the tree, stimulates growth. Ah, those autumn apples! Two-handers, as big as bowling balls and as meaty as chicken. I could have one right now. Better close the window before I catch pneumonia. Cold as a witch's tit out there. Blowing up a storm and no mistake. It did me good to think of the herd bedded down inside all snug for the night, keeping their moos warm. Ducked my head under the quilt and tried to do as well for myself. Haven't tented out like this since I was a kid playing

71

hooky with my pecker. Feet too large for this sort of crap now, sticking out like twin masts of a sunken clipper. Come on already, Alma. I can't stay up forever. There's work to be done tomorrow and no help for it. Someone pouring ice water on my toes! It's sad but true, as I've so often remarked to myself when a shade weary, there's no place to hide for a big man.

Who the hell's the wise guy? The window open and the chintz curtains snapping in the gusts. Goddamnit, what's the matter with me? Didn't I shut that thing? Threw off the covers and leaped out of bed, giving a wide berth to the piano this time. Always try to profit from experience is my motto. Grabbed ahold of the window and about to slam it shut when I notice someone on the other side looking in at me with a nasty squint. Must be near-sighted I figured. That coat. I'd know it anywhere, but it took a few seconds to dope out who was wearing it because the hat was a stranger. Resembled a World War I aviator's helmet, without goggles. But it was Miss Ellsworth's sister, Precosia, all right, three times the size of the other one and with as many more chins. Lost some weight since the last time I saw her but still cut quite an impressive figure. Last person in the world I expected to see out there considering she's been such a homebody of late. It occurred to me that maybe the sisters had but one coat between them and that's why Precosia had kept in these past three years. Got to hand it to those girls, they knew how to stretch a dollar.

"Good to see you again, Miss Ellsworth."

"You're destined for hell anyway, Newfield," she announced in a commanding voice. "I advise you to sign up without delay."

"But isn't it a little late for visiting?"

"I doubt it. Orientals regard sleep as a sensual delight, but you Puritans can hardly close your eyes without feeling guilty."

No question about it, she's a queer one. Played the violin in the town orchestra until one night at a performance in the school auditorium her music got away from her. Rose straight up off her stand and floated to the footlights. Hung in the middle of the air like Ezekiel's wheel according to reports. And her hustling after it and knocking over other people's music stands, playing her heart out all the way, the tears streaming down her cheeks. "The Blue Danube." They say she never missed a note. Got the reputation of a witch after that, but it's all a lot of nonsense. Farnum didn't know a solo from a snake in the grass. Staring at me with her eyes wild and glittering. A little nuts, that's all. Walking all the way out here from town on a night like this just to exchange pleasantries. Maybe she flew. I'd like to see the broomstick that could get that load off the ground.

"There's a touch of air trickling in, Miss Ellsworth, and I've got a busy day tomorrow. What's on your mind?"

"Yes, the wind's from the north. And no moon. I trust you know what that means."

"Snow and shoveling most likely."

"Be serious, Newfield! The meeting is scheduled for tonight. Ideal conditions for a merry get-together. The usual time."

"When's that?"

"Midnight, naturally. Everybody will be there and we'll be expecting you."

"In the woods I suppose."

"Don't be silly. At my house. Reverend Peaselee is especially anxious that you be there."

"Him, too! Told him this afternoon I couldn't make it."

"Things have changed since then. We've heard what you did to Carter. You need our help now. Of course you'll have to sign the register first, but that's only a formality."

"In blood?"

"Ballpoint will be sufficient."

"Much obliged, but you could have saved yourself the trip. I'm not a joiner."

"Everyone's a joiner, Newfield. Everyone. The news will be all over town by morning. We'll see how you feel about matters then. Sooner or later you'll need our help. We've waited a long time to get you. We can wait a little longer."

"Don't hold your breath," I advised her, frozen through and tired of humoring the old bag. Grieved though to see how far Miss Ellsworth had taken this witch business to heart. Seems as if some people will believe most anything they're told. No resistance. Poor old lady, batty as a barn loft.

"Who's there, Orin?" Alma whispering anxiously. The bathroom door was open a crack and her eye glued to it in alarm.

"Miss Ellsworth. Precosia Ellsworth."

"Precosia Ellsworth!" She couldn't believe her ears. Amazed, she stepped from behind the door to have a look for herself.

Maybe she's a witch at that, sprung Alma from the can. "Better put on your robe. It's chilly over here."

"Why didn't you ask Miss Ellsworth to come in?" Ignoring the cold, Alma leaned out the window, smiling as if she was overjoyed to have some company. Annoyed me to see such breakneck enthusiasm for a relative stranger.

Probably could use a few friends. "Where is she? There's nobody here."

Pulled her away and stuck my head out, the wind whistling past my ears. Too dark to see much beyond the light cast from the house, but she was gone all right. Wonderfully slippery for a stout lady. "She said she was in a hurry," I explained, not wanting Alma to feel rejected. And closed the window. And locked it this time.

"Couldn't wait I suppose."

"I didn't hear Ben," said Alma, giving me this peculiar look as I climbed into bed.

That's true. Hadn't noticed that before. "Must be off chasing skunks."

"He always barks at visitors, Orin." Nervously fingering the faded blue ribbon at the top of her nightgown.

"Maybe he's got laryngitis."

She came over and sat down beside me on the bed, her lips trembling. "Aren't you feeling well, daddy?"

"What are you driving at?"

"I don't know," she mumbled evasively.

Before I knew what was happening her arms were tight around my neck and she was telling me not to worry. Everything would be all right. If we could only get out of Farnum and start fresh somewhere else. Appeared so genuinely concerned about my welfare that I began to get upset. My head muddled. Teeth chattering as if I was still in front of the open window, goose pimples in the crotch. And outside, under the windowsill, the ground might be as smooth as a dance floor. Try to explain that to the medical profession. She's a sneak, Doctor, carries her footprints with her in a plastic bag. Maybe I do have muddy water on the brain. No. At fifty-seven it's not likely. Shape up, Newfield, you're in your

75

prime. Probably only a chill and they're putting you away in a padded cell. Less wife, less farm, less everything. Over my dead body.

"Can't we, daddy? Can't we get out of here? Sell everything and leave? We won't lose much."

"Over my dead body. Get into bed," I ordered her, and felt much improved putting everything back under my thumb.

Sulking, she didn't even say thank you for the warm sheet. Just pulled the covers up and turned her back on me. Disgusting. I won't hear of it, Alma. That way's for cattle. Put my hand gently on her shoulder to remind her which side I was on. In case she had forgotten. Make a decent woman out of her.

"I'm tired, Orin."

"So am I, honey. But it won't take a minute."

"Orin, please. I'm tired."

Refused to be daunted. Refused to take the easy way out when I knew she didn't really mean a word of it. Patience and consideration the order of the day. After a lifetime of loyalty, she has a right to expect something between her legs besides rashes. Show her that you love her, Newfield. Can't shirk your obligations at this stage of the game. From the night table drawer I took an Arabian Knight and covered the territory. Mohammed's revenge on Newfield. And the Pope. Everybody making sacrifices for what they believe in. It's not your fault, honey. Things change. Times change. Nine thirty-seven. And off with the light.

Where are you, Alma? Under her flannel the smell of brown soap and pot roast. Her ribs a xylophone and her hips no bigger than a weasel's. Pared down by time, poor thing. But still plenty of room where it counts. Our shadows squeaking against one another in the dark.

Sounding better than it feels. How I hate these damn things! Like wearing a pair of sneakers to go swimming. And missing the touch of the smooth packed sand at the bottom. Ah, the wholesome, natural couplings of my youth! The way it was on our honeymoon when we left Farnum for one day and lay skin to skin, tickling each other's fancy unconditionally. At the Hotel Coolidge in White River Junction. A wonderful place opposite the railroad station with a brown lobby and potted ferns that looked almost real. The name painted on the window outside in big letters that cast their shadow on the face of the only guest in sight, a rumpled old man dozing in a high-backed chair. Took him for a traveling salesman waiting to make connections. The Coolidge very popular with salesmen so you knew it had to be good. And genteelly quiet downstairs, but in the room next to ours on the second floor all hell was breaking loose. She giggling and he panting and Alma and I listening to them in stunned silence with our clothes off. Damned if they weren't newlyweds, too. Chasing one another around the room half the night, knocking over furniture and squealing hysterically. And me thinking then that was the way you do it. And all the while both of us getting more and more excited. Hotter and hotter. Until aching, I ran headlong at her expecting her to bolt but she didn't move. Only stood there. Arms wide open. Smiling me on with her eyes.

Next morning we waited hand in hand on the station platform and watched the Montreal-to-Boston express go by filled with well-dressed people. Then walked over and got on our bus. Hard seats and a bum transmission but it didn't make any difference. We stayed close and never noticed. Gears grinding. Bumping and backfiring. Banging together. All the way home.

I groped for the light and switched it on. Alma lying on her back like rigor mortis, her eyes wide open and a million miles away.

"It could save us, Orin." She spoke softly, staring at the ceiling.

Peaselee said the faithful husband learns it's a joy to love. Now I know. It's a joy to love. Nine thirty-nine and a half. Two minutes and thirty seconds. You can't do much better than that I imagine. Tried to wind up the Elgin and realized that I had done it already. Must be tired. I'll have to take care of everything myself tomorrow. Best get up a little early. There's snow in the air for sure.

7

At 4 A.M. breakfast is an athletic meal with no conversational frills. But at that hour I couldn't expect her to get up and make mine, so I crept silently out of bed and got dressed in the kitchen. Good-as-gold Alma, snoring her blues away inside. Let her sleep it off or she'll come apart at the seams. The penalty for trying to foot the bill for the world's misfortunes. Requires a little of my strength of purpose to set her straight. Buttoned up my mackinaw and stuffed a last thick slice of bread dipped in bacon fat into my mouth, licking the juice from my lips. Helps to keep the chill out. Delicious. Put on my gloves and taking the milk pitcher along to fill up before coming back, I closed the door softly behind me. Still pitch-black outside with no sign of the dawn and an eerie silence. Not even the wind now. Newfield feeling like the only man left alive on the planet. Civilization could probably do worse as far as that goes. For example, Carter. At least I've got standards and if success is the test of morality, I pass. Stepping off the porch into more than a foot of snow and it's still falling. Big juicy flakes coming straight down out of the sky and whacking the ground soundlessly. Stuck out my tongue the way I used to do when I was a kid and swallowed them down, sampling the day. Pure and promising. Snow meant work now, but with luck there'd be a slim runoff in the spring. Like most things, it wasn't all bad. A shame you couldn't say the same for people. As I trudged through the drifts to the barn, Ben came out of nowhere and plowed along beside me. Brushed the smudge of flakes off his muzzle and patted him.

By the time I had finished the milking, dug out the barn, and cleared the driveway behind it to the milk house, it was already well past eight o'clock of a dark, mean, broken-backed day. A sheet of steel stretched across the sky now and the snow still falling. The radio calling for two to three feet of it and no let-up in sight. Began to concern myself about Dutcher getting in to make his pickup when he finally shows up some two hours late, fur-wrapped and his mouth going a mile a minute to make up for lost time.

"Looks like we've got ourselves a little winter for a change. First big one of the season and it has to come right after a holiday when there's twice as much to load. Won't be so bad at that if the damn local plows would do the kind of job the state does on Five. Clean as my wallet all the way down from St. Johnsbury. And if you think that ain't clean after yesterday you've got another think coming. It seems as if Christmas gets worse every year. Had to buy presents for everybody and his cousin, but I guess it's worth it. The wife gave me this here jacket I'm wearing. Nice, eh? It sure comes in handy on a day like this. Practical, too. It's reversible and one pull on this zipper under here and the fur collar comes right off depending on the season. Did you see the zipper?

Anyway, it's a nice warm jacket. I like it. Morning, Mr. Newfield."

"You should have turned your truck up on the road and backed it in. Didn't you hear me hollering at you?"

"I saw you waving, but you can't hear a thing in there with the windows closed and the heater on and the wipers going. Nothing to worry about though. When I throw those gears into reverse, I could pull a dinosaur out of a tar pit."

Grunted and made for the milk house. Him strutting after me in his fur coat and high laced boots with the tops of his red woolen socks showing. The way they wear them in St. Johnsbury, no doubt. Quite the city dandy. And nosy, too.

"Where's Roy?" he wanted to know, as we started loading the cans in his truck.

"Met with an accident," I told him, which was the truth strictly speaking. "Careful with that one. The top's loose."

"Sorry to hear that. He sure is a funny old guy. Nothing serious, I hope."

"No. Nothing worth mentioning."

"I can't say I miss his help loading, but he sure as hell can tell a good story. You should hear some of the ones he tells about his wife. Wow!"

Expect he's told you a few about me, too, the sonofabitch.

"And dirty jokes! He knows them all. I'd give my left nut to be able to tell a joke the way that man can."

"Watch what you're doing there."

"I've got it." Pulling the rope out from under the tilting can, Dutcher straightened it out and came back to the tailgate for the next one. "He sure is full of beans for a

81

guy his age. Why he must be sixty-five at least. And still chasing after the young ones. A couple of weeks ago he was saying that the father of some kid in town wanted to shoot him for messing around with her. It sounded like bragging to me, but then again he's got a way with him. What do you think, Mr. Newfield?"

"I wouldn't know."

"You've got to hand it to him, that devil! Doesn't miss a trick. He knows how to live all right."

Didn't care to encourage the idiot any further, so I kept my trap shut. But I couldn't see that it made any difference to Dutcher. He hardly noticed. Running off at the mouth like an auctioneer with a million lots to sell and all junk.

"That's the last of them," I reported, after a final look around in the milk house.

"You really can toss those cans, Mr. Newfield. I thought it would take me twice as long when I saw what you had in there." Jumping down, he raised the tailgate and chained it. "See you tomorrow," he promised, and swung up into the cab of his truck as if it was some kind of achievement. The engine warming up and him removing his canvas gloves and putting on black leather ones for driving. Primping for the romance of the open road. From his toes to his fingertips, Dutcher was all style. The phony. Rolling down his window to say something as he started to back out. "Tell Roy I hope he feels better," he called.

"Look where you're going. Straighten it out."

I was watching his rear wheels and knew what was coming before it had even begun to happen.

"Damnit, straighten your wheels out!" I screamed, motioning frantically. Smiling and waving back, he ran his truck straight off the driveway into a drift and stalled. Started up again and gunned his engine, the wheels spinning and kicking a shower of snow into the air. Continued to hammer away at the gas pedal digging a deeper and deeper hole full of the smell of burning rubber. Finally gave up and got down, coming back to where I was to have a look. The truck wedged in up to its axle, the tires resting in crescent-shaped pits.

"In tighter than a bull's cock," he admitted good-humoredly. "I'd say it's there to stay." He glanced across to the shed by the silos. "Sorry to have to trouble you, Mr. Newfield, but would you mind giving me a tug with one of your tractors over there? I've got that rope in the back we can use."

Sorry to trouble you, Mr. Newfield. That's a good one. Thought I'd split my sides holding in the laughter. You couldn't care less, Dutcher. Imposing on others to pay for your own mistakes. Filching from the suckers and expecting to be patted on the head for living. Thinks I'm his mother. I wouldn't lift a finger to help him if my milk wasn't on the back of that truck. A blowhard without the brains to be decently ashamed of himself. No humility. It's gone out of fashion with chamber pots.

"Get in and put it in low. I'll push you forward."

"You'll push me!"

"That's what I said."

"By yourself?"

"Don't see anybody else around here, do you?"

It took the simpleton a while to digest my message. Looking me over as if he can't decide whether there's something seriously the matter with me or I'm kidding. When at last it dawns on him that I mean business, he shakes his head in amazement. Stalling for time while he tries to think of arguments against it, his mind laboring like a sledge hammer. Touched by Dutcher's concern, but stealing lollipops from babies is more in his line. Doesn't want anything to happen to me out of the goodness of his heart. Afraid I might sue.

"Don't get me wrong, Mr. Newfield. I don't mean to take anything away from you. You're a strong man. Maybe the strongest I've ever seen . . ."

Buttering me up, the imbecile.

". . . but the tare alone on this truck is five tons, and you can see for yourself it's full to the brim. You're not even going to budge it. No one could."

"Just get up there and don't race the engine. That's all you've got to worry about. Feed the gas slow and steady. We'll rock it out."

Dutcher shrugged his shoulders. "Have it your way," he said, giving up and hiking back to his cab. "Can't hurt to try, I suppose."

Showed more sense than I gave him credit for. Digging the toes of my boots into the snow, a firm foundation for the long thigh muscles that'll turn the trick, and pressing my hands and right shoulder up against the tailgate. Same form as always. It won't be the first time I've pushed something this big out of a hole. Nothing like experience for giving a man confidence.

"Dutcher!"

"Are you ready, Mr. Newfield?"

"OK, let it in slow now. Hear me, Dutcher? *Slow*."

He did what he was told. And Newfield straining legs and back and feeling the rhythm of the truck through every nerve in his body like a parade, easing off as it dropped back and pouring it on with the forward rock. Biding his time as the momentum built. Learning patience from dead weight. A seesaw motion, inching closer to the lip of the crescent with every heave. Newfield saving something in reserve for the home stretch when the wheels would crest the top, hang there, and not roll back. After that it's all clear sailing, cardinoo and blue skies. Snow inside my boots but feeling great. Damn colds and old age, I don't have time for them. Only two more falls now, three at the most . . . Suddenly the dumb jackass up front hits the gas and the truck skids sideways. Digs another crater. Stomping on the pedal when he should have been using a feather duster and nearly knocking me on my ass. Wasting my youth in the snow.

"Hold it!" I thundered. Clumping up to the front and wondering why it is there's always somebody else in the picture you have to depend on. Why, Newfield, why this uncanny knack for getting on teams? Mediocrities dragging you down with fumbles and interceptions. If there was only some way to do it all yourself. Drive and push at the same time. That'll bear some thinking, but meanwhile there's Dutcher. Probably so excited at the forward motion he couldn't control himself.

"Man, O man! Wasn't that ever something! You really had us going there for a minute, Mr. Newfield. But you see," he explained, the voice of reason, "it can't be done."

"What the hell's wrong with you, Dutcher? I said slow and I meant slow. I'm not straining my balls back there for pleasure. All right," I snapped, "let's try it again."

Went back and set myself against the tailgate once more. Concentrating like a shotputter. Nothing possible without willpower, but with it you could move a milk truck. Turning on my head full blast, primed with threats and promises, giving it all I've got. Plus a dash more to compensate for the numbskull. Not even thinking about my merchandise any longer, it was the principle of the thing. I don't lose gracefully.

"OK, easy does it. Go ahead."

Started slow and gradually picked up the pace. Rocking in unison, with a hatred for the damn thing that did my heart good. Grunting. Sweating. My aching shoulder wedged in its gut and my hands numb with the pressure. But less than halfway home when there's a snap at the knee and my bum leg buckles, knocking me on my can. The truck sliding back on top of me. Spun away. Just in time to avoid a nasty squashing. A close call. Sitting in the snow and freezing my ass off while mulling this truck situation over. "You lousy, dented, rust-pocked, slippery, broken-down motherfucker," I mused. Cursing myself slowly back into shape, but it wasn't easy. In fact, it took much longer than the knee. Clicked it into place without difficulty and dragged myself up. Snow in my mouth, my nose, my ears, and a few flakes trickling down into the heart. Brushing off the places I could get at when Dutcher comes running up, his face a national emergency.

"Jesus! What happened, Mr. Newfield? Are you OK? You look kind of pale."

"I'll do."

"What's wrong with your hand there? Is that blood?"

"Nothing," I said. The palm of my gray glove dyed reddish-brown. The wool soaking up most of it but a few bright red drops staining the snow. Out of place like the tears of pirates. "It's nothing."

"It looks like something to me. I bet you caught it on the tailgate chain."

"I suppose."

"Wait a minute. Hold on. I've got some Band-Aids up front."

Wonder it's not both hands, but there's no rush. This is only the day after Christmas. I've got till Easter for that.

"Here we are," said Dutcher breathlessly, running up with this small white can in his hand. "Let me see it." He was bending over, pawing at my wrist for some reason.

"What are you up to? Get the hell off, Dutcher." Brushed him aside and he stumbled back a yard or so, a dumber expression on his face than any man has a right to and live.

"The Band-Aids, Mr. Newfield. I only . . ."

"It's nothing I told you."

Knew what I had to do and it left a sour taste in the pit of my stomach. Feeling gloomier than the day as I went to get the tractor. On cold, dejected feet and all of the juice drained out of my legs. The aches and pains of old age settling in the bones like cancer. Brought around the tractor and Dutcher hitched it up to his front axle. One tug and the truck came away easier than a baby tooth. Depressed me no end. Haven't felt so bad in years.

"Thanks much, Mr. Newfield," called Dutcher, sitting high and dry up on the turnpike, his truck pointing toward town. "Sorry to have caused you so much trouble."

"Just a minute." Climbed down from the tractor and walked up to him. "Did you give me a receipt for the milk?"

"No, come to think of it I guess not. Sorry about that." Opened the metal covers of his receipt book and began scribbling. "It must have slipped my mind because I'm so used to giving it to Roy."

I'll bet you are. Slipshod or crafty, it makes no difference. They're all alike.

"Here you are. See you tomorrow, Mr. Newfield. And

I'd take care of that hand soon if I were you. You don't want an infection."

"Watch where you're driving."

I returned the tractor to the shed and on my way to the barn tripped over a pail buried in the snow. No need to ask who left that lying around. The old bastard trying to get back at me. Dumped the snow out of it and took the pail inside, feeling almost as empty myself. Thinking there was a day when I could have done it. When it wouldn't have mattered who was behind the wheel. When sooner than quit I'd have put that truck on my back and carried it out. By myself. Don't like the sound of this, Newfield. Don't care for it at all. In general you're not a backward-looking man. A sure sign of mortality. And the hand throbbing now. Tempted to look at it, but there was no sense in peeling off the glove just to satisfy idle curiosity and ruin a good clot. That's a little more like. Push on.

Busied myself by collecting the spilled grain and tidying up the stalls. Glumly battling the bacteria. The herd chomping away to cheer me up. Stroking the head of the one nearest me in gratitude when I heard a car coming up the road. "One of the widow's many admirers," I explained to her. "Not even a blizzard can cut down on attendance at the whorehouse." Shocked to discover it was Inga I was talking to, flirting with danger. She'd never let me pat her dome before. Must have been making an exception considering the way I felt. Wonderfully understanding animals, cows.

Through the window I could see the car go by the barn, but instead of continuing on it pulled off the road, stopping in front of the Carter house. It was Whiting's big Oldsmobile with its silver M.D. medallion bolted to the rear bumper. Watched his fur hat and galoshes pass in through the door and it was over an hour before he reappeared, whispering something to the missus on the threshold. A lot of fuss about nothing. Waited for him to leave before coming out and going back for lunch. Didn't want to run into him. Might think I was nosing around when I couldn't care less.

Putnam was next, arriving after lunch. I had just put away a loaf of French toast, changed into dry socks, and poured half a bottle of peroxide over the gash in my hand and was feeling considerably refreshed when the old man himself comes tearing along behind the wheel of his jeep, the bell on the bonnet ringing bloody murder. Only jeep I ever heard of that thinks it's an ambulance. Makes no difference whether they're hauling Ex-lax or penicillin, every Putnam delivery a crisis. But it wasn't every day that the old man stepped out from behind his two glass urns filled with red and blue and took the wheel himself. And in a storm to boot. Seemed like a whole lot of stir for a lousy case of dt's and a few minor lumps and bruises. It was beyond me.

After Putnam went jingling off, the cars started coming thick and fast. All that day and on into the next without a letup. A regular convention next door. Amanda Ellsworth was among the early arrivals, tooling up in the family coat. From the rear of her jalopy she brought out a steaming white tureen and carried it in like a gift of the Magi. Split pea was her specialty. A notorious do-gooder, even worse than Alma in that department. Then came Mrs. Otis in her station wagon. Not satisfied to leave Carter's bills by the roadside as usual, she had to present them in person this time. Collecting all of the latest tidbits so that she could hand them out along with the mail to her other customers on the route. Around about dusk Hatch's two-tone Studebaker put in an appearance. The self-styled mayor of Farnum come to aid an ailing constituent. Official sympathy oozing out of the janitor's mug even though he thought less of Carter than a mildewed turd. Damned hypocrite, trying to embarrass me. The same went for Russell.

The Senator came the next morning in a cloud of smoke after the snow tapered off and winter had snapped the lid down on Farnum. Distinguished straight back. Distinguished long gray hair. Distinguished huffing and puffing. His ears and cheeks pink with the cold, glowing like someone about to sit down to a banquet. Dropping by to sample the scandal. With a little time on his hands now that the election was over. Do well to spend some of it on his own farm, a miserable operation. It's a sad story. The year Alma and I got married Russell was sent to Montpelier for a single term. That was thirty-two years ago, and since then every two years faithfully packing his bags to be ready when the party calls him out of retirement. But the call never comes. His wife cautioned not to plant late-bloomers just in case. Couldn't take it when I told him he had no more chance of being returned to the State House than a Jew-black Mongoloid idiot. If he didn't want to know, why the hell did he ask?

And the pilgrims kept coming. Peaselee and the rest to view the martyr but I stopped paying attention to them after a while. Wouldn't give them the satisfaction. The whole goddamn town can come out here for all I care. Might learn something about the administering of justice. See that the resignation of my father and his father and his wasn't the entire Newfield story. Better yet, they could take Carter back with them, bag and baggage. Have him all to themselves and good riddance. Don't believe they'd care for that too much.

Digging into what counts and forgetting the traffic. The sudden freeze-up making everything twice as hard, not to mention the still tender hand and shoulder. Twenty-seven degrees registering on the barn door thermometer and the windows glazed over with thin patches of frost. Bathroom panes for the shy ones. I was heating the herd's drinking water to warm their bellies and keep their udders snug when a horrible thought crossed my mind. Namely, a cracked block. Broke out in a cold sweat, my heart falling to the floor and clinking like a tin earring. Across the road in the driveway where it had been all night, the new pickup truck was sitting helpless, freezing its radiator off. Where was the antifreeze to safeguard my investment? Blown clean out of my head by warm weather and rats and Carter. Trivia twisting Newfield's perspective, everything whittling him down to size. Really, a sensible fellow shouldn't be subject to these lapses. It wasn't like me.

Another trace of erosion beginning to creep in. Getting Newfield down. First his strength and then his memory and next . . . Who knows? His luck perhaps. A few mishaps putting all in doubt. Must a big man suffer for every inch above average? Would he be spared no indignity? Good questions but happily academic, the Ford kicking right over. Somewhat hoarse at first but it cleared up in no time, and so did I. Alma's Plymouth wasn't a problem because there at least I had taken precautions. Hadn't bothered to drain it out in the spring. Foolish to throw good money after bad. Squander too much on plates for it every year as it is. The annual licensing racket, and the fee probably never getting beyond Boyle's pocket in the town clerk's office. Enough loss without adding

Prestone. The old wreck coughs and wheezes regardless, another layer of rust in the radiator wasn't going to hurt anything. If only Alma was like other wives and would volunteer to drive into town and pick up the antifreeze for the Ford. What could be simpler? With me busier than an anthill right now. But knowing how she felt about traveling over ice and snow, I couldn't bring myself to ask for any favors. Especially when she still held Carter against me. The wronged man condemned and the culprit gone scot-free.

"I've got to go into town on an errand," I informed her as I came in the door. Went straight to the bedroom and took out my money clip from the top drawer. "Do you want anything?" Paused on the way out and raised my earflaps to show her that it wasn't a hollow gesture. Although gravely maligned, Newfield was willing to bury the hatchet.

"No, everything's fine, Orin. You go ahead."

Her voice so bubbly that I had to look twice. Suppressed excitement coloring her up. A touch of red on her lips and a clean apron over her sweater. A decided improvement. What do you know about that! A change not for the worse. It mellowed me to contemplate the imminent return of Alma's animal spirits. In bed and elsewhere.

"I'll see you later."

"There's another one!" she sang out, hearing Ben's bark. "They just keep coming. Have you seen all the cars?"

"I'm not blind. What's that I smell?"

"I'm baking something inside."

"Smells good. Something for supper?"

"It's burning. I've got to turn the oven down. Be careful driving, Orin."

Alma troubling me. Suspiciously on the go. Suddenly

I lost my taste for all her new-found energy. "We don't owe them a goddamn thing," I roared. "I'm warning you. I don't want you going next door. Do you hear me, Alma? Stay away from them."

Alma stuck her head out of the kitchen door and waved. "Good-bye, daddy. Drive slowly."

8

But could I trust her to keep her word? A revolutionary thought. Alma always did what she was told but recent developments made me wonder. And charity her weak point, being a charter member of the It's Good to Give society. Like the rest of them, dignifying her private urge as a general truth. Plunging the knife in my back in the name of a higher loyalty. Oh the skullduggeries of misguided allegiance were enough to make your head swim! Newfield in torment, doubting even his own wife now. Her, too? Then who's left? Tell me, who? Don't rush me, I'm thinking. God was out of the question. Lost somewhere in the gap between divine justice and the real world. And man is a moot point. But Alma . . . No, I won't hear of it. Zoomed into Dan's parking lot once more confirmed in the faith. Until proven otherwise.

The lot was crowded with comings and goings, everyone refreshingly speeded up by the temperature. All except Roger. Bareheaded with fuzzy red muffs clamped over his ears, he slowly wended his way in and out of the cars, chipping the ice with a lackluster stroke. So lazy he wouldn't even step up the pace to keep himself warm.

I left the engine running as a precautionary measure and got out. The kid standing still now and watching me like the main event. Remarkable that he didn't have anything snotty to get off his chest as I went by. That's more like it, fatty. Learning a little respect for your elders. If not for his arm coming up every now and again, I'd say it was a coma.

The Magic Dollar was alive with misshapen customers, swollen to three times normal by the weather. The narrow aisles clogged with bulky coats on top of bulky sweaters. Snow tracked in from the outside turning to brown mush on the floor. Overheated as usual. Obliged to open the neck of my mackinaw to prevent suffocation. At the check-out counter, Penny was barely visible because of the crowd around her. No great loss there. Her cackle dancing above the hubbub like a drunken fiddler. The line simmering down at the sight of me and nudging one another. Orin Newfield himself, ladies and gentlemen. I've got nothing to hide. From rags to riches and all by his lonesome. It sets a man up to be known by his neighbors, have a reputation in the community. Couldn't do without it.

Up the far aisle where kids home from school were messing around in the candy bins and getting under foot. Too many holidays. No wonder they never learn anything. Do better to send them out to earn an honest living and see how tough it is. Pale yellow streams dribbling from their noses and falling in the jelly beans. Snot in the winter and maple syrup in the spring. I love Vermont, always something happening. "Cut that out," I advised them, and they scattered like scraps of paper. One brave customer peeking back at me from behind the Campbell soups with his tongue out. Kids never ceased to amaze me. No matter what they did it was always playland.

Ah, the very thing! A shelf full of Brand X antifreeze

in one-gallon cans. Let someone else pay for the Prestone advertising, I wasn't that stupid. And at LaBombard's they do you a favor by putting it in themselves and charge accordingly. I can open my own petcock, thank you. Read the label from beginning to end, even the tiniest words. Most informative. Nothing flowery or self-serving there like the labels of some other companies I could mention. Two gallons would bring it down below zero and that was that. A pleasantly secure feeling as I marched to the cash register, a can under each arm. Admiring glances from all sides for the captain of industry who knows the value of a dollar.

Let me tell you, waiting on a line is a sobering experience. It makes you think. Of all the other things you might be doing to some advantage. Logical enough next door in the post office or down the street at the courthouse because the government isn't equipped to deal with individuals. Prefers to stack you up in tens so it doesn't have to see you. No reason for a line in this place though. I call it a goddamn sloppy system with Penny handling all the work herself. Get that kid in here to do the packing and let him earn his money. A little efficiency won't hurt. Moving up at a snail's pace and every time I closed the gap between us, the young woman in front of me turning around. Putnam's black-eyed daughter looking up at me in awe and admiration. So wise so young. She knows a good thing when she sees it. Drawing away and squashing the people in front of her to get a better view. Down flowering rod, this isn't the place. Newfield nonchalantly turning his head, studying the breakfast cereals, giving her the seasoned, craggy profile. Struck by the unusually grim expression on her face. Debating whether a friendly goose was in order to break the ice. Something definitely called for with such a thoughtful, serious girl.

"Can't you hurry it up, Penny?" she asked in an irritable voice. "I'm in a hurry."

And just when I thought we were getting on so well. "I'm doing the best I can, Miss Putnam."

Had she detected a smudge of gas in the air that was ruining our relationship? Could it be that she thought I was staling the line with leakage? And women like rabbits, with their keen noses to make up for what they lacked in muscle, priding themselves on their ability to single out even the faintest scents. Took a deep breath to make certain of my innocence and all I could smell was roasted coffee and barbecued chicken. Don't worry, Miss Putnam, when I fart you'll hear about it. Nothing more than a misunderstanding here, I'm sure.

"Give me one of those," she told Penny who was packing away three cans of tuna fish at the moment. Taking the can Penny gave her, the girl dropped it into a barrel on the floor at the end of the counter. Now what the hell's that all about?

"Thank you, Miss Putnam," said Penny, handing her back her change. "Sorry to have held you up."

Her bundle in her arms, the girl gave me a parting glance drenched with significance, and as she left dropped a second can into the barrel for good measure.

"Ring them up," I told Penny, setting the antifreeze down on the counter. "I'll be right back." She was a clever little thing and no mistake. Retrieved her two cans from inside the stuffed barrel and stepped outside.

"Hold on," I called to her. "You forgot something."

"Forgot something?" She seemed confused, annoyed, a real actress.

"Here," I said, and put the cans into her bag. "You should be more careful next time."

For a second the girl's mouth hung slack in bewilderment and then she began to splutter and fume. "Take those back where you found them," she cried angrily. "You had no right. I paid for them. It's none of your affair. I can do what I want with my things."

"What's the matter with you?" She looked as if she was about to cry. *Now* what had I done wrong?

"Get out of my way," she screamed. "You may think you own some other people in this town but you don't own me."

Running back into the store, she fiercely returned the tuna fish to the barrel, and, her head high, snubbed me as I held the door open for her on the way out. It beat the hell out of me.

"Something wrong with her?" I asked Penny.

"I really couldn't say, Mr. Newfield. That will be one dollar and sixty-five cents for the antifreeze."

It wasn't fair to keep the other folks waiting, so shrugging her off, I reached for my money clip. The price seemed right. As I thumbed through the bills, a sign stapled to the side of the barrel caught my eye. First I'd seen of it. "HELP THE CARTERS" it read. Some gruesome prank.

"What's that all about?" I inquired, trying to control my temper. "The sign. *This*." I toed it with my boot.

"Oh, that!" said Penny surprised, as if she didn't know what I meant from the start.

"Well? What about it?"

"We heard about Mr. Carter's accident. The poor man! A fractured pelvis and three broken ribs. Mr. Russell and some others suggested we take up a collection for him here. Real neighborly of them, don't you think?"

"None of their goddamn business. He's *my* handyman, not theirs."

"They only wanted to help," she explained weakly.

99

It was Russell's idea of a joke, the bastard. And everyone on the line holding his breath, waiting to see what I would do, meanness in every hooded eye. They hated me. The lot of them, they hated me. That's OK with me, you sons of bitches, because it's mutual I assure you.

"Wait, Mr. Newfield! Your antifreeze," she screeched excitedly as I kicked open the door. "Don't you want your antifreeze, Mr. Newfield? Mr.—"

The door slammed down on her voice like a guillotine, cutting it off. My only regret that it wasn't her neck in the jamb. It would be a lifetime before I'd set foot in that place again. A den of thieves and rascals. Left the taste of vinegar in my mouth and the blood bubbling in the fingertips. Itching for a brick to toss through the plate glass but the best I could do on short notice was a crate of navel oranges. Dipped into the crate for a juicy one and held it in the palm of my hand. All the way up here from the Indian River without incident, a little farther wasn't going to hurt it.

Afraid to come out, the customers stood riveted behind the door, watching, their noses squashed up against the glass. A comical-looking crew. So eager to see me make a fool of myself that their tongues were hanging out. Hefted the orange two or three times judiciously just to make sure they got the message, and finally, while they gawked squirming in their boots, took a big juicy bite. Spitting out the skin, smacking my lips, and laughing in their ugly faces. Put the rest of the orange in my coat pocket and drove off in high spirits. They'd never know how close they came to upsetting me. The taste of orange washing away the bitterness of the moment.

But they were plainly up to something, Russell and the others. Playing on people's sympathies. Getting them worked up against me. Probably trying to make out that

I was to blame for Carter's injuries without provocation. When, if there was any justice, they should have been taking up their collection for *me*. At last all the shit spilling out into the open like a broken cistern. And that broad-beamed hyena behind the counter behaving as if butter won't melt in her mouth because she knows I pay for what I buy. And the rest couldn't bear it. For if you don't owe anything to anybody in Farnum, they don't trust you. Our lunatic local bookkeeping. The mess of them wrapping their flab in the cozy upholstery of each other's debts. I'll pay cash and take my chances.

It would cost more at LaBombard's, but I didn't care anymore. Up Main Street, left on Wheelock around the Farnum House, and down to the corner of South where the friendly sign of the Texaco star was hung out to welcome me. Truly hospitable. LaBombard keeping open house for the suckers. Clean rest rooms to take your eye off the price per gallon. Shoving millionaire's oil in your crankcase while you farted around in immaculate surroundings, lulled into a false sense of security. A cardboard Santa Claus out front holding up a can of Prestone to show you what's in store, a broad smile on his face and a sprig of mistletoe in his hat to jolly up the bill. And "Merry Christmas" still hanging in the steamed-over office window even though it's long past. Any holiday on which it was better to give was one LaBombard wasn't going to let go of easily. I was on my guard.

Pulled up alongside a brace of streamlined red pumps and waited. The truck felt nice and warm, I wasn't going to set foot out there needlessly just to put a chill in my bones. For the prices he charges, he can come to me. It was a funny name, LaBombard. Canuck family. New in these parts. No more than twenty years at the outside but amazing the way he spoke English as well as I did.

101

Clever, and like the rest of those northern exports, full of queer ways and sharp practices. Impossible to make out anything more than still, gray shadows behind the cloudy glass so I gave them a taste of the horn to shake them up.

"Come on, LaBombard. I know you're in there. This isn't a parking lot." Nothing doing. Really leaned on the button then and the blaring horn knocking sparrows off frozen telephone wires and raising the eyebrows of the only person on the street, Tolliver's wife, scurrying by with a shopping bag. Roused everyone but LaBombard. Deaf and dumb, I decided, getting out and stomping toward the office.

"Didn't you hear me blowing out there?" I demanded, barging through the door.

Huddled together laughing and whispering and sipping coffee, the three people inside looked up at the same instant like some three-headed monster. The same twisted smile on each of their faces. Sort of a speak-of-the-devil expression.

"Oh, it's you, Mr. Newfield," said LaBombard matter-of-factly. He leaned back and ran his hand through his greasy black curls. "Quite a surprise. Long time no see."

I didn't care for his sarcastic manner one little bit. His wife, her pea jacket hung loosely over her shoulders and wearing pants the size of two parachutes stitched together, sat with her head bent over her accounts desk, fiddling with a paper clip. Archie Grubb was the third party. Used to keep turkeys before he was wiped out by his own bungling and since then all he did was bang around town collecting welfare and gossip. He sat propped up on the display shelf counting his feet. Stretching his mind to its absolute limit. Whatever lies they'd heard from Russell, I wasn't going to let it bother me. I didn't have time for them. Personality conflicts would be overlooked, self-restraint was the watchword. The portable gas heater in the corner had turned the office into a Turkish bath, the sooner I was out of it the better.

"Any other antifreeze besides that?" I asked, pointing to the pyramid of Prestone on the shelf near Grubb.

"Nope. You can buy junk that'll gum up your radiator anywhere. I only carry the best."

"Nothing cheaper?"

"That's it."

"All right. I'll take two."

"Quality may cost a little more but in the end you never regret it."

"Two is all I want."

"Two cans of Prestone?"

"Don't open them. I'll take them with me."

"I'd like to be of service, Mr. Newfield. Really I would, but unfortunately I just can't. Fresh out of Prestone at the moment."

"What do you call that? Tomato juice?"

"Oh, that. That's promised. Isn't it, Mary?"

Mary nodded to her desk, afraid if she looked at him she might break down in hysterics.

"Yes, sir, we've had quite a little run on the antifreeze today from our regular customers. It's the change in the weather. You understand, Mr. Newfield. Sorry I can't help you."

Face up to it, Newfield. You're *not* a regular customer. Be reasonable. You don't belong. Take my word for it, it has nothing to do with Carter whatsoever. LaBombard probably has long-standing orders from one year to the next. Or last-minute calls from old reliables to reserve a can or two. They'll be by on the way home from work tonight. The lucky names written in pencil on the back of each label. Or on 3x5 cards in the middle drawer of her

103

desk. Or memorized. What kind of bullshit was he trying to hand me? What kind of simpleton did he take me for?

"You might try Western Auto over at Brampton," La-Bombard suggested, clasping his hands behind his head and smirking at me. "It's not so far."

Is that right? As if I didn't know myself. But I thanked him kindly and turned to go.

"They say it's dropping all the way down to zero tonight," I heard him tell the others.

"That a fact," mumbled Grubb.

"Brrrrr." Mary pulled her jacket close around her. "That's cold."

I knew there'd be nothing to it if I didn't lose my head. Calm and collected. A twist of the wrist was all it would take. Simplicity itself. While they continued to jabber their nonsense, winking slyly at one another behind my back. Off with the burner to snuff out the flame and then I turned the key up and up and up. Let it blow its top, crack its sides, and leak its poisonous heart out. No pity, LaBombard, vengeance is mine. The valve wide open like the pearly gates. Hallelujah! Hallelujah! The gas shooting out like the hum of wings. Hallelujah! Hallelujah! Newfield nudging them across the threshold into Paradise. Who says he isn't willing to lend a helping hand to his neighbors? Liars! They wrong me by night and day.

"Two gallons of apple juice," Grubb was telling them in the background. "Filled to the brim and loaded with sugar. The covers screwed on tight as caskets. Somewhere he had heard that you needed heat, so he set the jugs up against the side of his furnace. A week later he came down licking his lips for some hard cider and there it was. Busted all over the floor."

Loud mocking laughter as I slipped unnoticed out the door, the burner key safely tucked away in my pocket.

There was no way for them to shut the valve off now. The office filling up like a murderous fish bowl correcting the error of their lives. With both hands locked around the door handle, I held on and awaited developments. They were not long in coming. First screams, then threats and wild, frantic tugging at the door. For God's sake, Newfield, let us out of here! For God's sake, somebody help us! Ground my molars together squeezing the juice out of the moment and turned a deaf ear to their mewling cries. Disrespect must be dealt with firmly. As they proceeded to choke on their own spittle, the scratching at the door gradually slackened off. The last faint groveling pleas in the twilight. A few feeble coughs. Silence. My hands soldered to the handle as if something was still going on, my mind shivering like a leaf. A touch of the nerves. Remember that it was the first time I had ever murdered three people. Yet it had to be done and I was never one to shirk my responsibilities.

On my right the rumble of the garage door rolling up overhead attracted my attention. "Lubrication," it said, and out came the grease ball, LaBombard. He rushed over and stared down at my hands.

"Is the door stuck, Mr. Newfield?"

Who asked for him?

"Can't you open it? Must be the weather. Here, let me try."

I glared at him and he froze in his tracks.

"I only thought you wanted . . ." He tentatively held out a large red plastic disk from which hung the key to the men's room.

"Get out of here. I'm warning you. Get the hell out of here. Get away, goddamnit!"

LaBombard fled, slamming the garage door down behind him.

Of course. It had been nothing more than a temporary lapse due to the heat inside. With the coast clear, I removed my hands from the door. A humiliating experience. My legs were as stiff as marble pillars as I climbed back into the truck. I must be coming down with something or how else explain why I hadn't called him to account then and there. The power of evil amazed me. Stamp out injustice in one place and it cropped up in another like guerrilla warfare. But let them twist right and wrong all they wanted, I was strong enough to bend them back into shape. Blowing my nose to root out the excess phlegm from my system. Clear the decks for action. Taking dead aim at the Prestone Santa, I sent the truck hurtling forward and smashed it to smithereens. "Put that in your Christmas stocking, LaBombard," I shouted triumphantly, skidding out onto South Street and away.

9

Patience, Newfield, patience. The river was the right place to collect your wits. Crossing over the Brampton bridge into New Hampshire, I pulled off onto the east bank's snowy shoulder for a look-see. Fir trees fringed with white hugged the shorelines. There was ice stretching from both banks like an arch in search of a keystone, the deep water in the center not yet frozen over. Another week of this and it would be solid through. The steel struts of the small bridge formed bold silver X's against the gray mat of the dark afternoon sky. Girders reeking with dependability. A wonderfully peaceful scene that did fine things for my nerves. And not even much traffic moving across the way on Five due to the weather. The whole of Farnum invisible beyond the hill with only its smoke showing. Forget it. Even before my great-grandfather's time it had disappeared from the river, dragging itself up onto the plain in search of more land for more people. Confusing numbers with prosperity. And when they finally saw it wasn't going to happen, they had become either too lazy or stubborn or indifferent to admit their mistake and go back. Blowing their chance to pollute the shore as the factories upstream had polluted the water.

Newfield's old hideaway saved by the bell. I had grown up down here, measuring myself against its silence the way some kids make marks on their doorposts. Pumping air into my lungs while clinging to the outside grillwork at the middle of the bridge and then no-hands into the soup. Plunging straight down through the cold murk in hope of touching something solid. Again and again, as if the bottom was the way out. Until staggering from the water and collapsing on the sloped bank still shy of my goal. Stretched out and fighting for breath to go back up yet one more time for another try. And wondering whether freedom was something you scooped off the bottom, or not having to dive again into that grimy river. A smart kid. Even then I knew. And never sick a day in my life.

The lump under my right buttock causing some minor discomfort. Surprised while straightening out my mackinaw to come upon a navel orange with a hole in it oozing inside my pocket. Of all things. Now why in hell did I take that? Provocation driving me to unexpected extremes. Dangerous deeds. Conspiracy warping my honest nature. When all I ever wanted was to lead a clean, simple life and be a good man. The question, ladies and gentlemen, then is this. How is it possible for a right-thinking citizen to avoid knocking up against the mob's cunning pieties, bunking into their Santa Clauses? It couldn't be done. Nevertheless, bitterness would not be tolerated at this end. Newfield keeping himself straight despite trial and affliction. With the strength of ten because his conscience is clear. The orange, naturally, would be paid-in-full. Although no doubt overcharged sufficient to redeem a crate of oranges, I made a mental note to send Hubbell an anonymous five-cent postage stamp on the first of the month. Start the new year off with a bang.

Since my orange was paid for, I couldn't see anything wrong in polishing it off. Give me the energy to deal with the Granite State crooks at Western Auto. Taking out my knife, I sliced the fruit into two perfect hemispheres, if you disregard the crater at the North Pole. Alma, now, preferred hers in quarters with a sprinkling of sugar and cinnamon. A complicated arrangement. Proves she's a born mixer. As always, the first half's tartness shivered my tonsils and the second was sunshine sweet. The one as unlike the other as the taps in the kitchen sink. As far as I was concerned, the initial coating of the tongue was the answer. An astonishing fact, nonetheless; one orange, two tastes. It suggested the possibility of another Newfield than the one you've come to know and respect. Some freakish copy prone to back-slapping, tear-jerking, poached eggs, and waste. The whole idea fairly turning my stomach. Though I imagine there are fools who'd call that freedom, too. That is, to live the life of the other half. Not realizing that you can't mix human beings and oranges willy-nilly. Take it from me, the only way out is in. Dedication and persistence stretching your possibilities like suspenders. If not for that, where the hell would I be today? Tacked down in front of some handyman's cottage for the boss to wipe his feet on. Enough to scare the shit out of anybody. And so taking charge of his steering wheel with a firm, free hand, Newfield drives on.

Brampton was a good-size town, but too crowded for my taste. It had a brick factory, a hotel, a Sears, a Piggly-Wiggly, and two furniture stores. The works. Not to mention an Armenian restaurant that advertised hamburgers wrapped in grape leaves. Damned foreigners creeping in

109

everywhere. Plus parking meters lining the main street with their greedy little red tongues sticking up. In the center of the snow-covered mall, the white bandstand topped by a scalloped roof was reserved for big-deal occasions like the Fourth of July and Arbor Day. And the rest of the year just looking pretty and gathering dust. I tell you!—there was a lot of show in Brampton. Circling the mall looking for a meter that still had some life in it, but it was a lost cause. Only one empty spot left and I wheeled in just ahead of this Nash that was trying to cut me out as if he owned it. The same to you, shorty. Shoved my nickel down the meter's throat and hurried inside Western Auto willing to settle for what I could get and go home to Alma and the cows.

Staggering variety of everything in that store including young swappers exchanging Christmas presents. Hockey sticks for switchblades and the like. Above the nuts and bolts and sockets, there were fan belts, thermos jugs, fishing rods, and stuffed dogs with unnaturally swollen heads and spaniel ears crowding the walls. Even three different kinds of antifreeze on the shelves. It pained me to see that they were all selling for the same price. Monopoly and collusion! But I was in no mood to argue after what I'd been through.

"Would you like a bag for that, sir?"

"Don't bother."

"No bother, sir."

"Give me that!"

Hustled back to my parking spot and there were only five minutes gone on the meter. Seemed like a shame to throw away the rest of the time when it was already paid for. According to the Elgin I still had a couple of hours before milking. By rights I knew I should get going, but the truth is I'd been under a little strain the past two days without Carter. Not sleeping well and my appetite reduced to moderate. Impulsively placed the two cans of antifreeze down on the floorboard out of sight and locked the truck. Across Main Street on the top floor of the two-story Fowler building hung the shingle of the Barnett Travel Bureau. "We Get You There by Land, Sea, and Air." And me with fifty-five credits at my disposal. Just time for a short vacation.

It was Barnett who had arranged my first trip a little over two years ago. After Duckworth and before Carter. Alma had been reading something in the paper about Puerto Ricans coming to New York and having the nasties. Unemployment. Prejudice. Tenements. Rats. Practically had her in tears. Of course that was long before she discovered rats of her own. She had more distance on their problem then. The article said that they didn't know English, but they were wonderfully industrious people willing to work for a song. And, after all, they were almost Americans. It gave me an idea. Duckworth had just walked off after five months and there was nobody else around who wanted the job. What the hell, I thought, I'll go down to New York and get me one. Nothing to lose but expenses and I could take those off my income tax. Besides, if I did get somebody, I'd be doing us both a turn. Alma couldn't get over it. Jumping up and down and clapping her hands and hugging me black and blue. So I should have known right there what to expect.

Barnett took care of everything. Round-trip train ticket, a place without frills to stay overnight, and the name of a nearby restaurant that could be trusted. Didn't charge me a penny for any of it either. That's what I call humanitarian. Private enterprise at its best rendering a solid service to the public. With Ben promising to look after the farm in my absence, I kissed Alma good-bye and was standing on the deserted station platform at five in the morning, my father's black Boston bag in hand, scratching my crotch and wondering what I was doing there. The train slid in at six-fifteen, right on schedule. A good omen. Barely had both feet in the door when it pulled out and I was free of Alma and Farnum at one stroke. Should have been having the time of my life but all the way down I kept worrying about Alma missing me and checking my watch to make sure Ben was doing his job.

The city was pretty much the way I expected. Big and dirty. But it was one of those particularly fine February days when even a pile of manure looks good. Flags twinkling in the sunlight and yellow cabs zipping in and out and armies of people every color of the rainbow doubletiming it up and down the streets talking foreign languages. Amazing. Not one familiar face in the crowd. The curse of overpopulation. I hiked up Fifth Avenue looking at everyone and everyone looking at me. Yes, ma'am, that's right. The Farnum Newfield. Word sure does get around fast. The smooth-cheeked men striding confidently in starchy shirts and black coats with velvet collars and the women tripping along beside them all nylon stockings and high heels, bouncing around inside their furs. On all sides luscious goodies jiggling like loose cargo in the hold. It wasn't in my nature to knock anything indiscriminately. There was a good deal of pep in this town that you had to admire.

But I didn't have much time, so I toted my Boston bag and went right to work. The East Harlem Protestant Relief House was about five miles from the station and the walk stretched the limbs and sweetened the brain after being train-cooped for seven hours doing nothing. Newfield combining business and sight-seeing. The houses becoming more and more glum and the sidewalks filthier as I approached 103rd Street. Barnett had written down the address for me. The Reliefers were housed in a narrow store on a block filled with fire escapes, their name stenciled in small, quiet letters on the window under a tiny cross. Protestants, all right.

Running the show was a gaunt, tic-ridden lady with pale green eyes that were set so far back in their sockets it was hard to tell whether she was looking in or out. Mrs. Kewell by name. Appeared as if she didn't bother to choose her clothes daily but just allowed them to accumulate on her by the month. The bun at the back of her neck was coming apart, and all the while we talked she kept jabbing at it with her pencil. I put it down to cooties. Should have thought she had enough problems of her own without bothering with other people's. Mrs. Kewell was a nice person to do business with though because she knew her stock. And when she heard there was a job in it, she really laid out the red carpet. Offered me a chair and Jesus. Didn't get the last name but Jesus was good enough for me.

"How do you," he said, grinning up at me like an idiot.

"Poorly, thank you." I had no intention of letting this puny runt charm me into a hasty decision. "How's your English?"

He leaned forward as if he thought there might be more and then turned helplessly to Mrs. Kewell.

"Oh, yes. Very good, very good," she said, nodding her head vigorously and him nodding right along with her. "He's learning new words every day. Remember, Mr. Newfield, Jesus arrived in New York only two weeks ago. I think he's doing beautifully for so short a time. Don't you?"

"Tolerable," I allowed, not wanting to step on her toes, but I couldn't make up my mind whether to take the gamble. He looked as if lifting one fork of hay might cause internal bleeding.

"He's a *very* hard worker," Mrs. Kewell added, sensing my dilemma.

"That so." I perked up my ears as she filled in the details. Ten hours a day in the sugarcane fields for forty cents an hour. Figured I could match that without too much of a strain. Mrs. Kewell really seemed to be in love with her work, pulling out all the stops.

". . . leaving his lovely wife and four young children behind on the island, but when he arrived here of course there was no 'employment agent' to meet him and no garment factory and the money he had given the man—his entire life savings—was gone. And *no one* is doing a thing to put a stop to this contemptible exploitation. It's horrible, Mr. Newfield. Perfectly horrible."

Might even throw in a bit more if he panned out. I didn't believe in taking advantage of anybody's hard luck. Coolly sized up the item one last time before committing myself. Small and dark with big soft brown eyes, a half-moon mustache, and thousands of dental sparklers. When he quit smiling, he seemed passable. And with what he knew about English at least there'd be no arguments.

"All right," I said. "I'll take him."

"You'll never regret it," Mrs. Kewell congratulated me.

Arranged to meet him at the train the next morning, shook hands all round, and left feeling uncomfortably as if I'd just been had.

Barnett's rooming house was way the hell at the other end of Manhattan on Sixth Avenue opposite a jail called the Women's House of Detention.

"Keep this closed," warned the manager, showing me how the contraption on my door worked. There was a four-foot steel rod with one end wedged into a plate in the floor and the other slipped into the lock to form a brace. Couldn't decide whether it was supposed to keep me in or the city out, but being a guest I asked no questions. Just followed the rules and went to bed. With Jesus on my mind. That plus the noise from down in the street and I didn't sleep a wink the whole night. Locked in and pacing. Until I finally wound down, thinking so escape isn't freedom either. While outside passersby shouted messages in to the prisoners. Throwing words back and forth like kisses, having a damn good time. Seemed as if there was never a dull minute in New York. I started for the station with the first streaks of light, glad to get out of there.

Jesus was already in the waiting room and on the look-out for me when I arrived. Cradling a battered gray suit-case held together with a brown strap on his lap. Appeared to be a punctual little fellow but I wasn't going to jump to conclusions. Might be that he sleeps here regularly. We sat side by side in silence all the way up on the train with him staring bug-eyed out the window and making an occasional faint burble of delight over more snow than he had ever seen before in his life. Tried not to get my hopes up but it was just possible I had picked myself up a bargain. When we got home the first thing I did was show him around. The herd, the barn, the pasture, and the handyman's house he'd have all to himself.

"Well," I asked, "what do you think?"

His eyes were glowing and he seemed sort of choked up. "I . . . I . . . I," he stuttered, wringing his hands.

"That's all right. Simmer down, Jesus. I understand."

"I love this thing."

"Thirty-two years of hard work is all it takes."

"I *love* this thing," he repeated, as if he liked the sound of it. Over and over, "I love this thing," turning every which way and pointing and smiling.

For a foreigner he had a real gift for the language. Began to grow genuinely fond of the little guy, and as for Alma it was love at first sight. She adopted him right off the bat, tossing his washing in with our own. To his credit, he returned the compliment by sweating for us around the clock and never once making a peep about it. Only helper I ever had who did more than was asked of him, and when Ben came by to tell me that Farnum was anti-Jesus, that they didn't care to have any dark-skinned stranger taking jobs away from them, I very nearly threw him out on his can. No one was going to ruffle my Jesus if I could help it. He worked for me like a demon for six days. For six days the only words I ever heard out of his mouth were "I love this thing." On the seventh he was gone.

I wrote an angry letter to Mrs. Kewell but all she said in return was that Jesus had been unhappy in Vermont and had gone back to Puerto Rico. Figured it was either somebody in town who had scared him off or a week of whiteness. Who knows? He didn't even come around to shake hands for the last time and collect his wages. It should have taught me something. You never can tell what's bubbling inside a pot until you lift the cover. Probably thought I wouldn't pay him for only six days. But I would have.

So much for Jesus, a thing of the past. Since then I've cut way down on my foreign travel, limiting it to an occasional visit with Barnett when time permits. Helps to take the edge off current events. It's a pleasure to hear that man go on about distant places you've never seen. So vivid you'd think you were actually there and with none of the wear and tear. At my age I prefer it that way.

Barnett was on the phone when I entered his office. Glanced up, smiled, raised one spick-and-span finger signaling he'd be through in a minute, and waved me to a nice-looking piece of furniture. Always polite. He never knew when it might be the real thing. Put myself down in his chair and it groaned under me and fought back. Newfield pinched by modern design. Shaped to hold a teaspoonful, it was getting a tablespoon of backside from me. Made for a generation of misproportioned lightweights. Sitting sideways, I rested one cheek in the cup and concentrated on the wall posters and the bubbles. Rising in the lighted green and blue candles on the small metal Christmas tree he had on his desk. Newfield on his best behavior, subtly conveying the impression that he wouldn't dream of eavesdropping. Why not? I could hear him perfectly well. Abandoned the ridiculous charade and felt much better with myself honestly staring at him.

"Yes, I see." Barnett muttering into the receiver and lifting his skimpy eyebrows to tell me he couldn't get rid of the pest. "Yes, all right." With his left hand, he nervously patted down the few remaining wisps of red hair he still had as he listened to the voice at the other end. Squirming about in his swivel chair. His belly rising up from between the folds of his brown suit jacket like a tweed medicine ball. Stuffed with beer and rice pudding. There was something optimistic about that comfortable belly that made you feel right at home. On the whole, the only reservation I had about the look of Barnett was that he wore cufflinks, but I tried not to see them. Nobody's

117

perfect. "And thank you for calling," he said cheerfully, hanging up. "Hello, hello, Mr. Newfield. Delighted to see you again. How are you?"

"Passable."

"And how's the dairy business?"

"Could be worse."

"And your wife?"

What was this, some kind of third degree? I wondered if Carter was at the bottom of it. Not way over here in Brampton, too.

"Well, where will it be this time? Skiing in the Laurentians or tiger hunting in the Transvaal? You call the tune and we'll pay the piper." Throwing his head back, Barnett howled merrily over the neat way he had put it, his belly heaving like a bag of chipmunks. An advertising mind. How could you be suspicious of somebody like that?

"OK," I decided, opening up on trust. "I'm thinking about someplace warm with flowers. Sunshine and a view of the sea. What have you got?"

Barnett didn't have to think twice. "Madeira," he shot back. "They say it's lovely this time of the year."

"That so. How do you spell that?"

Barnett spelled it out.

"Sounds OK."

"OK!" he gasped, and whipped out a brochure from his top drawer. "OK isn't the half of it. Listen to this. A tranquil green isle set in the blue Atlantic with an annual mean temperature of sixty degrees Fahrenheit. A lush tropical garden with over three thousand one hundred species of flora including the exotic frangipani, the bombax with its pink-colored blossom, and the blue agapanthus. Where the sun is a golden lamp suspended

118

from an azure canopy. Only three hundred and forty miles off the Northwest African coast—think of it, Africa! —and five hundred and twenty-eight miles southwest of Lisbon. Centrally located. Wonderful old wines. Heavenly scenery. Exquisite hand embroidery. What more could you ask? The Pearl of the Atlantic."

"Sounds kind of steep."

"When were you thinking of going?"

"Makes no difference to me. Say for instance the first week in January."

"The thrift season. You're in luck."

"Never thought of visiting an island before. Don't you get sort of choked up?"

"Were you planning on taking your wife?"

"Haven't decided yet."

"You'll be as free as a bird. Look, imagine yourself spending lazy hours in the sun lying next to some barefoot olive-skinned beauty with long, dark, tantalizing legs dimpled at the knee. Idly stretching out your hand, you pluck a passion flower and set it in her perfumed hair. She giggles. The sound of young berries falling into a crystal goblet. She takes your hands and marvels at their strength. With your rugged chin and great size and that distinguished-looking battle scar over your eyebrow, you remind her of the famous sea captains of the past who have come to Madeira. She thinks how splendid she'd look standing beside you on the quarterdeck, fondling your gold braid, as you sweep the horizon with your telescope. She calls you her lusty explorer and whispers unbelievable things in your ears that no one else can hear. And minutes turn to hours and hours days. Time has lost its meaning. The spell of the island is upon you."

As I told you, Barnett spins quite a web. Pulled a

clump of Lee's Big Boy overalls out of my hole and shifted cheeks in the chair. On second thought, if I ever do go anywhere I'd better take Alma along. She'd get lonely back here without me.

"I'm not so sure," I told him.

"Then a cruise is what you want. There's no reason to feel cramped on a cruise."

"But then again . . ." chuckling at the idea, "I wouldn't care to have that girl think I was neglecting her."

"Just a minute." Barnett hurriedly thumbed through a blue looseleaf notebook and found the page he was looking for. "Hmmmm," he muttered, tapping the page and rubbing a finger over his thick lower lip. It was soothing to watch him ply his trade. Did me a world of good. I had the sense I was in the hands of a professional.

"The American Export Lines New Year Cruise," he concluded. "It's short notice but I think I can still get you a booking. We'll have to work fast. First stop Madeira. You can combine the intimacy of a brief island adventure with a freewheeling panoramic sweep through the magnificent playgrounds of the Mediterranean. How does that sound?"

"Not bad," I had to admit, catching a little of his excitement.

"Now you're talking." He reached for his memo pad and began jotting down the information. "You'll leave from New York aboard the *Independence* on the first of January. Sailing time nine thirty in the morning. On the sixth you arrive in Madeira, spend the morning there, and then on to Casablanca, Algeciras, Palma de Majorca, Cannes, Nice, Naples, Genoa, Gibraltar, and right back home again safe and sound on the twenty-third of the month. More than three full weeks of enchantment in first-class luxury for the low-low price of—"

"Thanks," I said, getting up feeling rested and considerably broadened by foreign travel. Casually nudged the chair over to cover the puddle of melted snow left by my boots. Didn't want Barnett to think I was ungrateful for his hospitality. "I'll think about it."

"Do that, Mr. Newfield. And here's your itinerary." He handed me the slip of paper he had been writing on. "But remember I can't guarantee a reservation if you put off letting me know too long."

"Fair enough."

"Any time, Mr. Newfield. And if something comes up to alter your plans, don't hesitate to call again. The worst thing you could do is be a stranger. We're here to serve."

I think he meant it, too, so I didn't feel so bad. Of course he was pulling my leg about that girl on the island. There weren't really women like that. On the other hand, you never know. I've been surprised by a lot of things in my time. Quite a sizzler, and it was good to have her with me when I hit the street, a toasty thought to ward off the cold. Crossing over to the truck and speculating. By way of amusement. Whether there'd be enough time on that island to do her justice. Checking my itinerary to see, when the horns started blowing and the cars dodging around me. Hold your horses. Barnett should be a doctor, he's got the penmanship for it. The letters were jumping around in front of my eyes like cheerleaders. As near as I could make out, the paper said, "We've had enough of you, Newfield. Get out of town!" That couldn't be right. Looked again just to make sure and the message was gone. Along with everything else, my eyesight seemed to be failing, too. A temporary condition. The piece of paper was lying out in the middle of the street where I had dropped it. Went back to get the truth when this guy drives by tooting his horn and shaking his fist. Up yours, buster. I bent down for the paper and it had disappeared. Vanished! You wouldn't have believed it even if it had been done by somebody with a top hat and a wand.

"Hey, wait!" I shouted, starting after the car, "Hold on! Come back!"

One look at me in his rear-view mirror was enough. Fearing revenge, the driver hunched over his wheel and took off, his tires whirling away and my itinerary, pasted to his rubber, whirling away with them. The olive-skin darling of my dreams carried off by the chunky treads of a snow tire. Easy come, easy go. What hurt me most were her parting words, "Get out of town, Newfield. Get out of town." But not having the paper in my possession I couldn't go back and accuse Barnett to his face of inciting to riot. Wrong him on insufficient evidence. Kick the shit out of him without due process. That's not the way I do things. It must have been a relapse and just when I thought I was feeling so much better. Under the circumstances, the best thing I could do was cancel my trip. Simply filed away that itinerary as one more mystery in a long unbroken string of them that I would never get to the bottom of. The story of my life.

Drove back across the bridge, up the hill, and into Farnum. Historical markers along the roadside as thick as Burma Shave signs. On the playing field behind the school where the snow had been shoveled away in one corner there was a homemade ice rink and skaters in hoods and pompons were cutting capers. Must be after three I gathered and then recalled that it was a holiday. But it *was* after three and I hurried along. Past Hatch out in front of the school with a cigar butt in his mouth and a pail of sand in his hand surrounded by a noisy

122

bunch of kids. All of them fighting to help him sprinkle. The Pied Piper of Farnum. I could never understand what they saw in him. Past the white spire of Peaselee's First Congregational and Putnam's and the barber shop. Eppy dozing in his own barber chair under a No Shaves sign. Claims shaving interferes with volume trade but the truth is he's afraid to risk it anymore. Shakes like a tassel in a high wind. In the interest of public safety his sign ought to read No Haircuts, too. I wonder who clips his. Most likely his wife the way Alma does mine. Running my hand through the gray-flecked bush at the back of my neck and realizing that I hadn't been shorn in months. If Alma's up to baking again, I suppose I can ask her to trim me around now with a clear conscience. Lighten the load and brighten the spirits. My mother always used to say that. Poor woman, never knew a day's happiness in her whole life to judge by her face. My father did all the smiling for the family. That man had no sense of responsibility.

"Alma." Coming into the dark house and switching on the dining room light. "Alma." The place seemed deserted. What's happened to her? "Alma," I called anxiously.

"I'm in here."

She was in the living room. Sitting in the dark in her rocker by the window, her hands clenched in her lap.

"What's wrong now?" I asked, turning on the table lamp.

"Nothing."

"Did you go over to the Carters?"

She turned from the window and squinted at me curiously as if I was somebody in an old faded photograph she was trying to place. Must have been sitting in the dark for some time.

123

"You did, didn't you? Well, it serves you right if he's upset you."

"They've gone."

"Who's gone?"

"The Carters. Reverend Peaselee came out to help them pack. They're staying in town with him now."

It was too good to be true. "Did you check their house to see that none of our furniture was missing?"

"Orin."

The best news I'd heard all day. "What?"

"Orin."

"I'm listening."

"When Mr. Peaselee was here, I asked him to take me along, too."

I stared at her, not trusting my tongue to say anything for the moment.

"Didn't you hear me, Orin? I said I asked Mr. Peaselee to take me away from here. To take me with the Carters."

Waiting to see whether I was more miserable or furious. She had no right to air our dirty laundry in public. Embarrassing me all over Farnum. But I loved Alma. She was mine like this house and the barn and my cows. I'd be goddamned if I'd let any psalm-singing old fart take advantage of her.

"I don't believe you," I told her frankly.

"It's true."

"You're lying."

"It wouldn't have mattered to you if I had. You wouldn't have even noticed I was gone."

Good old dependable Alma. I knew she wouldn't do anything like that. "Don't ever lie to me again."

"Is your farm so much more important to you than I am, Orin?"

"What's that got to do with it?"

"For heaven's sake, look at yourself, will you! Can't you see you've changed?"

"I don't doubt it. Surprise me if I hadn't after what I've been through."

"Something's happened to you, Orin. You're not responsible for your acts anymore. That was a horrible thing you did to Roy Carter no matter what the cause. He's wearing a cast that reaches practically to his chin. He can hardly move."

"Ought to cut down on his dancing. Who's that?" I pointed out the window at the dim outline of a car parked near the barn.

"What's the use!" she groaned, and slumped down in her rocker.

"Whose car is that?"

"Mr. Tolliver's."

"Tolliver?"

"He's waiting for you. I invited him in to warm up but he said he preferred sitting outside in his car. Orin," she cried, "he didn't want anything to do with me. I don't think I can take much more of this."

"What the hell is *he* after?" Farnum's one-man police force and part-time chicken farmer. We were on his egg route, but seeing he wanted *me* not Alma I gathered it wasn't a delivery. I had a hunch, though, what it was that brought him out here and went outside to learn the price of his visit.

In his round knit hat pulled down low over his ears Tolliver resembled a small woolen tit with steel-rimmed glasses. He must have gotten out of his car when he saw the truck drive up, expecting me to come right out. Shivering his ass off and stomping his feet in the snow to keep warm.

"I've been waiting for you, Mr. Newfield."

"So I heard. Why don't you come back in about a week. We've got enough eggs for now."

"I didn't come to talk about eggs," he said grimly. "I'm here as the police chief of Farnum, Vermont."

"Stick with your chickens, Mr. Tolliver. Poking into other people's business is dirty work."

"Well now, I don't look at it that way, Mr. Newfield. It's a job like any other. And when a crime has been committed, somebody's got to pay for it."

A subtle hint that I ignored. Enjoyed seeing him sweat for his money. If he wanted to chat, he'd have to catch me first. Tolliver trailing behind like a caboose as I strode back to the truck and emptied out its radiator. With the temperature sinking, I wanted to get the antifreeze in before milking.

"Regardless of who it is. Regardless of how I may feel about that individual personally. I can't allow it to make any difference to me. I just do my duty, Mr. Newfield. Justice is blind, you know. It's not my idea. I'm only a servant of the people."

"At the beck and call of society, eh Tolliver? Tough shit. Give me that other antifreeze." Took the can from him and, slamming two holes in the top with my screwdriver, poured it in.

"You won't get angry?"

A squeaking voice and a wheedling manner. As far as I was concerned, he had worn out his welcome. "All right," I said, replacing the radiator cap. "How much is it going to cost me?"

He ran his hand over his mouth and, closing one eye, peered at me suspiciously. "You wouldn't be trying to bribe me, would you, Mr. Newfield?"

"When I break something, I pay for it. That's only right. How much?" I asked, and reached for my money clip. "A dollar ought to more than cover expenses I should think."

"A dollar!" Even in the gloomy darkness of that late afternoon, I could see Tolliver's eyes bulging white in disbelief.

"What the hell does LaBombard want for a cheap piece of cardboard? He probably got it for nothing anyway."

It must have dawned on him then that he couldn't make a sucker out of Orin Newfield. Hemming and hawing and clearing clutter from his throat. "Mr. Newfield," he said, scratching his cheek, "you're too much for me. I can't figure you out."

"A dollar and not one cent more. Take it or leave it."

Tolliver took a deep breath and reached into his back pocket. "I'm sorry about this. But like I say, it's my duty." Thrusting a folded paper into my hand, he headed quickly for his car, not running but not walking either, and looking back over his shoulder to make sure he had a good head start just in case.

What's this all about? Held the paper up and caught the dim light from the house. It was the size of a small menu. Summoning me. Newfield to be served up in two days for the assault and battery of his handyman, Roy Carter. Sons of bitches, they were going to try the wrong man! Chop off my head, boil it in oil, and smoke the rest for the Farnum fair. Not a chance. If I could help it. Which I doubted. Ripping the paper into tiny bits, I stuffed the pieces into my pocket. Neatly. Upsetting, yes, but no reason to litter the front yard with trash.

10

The Green County Courthouse where justice will triumph. A white clapboard thresher with green shutters dedicated to separating out the truth from the slander. Public vindication beneath its gold crowned bell tower. Aside from the waste of time involved in a trial, there was really nothing to be uneasy about. Rather it was an opportunity to set the Newfield record straight before his Farnum friends and neighbors. Draw the line between popularity and innocence and rub their noses in it. Shove it up their sentimental asses.

The dirt parking area in front was jammed with cars for the occasion. Their snow-covered hoods facing the rectangular green and their rear ends sticking out disrespectfully at the courthouse. Happily, according to Tolliver, justice is blind. Spectators crowding up the front stairs so as not to miss a drop of the proceedings. All of Farnum pushing through the wooden slab of a storm door framed by two fake columns. Above it, a purple globe for night cases. Off a narrow hallway with freshly painted gray floor planks were the offices of the town clerk, the clerk of the court, and the local draft board. A circular wooden staircase, creaking eerily under the traffic, led upstairs to the courtroom. As Alma's husband preceded her up the stairs, he noted a small round opening at the top of the stairwell. Hanging down from it and stopping in mid-air was a thick bellrope, knotted at the end like a hangman's noose. It meant nothing. Hopefully.

A loud buzzing throughout the packed courtroom as a big man enters followed by a trimly dressed little woman wearing tan oxfords and a pillbox hat with a black half-veil shadowing her eyes. She walks stiffly as if this is her first day out after a long illness, the exposed lower part of her face porcelain-pale. Down front a low wooden fence separates the visitors' gallery from the two tables reserved for lawyers and their clients. Holding the gate open for her to pass through, he scans the room disdainfully, taking on all challengers. If the world is filled with two sorts of people, those who think others are infinitely better than they are and those who think others are infinitely worse, it was plain where he stood. His long face rigid, he counts the house which grows quiet under his fierce gaze. Struck dumb by the large assortment of razor nicks on his smooth-shaven jaw. The graying hair soaked through with water and pasted down to hide the need for a haircut. Removing his red and black checked mackinaw, he reveals the well-brushed dark blue suit he was married in. A trifle snug across the chest now with the weight of years and heavy wrinkles around the button-holes. Beneath the jacket he has on a white dress shirt closed at the neck and tieless. The audience bubbling, breaking out in gapes, gasps, and stirs. This Newfield making quite an impression on them. They had never seen him dressed up before.

"You're looking fine, Orin." My lawyer, Billings, congratulating me loudly with an athletic handshake and a smile brimming over with optimism. An intense, sharp-eyed shyster, medium-rare cleft chin and a nose like a drill. Never set eyes on him before yesterday and already we were on a first-name footing. Where the hell does he get off?

"Allow me, Mrs. Newfield." Ceremoniously pulling a chair out for Alma. If he thinks he's going to get a tip for that, he's mistaken. Didn't want him in the first place. You shouldn't need anybody if you tell the truth, but the judge insisted and threw him in for free. Said he was high-minded, too. Court-appointed Billings from Windsor, a legal giant dedicating his services to the preservation of a fair, free, and impartial judicial system regardless of the accused's status in society, high or low. Another pious philanthropist, but I wasn't inclined to be unreasonably prejudiced. As long as he got me off, I didn't give a damn about his queer motives.

When we were all seated around the table, he leaned over and whispered, "Glad to see you took my advice. Half the battle is making a good impression."

"Don't know why the hell I bothered. They know who I am." Putting one finger inside my shirt collar to ease the chafing. "I'm not much for window dressing."

"That's not the point. First and foremost a judge is a man, not a mind reader. Look like a bum and he'll treat you like a bum. He's only human."

"Mr. Billings," I told him flatly, "I believe that it's possible to get justice in a court of law no matter what the trappings."

"Shhh, not so loud. Yes, of course. Don't get me wrong. So do I. But I'm sorry to say that I've seen cases where innocence wasn't always enough. There are times, Orin, when a judge's mind can become muddled by a shrewd, smooth-talking attorney. If by dressing confidently you aid him in seeing the truth, then that's what must be done. He needs all the help you can give him."

Without a doubt, Billings was the most thoroughly cynical individual I had ever met. More like a disease than a man. With a strong smell of perfume, or toilet water, or lady's powder. Intended to have as little to do with him as possible under the circumstances. There were few enough things left for me to believe in, I wasn't going to risk justice. While he carried on, opening his briefcase and covering the table with papers and small talk. Indifferently resting my ear in my hand, I noted: the fancy golden eagle on top of the flagpole to the right of the raised and empty judge's bench, the dark oval portrait on the wall of somebody with a full beard, and, sweeping his goddamn white papers to the floor from in front of me, the honest warm manure brown, the sincere brown of the tabletop.

As a wave of sighs and groans washed over the courtroom, Alma placed a hand on my wrist.

"What's the matter?"

She was looking toward the rear of the room and I tried to follow her gaze. Couldn't make out anything but the backs of a lot of thick heads. Notably Mrs. Otis in curlers and a white bandana. Wants to look her best for the party tonight. When they hang me. On your way, sister, stop holding up the mail. But nothing to cause a commotion other than Plunket and Peaselee sitting uncomfortably close together playing footsy. Then I saw what she had in mind. Carter coming down the side aisle in a wheelchair, his head lowered and his arm in a red and white polka-dot sling. A high-visibility sufferer that one. Thought they said it was his ribs that were busted.

The chiseler throwing in the arm for good measure. Pushing him at a snail's pace so that everybody could get an eyeful was our retired local ambulance chaser, Pierce, and that straightened out a few things for me. Here was the party who had put the old bastard up to making a case out of it. Carter wouldn't have had the nerve to do it all by himself. Bringing up the rear was his missus dressed in black and their oldest kid, scrubbed up and with a haircut. The only thing Pierce seemed to have overlooked for the two of them was black armbands.

Playing the man, the kid all of a sudden put his hand protectively around his frumpy mother. That did it! There wasn't a dry eye in the room. Sympathetic purrs from every side for the innocent victims of the tragedy. A sickening spectacle.

"Look at that!"

"Take it easy," whispered Billings. "It could be worse. The boy might have been a cripple."

Pulled in my legs and crossed them. Watch your language, lawyer, or I'll hammer that pointy chin of yours right through the floor.

"Oh!" Billings reddened and shifted about uncomfortably in his chair. Ducking his head, he began busily shuffling through his papers.

Apology accepted. Up till now mine had been an open-and-shut case, but with the arrival of the Carters I began to see that the law business might be more complicated than I had thought. Still, there was nothing to worry about. Stick to the truth, Newfield, and the truth shall set you free. Barring slip-ups.

Billings was nudging me. "The judge," he said. "Get up, Orin."

Everybody in the courtroom standing so I joined them

as this young freckle-face in a baggy black gown came in and took his seat. Looked to be about sixteen with big ears and a crew cut. Wouldn't have thought he was old enough to have an erection much less be a judge of men. Wiggins by name, from White River Junction. Hard but fair, according to Billings, and with a reputation for having some brains. If true, the first thing he ought to do is shout "FIRE" and watch Carter hop up out of his wheelchair and dash for the exit. Case dismissed. Instead, he glanced sourly down at the room like a plate of leftovers and instructed Tolliver to clear the aisles.

When that was done to his satisfaction, he turned to Carter's lawyer and addressed him in a husky voice, low down, deep, and knotted. "All right, Counselor," he said, "you may begin."

Pierce got up and came forward slowly. A shaggy, rumpled character, tie one way and collar another, thick horn rims sitting on the edge of his broad nose, and a fine head of skin polished like a hubcap.

"Dr. Whiting, please," said Pierce quietly. While waiting for the doctor to take the stand, he pulled out his green tie and cleaned off his glasses with the tip of it. Returned them to the edge of his nose and peered over the top at the clerk who mumbled some words that Whiting swore to and sat down.

"Now then, Doc," said Pierce, hunching forward to suggest the importance of the question he was about to ask. "Could you tell us the shape you found Roy in when you went to see him out at Newfield's?"

"Naturally. That's why I'm here. As I told you yesterday, Mr. Carter had some ribs fractured, a pelvis, and one or two other complaints of the garden variety. Nothing to write home about. Just the sort of things you'd expect from a beating."

Billings' hand flew up. "I object, your Honor. That's merely conjecture on the part of the witness."

"Sustained," rumbled Wiggins. "Please confine yourself to the facts, Doctor."

You tell 'em, Billings! Appeared to be on his toes. I liked that. He was liable to come in handy after all.

"All right, Doc," said Pierce, picking up where he left off. "Exactly how many of Roy's ribs were busted?"

"Three," Whiting snapped angrily. Plain to see he had taken an aversion to the judge and wasn't going to volunteer more than was called for. Good.

"Three busted ribs, you say. And the pelvis. What was wrong with that?"

"Mr. Carter's pelvic arch was *slightly* tipped back."

"No fracture?"

"Definitely not!"

"I see." Pierce sounded disappointed. "And those two or three other injuries you spoke of?"

"Contusions covering the right side, dislocation of the right elbow, and possible ankylosis."

"Possible ankylosis!" Pierce clucking in shocked disbelief, giving rise to a chorus of nasty mutters and groans from the onlookers. Damnit, they didn't know what that meant anymore than I did. Smartest thing I ever did was turn down a jury trial.

"Well, well, well. Ankylosis. You don't say."

"Medically speaking, common as grass," blurted the doctor, unable to restrain himself.

Just as I thought. Despite his slow, folksy ways, Pierce was a cunning bastard for sure.

Rubbing the back of his scheming head thoughtfully, he said, "Not to my mind, Doc. I don't see it that way at all. But let's backtrack a minute to those ribs. In your expert opinion would you say that it's possible because of his age that those busted ribs of his won't ever heal properly and that Roy Carter will never again be able to do heavy manual labor?"

"It's possible."

"In other words, his livelihood will have been taken from him. And would you say, Doc, that as a result of what happened to his pelvis that Roy's sexual powers might have been insulted or damaged in some way?"

"I saw no immediate evidence of that, but it's possible."

"In other words, his sexual life may now be in jeopardy, not to mention his marriage."

For crissake, he's sixty-four with a regiment of kids! What more does he want? His wife could use a vacation.

"In short," concluded Pierce, turning to his client in the wheelchair and shaking his head sadly, "Roy Carter here has been transformed from a strong, vigorous, healthy, robust older man in the full bloom and ripeness of his powers into a hollow shell, a human wreck in constant pain, a chronic, suffering, and perhaps, heaven help him, even impotent invalid. Thank you, Doc. That will be all."

"Goddamnit, Pierce!" I shouted, jumping up. "He was damaged when I got him."

The judge smashed down his gavel. "Sit down," he growled, glaring at me. "Mr. Billings," he said, "I advise you henceforth to control your client's tongue. This is a court of law, not a gymnasium."

Young Wiggins apparently had no taste for language. Some sort of Puritan fanatic. Felt like taking him across my knee and spanking some sense into him.

"Easy, Orin. Don't antagonize him. We'll have our turn."

Sat down and the judge kept staring at me as if he was

trying to prove something until I looked away. Then he turned to Billings.

"Do you have any questions to ask the witness before we excuse him, Counselor?"

"Only one, your Honor. Is it possible, Dr. Whiting, that Mr. Carter's injuries might have been the result of an accident suffered while, for example, in a fit of dizziness . . . or experiencing a momentary loss of consciousness . . . or even perhaps under the influence of alcohol?"

"I object, your Honor," Pierce drawled loudly. "That's all a lot of hypothetical poppycock."

"Your Honor," said Billings, appealing to the judge. "I intend to show that my client had nothing substantive to do with the injuries suffered by the plaintiff, but rather that they came about in another and quite different fashion than attorney for the plaintiff would have us believe. My question is directed to that end."

Liar! I had plenty to do with those injuries. He deserved them and more. What the hell was Billings trying to do, lose the case for me?

"Objection overruled. Dr. Whiting may answer the question."

"I suppose," said the doctor, not putting much stock in it, "*anything* is possible. Men have slipped in bathtubs and killed themselves. However, it's not likely."

"But you agree that it *is* possible." Billings ran his tongue over his thin lips in quiet satisfaction. "That's all."

As soon as he got back to the table, I let him have it. Warned him in no uncertain terms that unless he stuck to the truth the way I had explained it to him he was going to be out of a client. Nothing to worry about, said Billings and began scribbling so hard that he snapped off the point of his pencil. Whipped out another one from his briefcase, barely breaking stride, and went on with his work. For one reason or another, he didn't want to talk to me. Sincerely hoped for his sake that there *was* nothing to worry about.

The next witness to be called was Hatch in his Sunday suit. Hardly recognized him without a cigar in his face. Sitting up there scowling as if he owned the place and weighing and measuring each answer like war and peace hung in the balance. Pierce asking a lot of nosy questions about what he knew of my relationship with Carter and the fights we had had. Billings objecting to all of them.

"Irrelevant, incompetent, immaterial," he shouted repeatedly, jumping up again and again.

The judge overruling him every time. Claimed information about quarrelsomeness was relevant for rebuttal in a possible plea of self-defense. Couldn't make heads or tails out of the whole business. The only thing clear was that by the time Pierce had finally finished with the pompous ass I seemed to be losing.

Poured myself a glass of water from the pitcher on the table, wiping up the wet stain it left with one of the sheets of paper at hand, and gave Alma a drink. Looked as if she could use one, too. Our fingers touching as she took the glass. Exchanging glances, her eyes tear-bright prisoners beneath the dangling cheesecloth of her veil. Stroked the back of her hand to get some color into it and felt closer to her than I had in years. When this is all over, Alma, we're going to go away. To Madeira. Where I'll pick flowers for your lovely hair and cover those fine points of yours with coconut oil until they blossom and hang my ass from some treetop naked in the sun to make you laugh. It's a promise. Anyway, I'm thinking about it.

"On Christmas Day, Mr. Hatch," Billings was on his feet and addressing the witness, "the day Mr. Carter received his injuries, would you tell the court whether he had been drinking?"

That's the stuff, lawyer. Now you're making sense. Put it to him.

"Hmmm, well . . ." Hatch frowning and pinching the end of his nose, "that's hard to say. Maybe yes. And then again, maybe no. I couldn't rightly comment one way or the other."

"Come now, Mr. Hatch, you can do better than that. What would you call it when someone is stretched out on the floor at the back of Dan Hubbell's market with a beer bottle in his hand, drooling all over himself and talking gibberish?"

"I see . . . hmmm . . . yes. I'd say he'd been drinking."

"Very good," Billings said patiently. "And—"

"But I don't recall Carter being in that condition, if that's what you're driving at."

"You lying sonofabitch! That's not so," I roared, nearly knocking over the table in my eagerness to get at him. Hatch blanched, seeing me coming.

"No, no, no," moaned Billings, his hands on my chest trying to hold me back. Tolliver rushed up panting and fastened his light fingers around my arm like a pink bow. "Take it easy, Mr. Newfield," he said mildly. "Now, take it easy. This is no way—" Somebody else climbing on my back and the spectators screaming bloody murder while Wiggins' gavel banged in my ears. "Order!" he bellowed. "Order in the courtroom. I want order."

Shook off the people holding me like so many flies and

leveled a finger at Hatch. "I . . . I . . ." so angry that I couldn't think of anything to say. "You tell the truth, janitor," I warned him, and marched back to my seat.

Suddenly grew so quiet you could hear Carter's wheelchair squealing, Alma studying her lap in embarrassment. Tried to whisper something to Billings but he turned away from me as if stricken with a great pain. I guess I did it that time. Don't let them get the better of you, Newfield. More self-control. The judge, red-faced, laid aside his gavel. Leaning forward, he aimed the black pupils of his pale blue eyes straight at me like two gun barrels.

"Another instance of such behavior, Mr. Newfield," he said firmly, "*one* more time and you will be cited for contempt of court. Is that understood? Now I think you owe the court an apology."

Let Hatch apologize, he started it.

"I hope you mean it," said the judge approvingly. "You may continue, Mr. Billings."

The best Billings could do with Hatch was get an admission that Carter occasionally liked to take a drink. Once a year on Independence Day. When Plunket and Hubbell were called to the stand, try as they might they also couldn't dredge up a single recollection of Carter being drunk. Had no trouble recalling a lot of other things though, even some that never happened. It was a conspiracy.

"And you mean to tell me, Dan," said Pierce, going over the ground slowly in amazement, "that the defendant actually threatened you that afternoon?"

"I ob—"

"Overruled!" snapped the judge, seeing Billings' objection coming. "The state of mind and behavior of the defendant on the day the plaintiff received his injuries is germane. You may respond, Mr. Hubbell."

"Yes, sir. He threatened me. That's a fact."

"And why did he threaten you, Dan?"

"Mr. Newfield sometimes gets pretty excited," said Hubbell smoothly. "Maybe he just doesn't like the way I run my store. I honestly couldn't tell you why."

Like hell you couldn't! Afraid to lose your beer license, Hubbell? Just wait till I get up there. I'll give them an earful about you and your store.

"So Newfield gets wrought up, you say, Dan? Has a little temper, does he?" Pierce turned and squinted in my direction. "I can hardly believe that. Why he's been as quiet as a mouse since he came in here."

The courtroom exploded. Spectators hooting and splitting their guts, they thought this was so comical. Tears of laughter soaking the floor. Wiggins gaveling the room back into shape, but even he had all he could do to hold back a smile. I can take a joke as well as the next man. But don't mock me, Pierce, I won't be mocked.

"As I said, Dan, it's hard to believe that calm *Mr.* Newfield over there has a temper. Could you give us an example of what you mean?"

"Yes, sir. Two days ago he was in the store with Miss Putnam and for no reason that I could see he began to curse her out. Threw a regular fit. Then he ran outside, stole an orange, and dared me to come out and take it away from him. You can see I'm pretty good size but then so is he, and in his condition I can tell you I wasn't about to argue the point."

"He's a big one, all right. Probably strong, too. I don't blame you a bit, Dan. Not a bit. Thank you."

Pierce called Miss Putnam next. I expected big things

141

from her when she took the stand, but she only stayed up there long enough to lie.

"Yes, he did," she said, pulling on her handkerchief.

"Could you give us some idea what they were?"

"I couldn't repeat them here. I just couldn't. They were . . ."

"I see. Say no more, Miss Putnam, we understand. So that's the sort of language he uses to a young woman. Well, well."

Taking her arm, Pierce led her back to her seat, her nose buried in her handkerchief. Weeping for the truth, I imagine.

"Your Honor," broke out Billings, exasperated. "Whether or not my client used such language to the witness seems hardly to the point. All of this allegedly happened two days *after* the event in question. What possible bearing can it have on the case?"

"The court is quite aware of that fact," growled Wiggins, his young feathers ruffled. "Certainly as aware as Counsel for the defendant. Proceed, Mr. Pierce."

"Exception," cried Billings, and threw down his pencil in disgust.

"Noted. Proceed, Mr. Pierce."

Wiggins appeared so cocky and sure of himself that it made me wonder. Did the girl and those others know something about what happened that I had missed? That I wasn't letting myself see? I couldn't believe it. Fact is they were all in it together. Maybe even the judge, too. And as the trial went on, the outlook began to seem bleaker and bleaker.

LaBombard came forward and claimed I was trying to break off his doorknob because he didn't have any anti-freeze. Carter's wife held that her husband never got along with me and that she was always expecting something like this to happen. Only reason they stayed on, according to her, was that Alma was so nice to them.

"After what happened, Mrs. Newfield even brought over some peanut-butter cookies," she revealed, and you just knew from the sounds in the courtroom that everyone there was thinking how could a nice woman like that bear living with Newfield all these years. I warned you about going over there, Alma. See what they're trying to do to your husband? That's the way they repay kindness.

The Carter brat was on stage next, dazzled by the limelight into having an opinion about everything. Swore that he believed I hated his father and hated him, and anybody who hated kids probably hated himself. Added, by the way, that he was there when I beat up his old man. But Billings wasn't going to let that get by him unchallenged.

"Tell me, young man," he asked during cross-examination, "did you actually see Mr. Newfield strike your father that evening?"

"Yes, sir. I was there when he did it."

"I didn't ask you whether you were there or not. Pay attention. This is important, so I want you to think very hard before you answer me. What I want to know is did you actually see Mr. Newfield *with your own eyes* lay a hand on your father?"

The boy hesitated, glancing in my direction and then away. "Well, no," he admitted, shamefaced. "Not exactly."

"That will be all, young man," said Billings, and sat down.

"But I saw him turn him over with his foot looking for his gold tooth. He was trying to steal it. Would have, too, if I hadn't grabbed it away from him."

"*That,*" repeated Billings sharply, "will be all!"

Then Carter himself was rolled out to put in his two cents and the finishing touches on me. Made an effort not to listen too hard. Didn't want to get any more upset than I was. Concentrating on the wheezing of Russell who was seated right behind me on the other side of the fence. . . . *into Dan's and began working me over without cause.* Russell snorting angrily, so I shifted to Billings who was toying with his pencil and taking notes. *Thinks just because he's rich he can get away with murder.* Solemn nods of agreement from Carter's fan club, their eyes covering the back of my head like mealworms. Couldn't imagine who he was talking about. Didn't sound like anybody I knew. . . . *all it was. Them two lousy cans. And I told him about it soon as it happened.* Even without looking at Alma, I could sense what she was feeling. Like in the old days. Supporting me right down the line. We'll make it, honey, don't you fret. Just a matter of time before I straighten this business out and we can go home. *Well, he went clean out of his mind then. Cursing me out and spitting on me and punching me and you name it.* Holding on to the edge of my seat as if it might shake me loose any minute. I'll throttle you yet, Carter. Why don't you tell them how you were soused? How I told you to go home and sleep it off? How you banged around my machines to aggravate me? How you belched at my cows? How you deliberately spilled that milk to get even with me for having to work on Christmas? Why don't you tell them that, big mouth? The judge leaning forward and spooning up Carter's slop as if it was whipped cream. This Wiggins was no Solomon, by a long shot.

When Pierce was through with Carter, Billings had a go at him but without success, and the judge declared a short recess for lunch and left. He was about the only one. Practically everyone else keeping their seats for fear they might lose them to the crowd waiting just outside the rear door at the top of the stairs. Brown bags filled with sandwiches and apples popping up all around the room. Archie Grubb watching Plunket crack walnuts between his teeth and laughing. Making a picnic out of my execution. Always a joy to see people or animals taking nourishment. Without choking. Or otherwise souring their intestinal tract. But I know such things can happen. On a good day.

As for me, I had lost my appetite, which was unheard of. Alma pushing her veil back in disbelief, the upper part of her face a shade lighter even than the lower, two-tone, like when you take off a bathing suit.

"But bring *her* back something," I instructed Billings, handing him two quarters.

"That's not necessary. It's on me."

"Take it." Thrust the money back into his hand. "I don't need charity."

Billings took the coins quickly, not wanting to make a scene. "Don't lose heart, Orin," he said, making an effort to cheer me up. "When court resumes it will be our turn. We're not through yet." On his way out through the gate he paused. "And if Wiggins finds against us," he added, with determination, "we'll appeal."

Most reassuring. I didn't need him to tell me how bad things were going. Not only could the judge charge me damages for Carter's pelvis and each broken rib and general wear-and-tear plus interest compounded quarterly but he also had it in his power to put me away for a long, long time. But Billings wasn't breathing a word about this. Afraid I might panic and do something indiscreet like blow town. Flee behind the Iron Curtain. He

145

didn't know me very well. The handyman had been punished fair and square and sooner or later they were going to have to acknowledge it. If I lived that long.

Standing by the window with my feet tucked under the accordion-pleated radiator and flashbulbs exploding in my brain. Some reporter from the *Valley Gazette* taking pictures. Gave him the small of my back and listened to the steam. Forehead resting against the cool glass. To reduce the swelling caused by prolonged exposure to crap. Twelve panes in the upper frame and each one filled with the same account. Good old glass! You could always depend on glass to give you a straight story. The flat top on the post office, a modern, one-story, red-brick box. Beyond it the pitched roof of the Magic Dollar. And towering over both of them the mansard of Farnum House with its twin stacks. Hardly any serious snow to speak of on the last two, but on the post office it was piled high in perfect mounds. That flat roof troubling me. Thought about it for quite some time. It was a mistake. Bearing the full weight of a few of our winters that roof was going to go. No doubt about it, only a question of time. In Farnum you can't risk offering too much exposed area to the elements. Whatever it is, they'll wear it down and do it in. Just like the government to build something wasteful like that. Tolliver tiptoeing around my elbow trying to tell me that the judge was on his way. Let him look, too, it's a free country. If I could face up to reality others were bound to enjoy it too. A dirty sky and impending doom. Nothing really new there, egg man, if you'd been focusing properly all your life. The secret is not to let it get in your way. To put together something in spite of. Like sixty-three hydraulic Holsteins on three hundred and twenty-seven choice acres. Before it's too late and you're washed up, packed in, and down the drain without leaving so much as a healthy turd behind to be remembered by.

"Please, Mr. Newfield. The judge."

Billings had come back and was huddled with Alma, pointing to one of his many papers and hurriedly explaining something. And her listening with eyes wide open and innocent, nodding gravely. Hanging down from the hem of her skirt a long curly black thread undermining her dignity. Poor Alma.

"What are you doing, Orin?" she asked, alarmed at seeing me bending down beneath her chair.

"A thread." I tore it off.

"Would you like some coffee? I've saved you some."

"Not now." Drinks too much damn coffee, Alma.

The judge gaveling and the court coming to order. Placing a reassuring hand on my shoulder as if to say, here we go, over the top, GERONIMO, my melodramatic jackass of a lawyer rose and called his first witness. It was Dutcher. Saw him sitting on the aisle when we first came in. Wondered what he was doing here.

"Your name, please."

"August Dutcher. But if you like you can call me Augie because that's what most people do. August, Augie, either way. It makes no difference to me."

Goddamn windbag. What the hell does Billings think *he* knows about this? He wasn't even there.

"That's fine. I understand, Mr. Dutcher—"

"Suit yourself. If you're happy, I'm happy."

"Fine, fine. Now, Mr. Dutcher, I understand that on the day after Christmas you went to Mr. Newfield's farm as usual to pick up his milk. Will you tell the court what you told me of your conversation with Mr. Newfield that day?"

"Glad to. You see it was snowing something fierce and

that, plus the double pickups after the holiday, held me up for a couple of hours so I was a little late getting to Mr. Newfield's place. It had nothing to do with my rig, though, because I've got one of the best on the road. An International with a "

"That's all very interesting. But could you get to the reason Mr. Newfield gave you to explain why Mr. Carter wasn't able to work that day?"

"Right. I was coming to that. Mr. Newfield told me that Roy—that is, Mr. Carter—had an accident. And I couldn't see that he was mad at him or anything like that, which he might have been if there had been a fight. Even said he'd send my regards."

"An accident, you say."

"That's it. Heard it with my own ears. He said Roy Carter had an accident."

Idiot! I said it but I didn't mean it. It was a joke. Pierce saw that right away, but he couldn't get Dutcher to agree with him and passed.

Billings' next witness was a real surprise. Out of the blue came old man Spooner, waddling up in his overalls and plunking himself down on the witness stand like a permanent fixture, his cane between his legs. Might have been sitting there all his life. Small bright eyes in a glowing face wreathed by a kinky white beard. The picture of health. Remarkable the way it resembled the negative of the one on the wall. Spooner came into town rarely and he looked the better for it. His appearance causing quite a stir in the courtroom and when he told what he saw Christmas Day the noise grew louder and more nasty with every passing word until the judge, fearing that things might get out of hand, put it down with a few raps.

"Drunk as Noah, he was," chuckled the old man, eyes

148

a-twinkle. "Weaving back and forth cross the road and howling at the top of his lungs. 'Silent Night' was the tune if I remember rightly. Scared the hell out of my dogs, I can tell you that."

Now we're getting somewhere! But just when I thought things were looking up, Pierce dug his hooks into the old man. Asking him if he didn't like to take a drop now and then himself and slyly making out that maybe he was the one who had the Christmas staggers. Besides, everybody knew his boy Wayne. "Basically a good boy, I'm sure," Pierce sympathized in an oily voice, "but with an unquenchable thirst. Not to mention a police record going back to grade school." The lawyer hinting that the apple didn't fall far from the tree. Chewing nervously on the ends of his beard, Spooner appeared a mite crestfallen. He wasn't the only one.

Queer loud reports in the courtroom that I finally pinned down north of my navel. An empty belly is a social handicap. Mine clattering like a wagonload of pots and pans, creating an unfavorable impression on the court. Busy tightening my stomach muscles so as not to be held in contempt when I spied this little girl sitting primly up in front of the room with her knees together, hands folded calmly in her lap, and a black pancake on her head. How did I get her into this? Come back, Alma. She seemed so small up there, so helpless. If Pierce does anything to upset her, I'll wring the tongue out of his head and use it for a cowbell clapper.

But Billings was asking the questions now and she was speaking so softly that I had to strain to catch her answers.

"Yes, that's right," she said simply. "Mr. Carter was drunk."

Stunned silence in the courtroom. The way she said it

even Carter's own mother would have had to believe it. Wonderful! That-a-girl, Alma. Give it to them.

"No. He never insisted. When Mr. Carter came into the barn that way, he said not to. There had been some accidents and he didn't want any more. He told him to go home and lie down."

The truth, at last! You tell 'em, Alma. Make them bleed. Gloating, when it suddenly occurred to me how the hell did she know that?

"Mrs. Newfield," said Billings gently, so as not to frighten her, "how is it that you know that?"

"I was there."

"You mean you were actually an eyewitness to what went on that day in the barn?"

"Yes, that's right."

Pierce frowned and excitedly began to exchange words with Carter. Alma, what are you saying?

"I see. Well then, could you tell us exactly what it was that happened there as you remember it?"

Don't do it, Alma! You can't. I won't let you. Gripping the edge of my seat and holding on for dear life.

In a calm, matter-of-fact voice Alma laid out her version of the events of that day and neatly stitched them together into a handsome piece of merchandise. Carter was drunk, the milk was spilled, he was asked to leave, he refused, a few angry words, there were no blows, he was shown the door, he reeled drunkenly out of the barn, he tripped, he fell, he hurt himself: and no, Mr. Newfield, and absolutely not and in no way was he responsible for what happened.

It was horrible. She couldn't possibly have dreamed this up all by herself. You can bet Billings had a hand in it somewhere. Other than the angry rumbles from my

150

belly there wasn't a peep in the courtroom. The judge must have heard the noise and known where it was coming from. While Alma filled in the particulars he kept glancing suspiciously in my direction, his gavel poised, as if he expected trouble any minute. He needn't have bothered. What he heard was only me eating my heart out. With dry lips and a flannel tongue. Newfield crippled by good intentions. I'll come quietly, your Honor. Limping to the gallows.

"Yes, indeed. I certainly do want to ask that witness some questions," announced Carter's lawyer, and he went at Alma as if he was going to tear her apart. I almost wished him luck. But Billings had coached her well and she stuck to her story like the truth. Pierce couldn't do a thing with her and he seemed to be getting more ruffled with every soft-spoken answer she gave. The way he was rubbing at his scalp there wouldn't have been anything left of his hair if he had had any to start with. Rubbing away and puffing out his cheeks in exasperation. It amazed me that Alma could be so strong. I would never have believed it. Sold a bill of goods by the lawyer, she was determined to see me through and wasn't going to be budged for anything. Misguided, sure, but in some mixed-up way she probably thought she was helping me. Who the hell asked her to stick her neck out when the truth would have been sufficient? Take it from me, it's not a woman's eyes that should be veiled but her mouth. And yet, though I hated to admit it even to myself, I felt a sneaky sense of pride in Alma's sweet mulishness. She wasn't about to let Pierce get the better of her no how. Nice to see a little grit in that small container for a change. Unable to crack the defense's eyewitness, Pierce finally gave up in frustration and slumped back to

151

his seat to lick his wounds and figure out some new line of attack. In like a lion and out like a lamb. Shorn to the bone.

Billings so elated he had all he could do to keep from breaking out in a strut as he approached the judge. "The last witness I should like to call is Orin Newfield."

"Orin Newfield," shouted the clerk of the court. "Orin Newfield to the stand."

Heard him the first time. Scowling at Billings as I came forward. Quite the little schemer, aren't you, lawyer? Almost as bad as the other one. Didn't even bother to tell me what you had in mind. Afraid I wouldn't be a party to it and counting on backing me into a corner with Alma's testimony. Pretty damn clever, but I can see through you like a moth-eaten sweater. You never should have done that to Alma.

Shoving a book at me, the clerk was mumbling something. He raised his right hand. He put it down. He pointed to mine. Why not, I thought, and stuck it up.

"Do you solemnly swear to tell the right, the wholesome, the deep regardless of immoderate laughter and low titters so help you God?"

What's this about tits? Slow down, goddamnit! Way he rushed his words together it was impossible for a careful man to keep track of all of them.

"Well do you?" he asked, annoyed.

"Do I what?"

The snot looking at me as if he couldn't believe it. A typical petty bureaucrat. They learn to sneer that way in their cradles.

"Mr. Newfield," irritatedly broke in the judge, "let's get on with it. Do you swear to tell the truth so help you God?"

"I always tell the truth."

"How refreshing. Then swear it."

"Can't do that."

"Why not, may I ask?"

"I'm not a believer." It wasn't exactly a secret but Farnum couldn't take it out loud. Widespread gagging in the gallery and Peaselee stiff as a plank.

"That's not necessary in a court of law. Read him the other oath, clerk."

Had no notion that they'd have a special one for people like me. Pleasing to think that somewhere in the state of Vermont there might actually be somebody else to talk to with a little intelligence.

"Do you solemnly affirm and declare that what you are about to say is clean, neat, and free of the sour taint of spoilage under the pains and penalties of perjury?"

Sounded sensible. At least those parts I could make out. What the hell, I figured, I'll humor him. "Sure," I agreed, and Billings jumped right in. Sweeping under the carpet any bad impression that my godlessness might have made with a lot of quick questions and fancy footwork. He was shrewd, all right. Asking only what he was sure of and cutting me off when I tried to tell him the truth. "Yes, Carter was drunk and—" "Yes, he spilled my milk and—" "Yes, I removed him from the barn but . . . but—. Now hold on! Just a minute!"

"Your witness," said Billings politely, and washed his hands of me.

Wouldn't give me a chance to tell him anything. But no matter how he had boxed me in, the difference between right and wrong couldn't be sloughed off that easily. I had my conscience to think of. Setting up such a racket that my teeth were beginning to ache. Somehow or other I was determined to get the news out. And when Pierce ambled over, licking his chops, I could hear opportunity knocking at the door.

The first ten minutes dragged by without an opening. A lot of stupid, beside-the-point questions about my health and the farm, most of which Billings objected to with not much success. They were warm-up lobs wide of the mark. Popped them right back to him, keeping my eye out for the big one. Then Pierce, who had been pacing back and forth, came to a halt in front of me and drew himself up. Uh-oh. Here it comes.

"Now when this milk of yours was accidentally spilled —Am I boring you, *Mr.* Newfield?"

"What?"

"I see you're yawning."

"Sorry."

"As I was saying, when that happened . . ."

Must be nerves. On your toes, Newfield.

". . . did you willfully lay hands on Roy with the intention of teaching him a lesson, so to speak?"

There it was. A fast ball right over the plate and all I had to do was lay the truth to it and send it flying. But right before my eyes it splintered into a half-dozen smaller balls that curved, sank, slid, and jiggled. There was justice and truth and right and wrong and putting Billings in his place—but most of all there was Alma. After what she had done for me, how could I make a liar out of her? Perjury! The Women's House of Detention! Terrible steel braces on the doors and bathrooms in the hall. Even with me calling to her through the bars every day she wouldn't last a week.

"Well, did you?" repeated Pierce, with a show of impatience.

What will it be, sport? Swing for the fences and risk

striking out or lay down a sure lie and advance all runners. You *are* a team player, aren't you, Newfield?

"No." I won't do it. "No, I didn't do it." And suddenly it wasn't only my teeth that were aching.

Seemed to take the heart right out of Pierce. I suppose he thought he had been dealing with an honest man. He had no interest in a liar. A few more questions to make sure and then he dismissed me with a wave and a grunt. I couldn't see that I was worth even that much. Slouched down in my seat, as small as possible, and ignored the cheerful whispers of Alma and Billings. Shut the door and turned off the lights. Brooding on the inside. The breath of hecklers an icy wind gusting, swirling, blowing through my mind. Freezing my pipes and canceling all vital signs. Tempting me not to live forever.

Frankly I didn't much care about the trial after that one way or the other. It wasn't going to prove a thing— even if they sent me to jail. And Alma along with me. Which they might very well do because Pierce put Carter's wife and kid back on the stand to give her the lie. The missus didn't have too much to add because she disremembered exactly when it was that she had first noticed Alma at the barn, but the boy swore black and blue that Mrs. Newfield couldn't have seen anything because she didn't show up until after it was all over. Had to admit that for the truth it sounded pretty convincing. Suddenly all I could think of was penitentiaries. They had cement floors. And with her Mortinson's toe . . . Poor Alma.

"May we take your case to be concluded, Mr. Pierce?"

"I guess that's it. I have nothing more, your Honor."

"All right. Then may we hear your closing argument?"

Pierce let him have it. Saying that the defendant must not be allowed to get away with this brutality just because he happened to be one of the wealthiest farm owners in the area and his client was only a poor workingman. Going over and over Carter's injuries, rubbing them into the judge like a massage, and holding that no reasonable person could imagine that they were acquired accidentally. Newfield's temper was well-known throughout Farnum and had been established beyond question by several of the witnesses. An unbalanced man, he called me, and a real danger to society. Which was probably true, at least the last part. Finally wrapped up his case by talking about the irony—the irony, your Honor!—that that big ox should have chosen of all days, Christmas, on which to brutally attack little Roy. With that, there was such general carrying on in the court you'd have thought it was a funeral. Eyes welling up and noses dribbling. Made me wish I had the handkerchief concession.

To his credit, Billings was brief and to the point when he got his turn. Those were about the only virtues I could find in what he had to say. Otherwise it was pretty much all quarter-truths, half-truths, and out-and-out lies. That I had sworn to, so I couldn't even feel sorry for myself. According to him, drunkards were always busting themselves up, and Roy Carter was a drunkard. Old and frail, he was more susceptible to serious injury than a younger man would have been in a similar situation. It was an accident, pure and simple. Just for the hell of it, I glanced over my shoulder to see if anyone behind me had been stupid enough to swallow Billings' story. Couldn't say that I blamed them. Looked to me as if they had their minds pretty well made up.

Then it was the judge's turn. Apparently it wasn't necessary for him to retire to mull over the facts and empty his bladder. Came to a decision right away. Though he didn't seem to be rushing to let anybody know what it was. Enjoyed hearing himself talk and long words billowing from his lips like streamers. Spellbinding his listeners with heinous and derogatory and stipulation and pointing in my direction. Got the impression that he didn't think too much of me. Especially when he rambled on about bad manners in the court and parties with wicked tempers. Finally came right out in the open, making no bones about it. Stating flatly that he'd like to throw the book at me, and the courtroom held its breath.

"There is no question of the grievous and lamentable damage suffered by the plaintiff. Unfortunately, however," and here he looked at Alma, "there does seem to exist a reasonable doubt that battery has actually occurred in this instance, and inasmuch as assault requires intent to do bodily harm and no such intent has been conclusively proven, we must, though with considerable reluctance, find the defendant not guilty."

I wasn't expecting that, but there it was. Not exactly a vote of confidence, but I had won. Dutcher patting me on the back and Billings congratulating me and shaking my hand and Alma in tears. Made me feel sick to my stomach. As if I was standing head and shoulders above the crowd waving from the top rung of a ladder fifty feet in the air. And it broke.

My ears detecting a low ominous rumble in the background. The thwarted gripe of the sore loser. Complaints turning into rage and gathering momentum. Filling every nook and cranny of the courtroom, pushing the walls out, busting open the doors, shooting up the bell tower, spouting out the chimney, spreading over the whole of Farnum like a thick black storm cloud. And all because of me.

The cripple limping slowly up the aisle with his faithful wife clinging to his arm when this young assassin jumps out and pokes a lens into his bloodshot eyeballs.

"Give us a victory smile, Mr. Newfield."

I didn't feel very smiley at the moment.

"Go ahead, big shot. Don't be shy."

"It's not going to cost you anything. Give the kid a smile."

"Yeah, while you still have all your teeth."

Whirled around and there was Hatch flanked by Grubb and Plunket, looking on with blank faces and their mouths buttoned up tighter than my suit jacket. I must be hearing things.

"Please, Orin," said Alma, tugging at my arm. "Let's go."

She was right. Besides there were more important things on my mind. Brushed the kid halfheartedly to one side and led Alma out the door thinking. Of how under the circumstances I had tried to do the good thing, but got distracted.

11

"Ask Ben to stay for supper," said Alma, the first words either of us had spoken since leaving the courthouse. I was in no hurry. Waiting to pick just the right time to have it out with her. Pulled up the driveway and around his station wagon to avoid blocking it. Choosing not to throw any unnecessary obstacles in the way of his departure. The brake light on the right side told the whole story about her brother. It had been smashed five months ago when he backed into a tree stump and was still the same. Not that he was lazy, which he wasn't, just easily satisfied. Bachelors tend to be that way in my experience.

Alma hobbling off. Hobbling because she didn't wear the tan shoes often enough to break them in. A perfectly good pair in her size and she was hobbling. Quickly into the house so as not to give me a chance to say no. Trying to use company to put off what she knew was coming. That's all right, Alma, I'll see you later.

To the barn to see how that brother of hers was taking care of my beauties. Co-co looking somewhat peaked as if he had left the tubes on her longer than necessary but other than that I couldn't detect any wrongdoing. On the surface. Just easy munching on both sides of the alley. By and large, he did an adequate job. Which he owed me, since I never charged him a penny for the annual loan of one of my tractors. But to give him his due, he was always ready in a pinch to fill in for me. That and the fact that he had no sense of humor I'd say were the two qualities that showed him to best advantage. Slim pickings, but then it's a wife you choose, not a brother-in-law.

"I had an idea it might take you longer than you thought," he said, putting the plugs to Camille.

And her turning her head to give me the glad eye as I came up. Patted her on the pinbones for thinking of me.

"What's the matter with Co-co?"

"Nothing so far as I know."

"She doesn't look good to me."

"I didn't notice anything."

"She seems worn out."

"I'm a little tired myself."

"OK, I'll do the rest. Thanks for getting started."

"This is the last one," he said, uncramping his legs and straightening up. White hair parted down the middle and permanent red welts on the bridge of his nose from the clip-on glasses he used for reading the sports pages. Might have passed for a banker except that he didn't have the money. He looked me over glumly, his normal expression. "Besides you've got your good clothes on."

"Mind those plugs. She tends to pull." Grabbing the hand truck, I began rolling the cans out to the milk house. At the top of the ramp I called back to him, "Alma wants you to stay for supper."

"For supper?"

"If you're free that is." But it was so hopeless I didn't bother to wait to hear his answer.

After the cans had been put away and the machines taken apart and scrubbed up, I closed shop and we walked across to the house. Him giving me these funny sidelong glances all the while and when he saw I wasn't going to say anything finally coming out with it.

"How did it go for you in town?" he was dying to know.

"Not bad." And that's all he'd get from me. Ben was a blabber with friends, it didn't pay to tell him too much.

"Oh, that's fine. Carter should have never taken it to court. That's no way to settle things."

It was better than I expected from him, but then he hadn't had an opportunity yet to talk to his chums in town. They'd set him straight in short order.

As we came up the driveway I could hear the telephone ringing in the house and the light went on in the living room as Alma came in to get it. I yanked Ben toward me.

"What's the matter?" he asked, alarmed.

"Stay on the path. She's got something growing there."

"Oh . . ."

We went inside and I took his coat while he struggled out of his boots. Hung it up on a peg in the hall along with my own and wandered into the living room. Alma standing there motionless with her back to the door holding the phone.

"That for me?" I asked.

Thought she'd jump right out of her slippers. "You scared me!" she cried, flushed as if she'd just stepped from a hot bath.

"Who is it?"

"Oh, nothing," she replied, her voice back to normal. She hung up the phone. "A wrong number. Is Ben with you?"

"He's inside."

"Why don't you both go in and wash up? Supper will be ready in a minute."

Now Ben is one of those people we all know who never seems to get dirty, a little like the kid Roger in that respect. I couldn't see where he needed any improvement. But when I had toweled off my hands and opened the bathroom door, there he was waiting his next. Sent by his sister to touch up perfection at the expense of my well. As usual she was treating him like visiting royalty. And this time there was even a fresh white cloth on the table and linen napkins. Alma sparing no expense. Going to amazing lengths to make something special of this meal. Called Newfield's last supper. Serving up my favorite food in all this world. Boned chicken sautéed in tomato soup with pimientos, green pepper, and a sprinkling of basil. And scallions, mustn't forget the scallions. Oh, those delectable sweet shoots, those tender little crunchy whorls that melt in your mouth. And there it all was under my nose, so to speak. Pale red bubbling in a dark red casserole on a rectangular field of white. After what had happened in court, I was in no mood for a celebration, but the smell alone was dissolving my mouth into a helpless pool of juices. Don't imagine that you're going to get around me that way, Alma. Mark my words, there'll be a full accounting when the coast is clear. Meanwhile, however, I'll just dig in. The way she was dishing it out to that freeloader you'd think there were only the two of them. One side, wife. Never let it be said that good manners blinded Newfield to reality.

The meal crowding out all the ugliness in my life. Each mouthful stuffing the sack with joy, with fragrance. Leaving my mind a better place for having had the experience. And the good effects not only limited to this side of the table. Even that great sow's ear over there had for the moment been turned into something fit for a human being to associate with. His chronic frozen face now featuring a kindly, bless-you-my-children expression. Oh I was fooling fine. It was a chicken to remember, a night to remember. With brother-in-law glowing pink in the firelight like a belt buckle. And Alma all stardust and angel. And me mellow.

Over the dirty dishes I lazily picked my teeth and marveled at the resemblance between those two. The older they got the more they were growing to look like one another. I thought that was only supposed to happen to married couples. Ah nature, you cunning witch! Full of all sorts of tricks, aren't you? But then they were unusually close.

Ben opening the three bottom buttons on his sweater and leaning back in his chair to say, "That was a first-rate dinner, Alma. A *first-rate* dinner."

"Have some of these," she said, offering him a bowl of mixed raisins and almonds. He took a handful and chewed with his mouth closed, the fancy way. Right there my good humor began to lose its sheen. Alma watched him with complete satisfaction. The fire crackling down and Ben crunching and Alma smoothing out the apron covering her dress and me tapping my fork on the table like a blind man's cane. Waiting for him to swallow and go home.

Alma leaned forward on her elbows. There was something on her mind. "They say," she cleared her throat, "they say Mr. Truman's daughter is taking singing lessons."

"I read about that." Her brother reached for the bowl again.

"She wants to become an opera singer. She wants to

163

have a career of her own."

"Seems to be an ambitious girl."

"Damned Democrats! Turning the White House into a burlesque theater."

"Now be fair, Orin." The small farmer rising to the defense of his price supports. Carrying on as if his old man had been one of the original mugwumps. "No matter what you may think of the Democrats, you can't say that Mrs. Roosevelt was ever musical."

"What the hell is that supposed to prove?"

"Go ahead, Ben," said Alma gently. "Have some more."

Her brother mumbling over his nuts. He knew when he had enough. Should be leaving any minute now. And there he goes, pushing his chair back from the table.

"Only three more days," he reported. "Who do you pick in the Rose Bowl?"

A false alarm.

"The football game," he explained, talking as if to some kind of dunce. "You know, the Rose Bowl."

"I don't go to football games."

"This one is in California."

"I wouldn't go if it was in my backyard."

"I've never seen California," said Alma wistfully, staring at the dying fire.

"I was to Los Angeles." Ben shook his head to verify the fact and lighted up a cigarette.

Now I'll never get rid of him.

"I was there for about a week in the Army. It's got a nice climate. Mild in the summer and mild in the winter. That's why they hold the game way out that way."

"Someday I'd like to see Los Angeles. I'd like to see Los Angeles before I die."

"What's so damn special about Los Angeles?"

"It's got a nice climate," said Ben.

"Orin," said Alma, catching at my sleeve. "I want to go away."

She was on to that again. "What's wrong with this plooo?"

"Not permanently, just a vacation."

"That's a good idea, Orin. Alma looks as if she could stand a change. Don't worry about the farm. I can take care of yours and mine both, and I'll get in the boy I use in the summer to help."

Have it all figured out, don't you? They seemed to be in this thing together. I was just about to tell him I'd be much obliged if he'd keep his fuckin' nose out of my affairs when the telephone rang. Alma started to get up but I put my hand on her shoulder.

"I'll get it." Let her listen to his drivel, he wasn't my brother. As I left the room he was explaining to her that the herd would be no trouble. They knew him as well as if they were his own. They'd never miss me.

The damn fool. "Hello!" I shouted into the receiver. "Hello. Who is this?"

"That you, Newfield?"

The voice sounded familiar but I couldn't place it. "That's right."

"We're still waiting. Didn't your wife give you the message?"

"What message? Who is this?"

"Why don't you come down to the green right now, Newfield? We've got a little bone to pick with you."

"What's this all about?" The smell of liquor so strong it was coming through the line. "Who is this?"

"Let's just say a few of Roy Carter's friends want to teach you a little lesson."

165

"Why you sonofabitch! Is that you, Plunket?"

"We'll be waiting."

"As far as I'm concerned you can wait there until your asses freeze off and roll down the green like bowling balls. Did you hear that, Plunket? Plunket, is that you?" I roared, trying to put the finger on him, but the line was dead. With only a faint humming left in my ear to mark his hideout. A memento like Plymouth Rock. Under which they say there are also many snakes. Not to mention mushrooms.

When I went back inside to join the party the fire had gone out. Alma and her brother staring from cold white upturned faces as I entered the room. Making me feel like a TB carrier.

"Who was that?" she asked, sounding out of breath.

"Wrong number."

Ben looked as if something he had eaten disagreed with him. His old self.

"What's the matter?" I asked him. "Don't you believe me?"

"If you say so, Orin."

"Probably the same party who called earlier," I added, looking squarely at Alma. She lowered her eyes. I should hope so. Seemed to have more secrets than I ever imagined. Round ones and square ones and tiny green triangular ones with razor-sharp edges buried at the bottom of a trunk in her attic. It shook me more than the telephone call. How many other times had she lied to me I wondered. And one leading contagiously to another. We're going to do some serious talking, you and me, Alma. But all in good time. Stuck my foot into the fireplace to see if there was any heat left in the back side of the log and it flaked out under my shoe. For crissake, was he planning to stay all night?

"I don't know about you," I told him point-blank, "but I've got to work tomorrow. I'm going to bed."

" 'night, Orin," he said.

I had to go. The idiot couldn't even take a hint.

But Alma caught me before I got to the door. Filling my arms with sorrow and bad breath. Reminding me of my mother's mouth when I was a kid. That foul smell again. Mortality shrinking the gums from the bone. She said she couldn't bear any more. She said she was exhausted. She said she needed peace and quiet. She said what she had done for me at the trial was more than anybody had a right to expect.

"Who asked you to do anything but tell the truth?" I bellowed, and all I could think of was not now, Alma. Not with him here.

"He said you'd go to prison otherwise."

Damnit, what's the matter with you? Can't you understand I'm waiting to pick the right moment?

"Who said that?" Ben wanted to know, his eyes round and his cigarette burned down so close to his fingers that the flesh seemed to be smoking.

Keep out of this, you nosy bastard.

"His lawyer. He said—"

"Shut up, Alma," I whispered through clenched teeth and grabbed her wrist.

"You're hurting me. Let go."

"You don't want to do that, Orin," suggested her brother, giving me the benefit of his advice.

"Shut up."

"Well stop that. Leave her be," he cried, coming around the table.

She was trying to pull away when there was the snap of dead wood breaking. "Now look what you've done," I shouted at him for no particular reason.

167

"What's the matter with you, Orin?" Red-faced and wheezing, he struggled to undo our hands like some complicated knot. "Have you gone crazy?"

An interesting question. However, this was no time for it. "Get out of here," I warned him, yanking his hands away, but they stuck fast to mine.

Newfield the king of the dance. With two partners, one dragging her tootsies and the other trying to lead. Stumbling around the room upsetting chairs, colliding with tables, and slipping dangerously on butter knives. While also engaged in a spirited, free-style, three-dimensional hand-wrestling contest. Brought to a satisfactory conclusion by bending back his opponent's fingers into the shape of a coat hook.

"That's my sister," he complained bitterly, winded and gulping down air.

"And this is the door," I said, letting go of Alma and holding it open for him. "You heard what I said. Beat it. And don't come back."

"Do what he says, Ben." Alma rubbed at her wrist. "I'll be all right."

But he wouldn't leave until he had examined her for broken bones and despairing tissue. As if he could tell. Playing the devoted brother and making me look bad in the process. Didn't she say there was nothing wrong?

"Where do you think you're going now?" I called exasperated, as he went inside. He returned from the hall with his coat. In silence, he sat down and pulled on his boots. Hurry up, goddamnit, I'm not going to hold this thing open forever. Even with the storm door closed it was still cold where I was standing. And goose pimples crawling up my legs. Don't you know when you've been shown the door, meddler? I shut it until he was finished. Noting a long, angry-looking scratch down the back of his right hand. Self-inflicted, most likely, to soil my good name. I wouldn't put it past him. Who eats your food and picks a fight.

"I'll be by tomorrow," he promised Alma in leaving.

"Don't do us any favors," I said.

Alma sat down limply and spread her fingers wide on the tablecloth. Staring at them. Her wrist a delicate shade of blue edging off into buttercup yellow. Looked at abstractly it lent a nice touch of color to the room. Sorry about that, Alma, but you should have known better than to bring up private family matters in front of witnesses. Still, I'm not one to hold a grudge. Let's sit down and discuss this business like two sensible people. I pulled up a chair.

Now first off why did you let Billings fondle your testimony and tamper with your spotless bloom? I see, it was done for me. Perfectly understandable. But still there's the matter of that phone call. A secret admirer perhaps? Of course not, you say. Daddy mustn't be upset by every anonymous crank with the price of a telephone call in his pocket. Done for me again and well done. Most thoughtful. But then what of the rest? The threats to run off with ineligible clergymen. The sweet treats taken to strange beds behind my back. And the hundred and one other God knows what. You don't mean to say . . . for me? All, all, all done for me. It was true. I could see that now. She hated me because I refused her sacrifices and she hated me for those she had made. I ask you, how can you talk reasonably to somebody like that? Newfield cracking under the strain. Making gargling noises. Releasing gale-force winds. Removing his shoe and banging it on the table. So to speak.

"Will you stop trying to do me favors, Alma? I don't want to be protected. Can you understand that? Can you get that through your head? I want to know what's happening to me. I want to know that I'm alive. I'm a man, goddamnit, not a grapefruit!"

Alma began carefully, laying each word out like an operating instrument "If you won't go," she said, "I'm going to leave without you."

"What's that?"

"I mean it, Orin. You'll have to decide."

"You don't know what you're saying."

"One way or the other," she declared without emotion. Pushing herself up with one hand, she removed her apron and dropped it on top of the dirty dishes. "I don't care. I'm too tired. I'm going to bed."

"A good idea. Get some rest. You've had too much excitement today. It's bad for your condition."

"I can't live up to you, Orin. I'm not that strong. I don't want to have to fight the world. I want to get along with people. I want them to like me."

"Of course you do. Off you go now. A good night's sleep is just what the doctor ordered."

"Either way," she said as she trundled off to bed holding her wrist, "I don't give a damn."

The gentle breeze of her passing causing a trembling in my extremities. My God, what's got into her? And where does she get these wild ideas from? That brother of hers a likely source of pollution if I ever saw one. Why she could barely cross the room without my help and here she wants to run away all by herself. To wander alone in foreign cities where small dark men in pointy shoes wave briefcases and shout halloo. She'd die. But tomorrow was another day. A clean page to scribble on, wide margins for corrections. She'll be up with the sunbeams and everything OK. Letting bygones be. I cleaned up the dishes for her and went around the house cheer-

170

fully shutting off the lights. Throwing a chill into the heart of the Central Vermont Public Service Corporation. Then a few healthy yawns to flush out the fumes of the day. Then into bed. And the cold sheet on my side. The kiss of the hops, a bare ass on a frozen fender. Wiggling my toes to keep the blood flowing down there in the deep water. Look out below, here comes Newfield. Going under while thinking things. Like how you could never count on people to go according to plan. And how I preferred cows.

A million-dollar smile was Newfield's nogginnote when the judge came in on metal crutches. His black cape aflutter and the brim of his pearl gray fedora turned flapward against the elements. Reminding the defendant of one who shall remain nameless because of the difficulty of making suitable connections on short notice. Until said judge sat down and inserted his legendary ivory cigarette holder at a jaunty angle between his world-renowned teeth, the flame from his phosphorus a set of matching lamps burning in the windows of his specs. Rimless, to be sure. Carefully regrouping the givens and reducing all fractions to their l.c.d.'s, what could you expect? After all, numbers never lie. O that sonofabitch! He was back from the dead for a fifth term. Go quickly and tell his disciples if you want to, but it's all done with mirrors, trapdoors, and synthetic fibers. Under such parlous and bile-begetting circumstantiation, Newfield did what any right-thinking Green Mountain boy would do. Extending thumb and index finger, he pincered a dilled cucumber—medium sour—and ground it up into satisfaction. Delightful. Yet it was an aggressive act and as such not calculated to win universal approval. Rumor had it that the defendant was flouting the law with malice aforethought.

BARRABAS demanded the gallery. And likewise up yours cried the bold Newfield. Undaunted despite the Oriental sneakery and redskin ambuscados of his timorous wife trying to whisk the cukeplate out from under his very nose. Not on your life, little woman. The judge industriously taking note of all this in octaplicate but otherwise beaming. By Jesus, it was impossible to insult the man. The first witness called and duly sworn into her seat and invested with all the rights and privileges assigned thereto. The widow Bromhower immediately stripping to the waist. Well, well, well, what have we here? Two tits of uneven size and dangle. Hardly conclusive evidence in itself when one considers the asymmetrical male ball or the notorious irregularity of the foots. Snagging a cuke, Newfield munched unabashedly while waiting for her to make her point. Which the widow did by moving her finger nippleward and yes, O yes, no doubt about it, there were indeed teeth marks in this tissue. Remarkable. Of course she had every right to be proud of the little bastard. Only a few months old and he had already cut a full set. The judge promptly entered them into the record as Exhibit A. But that was only half the story. Placing her pocketbook under her arm, Mrs. Bromhower stalked off the stand and shook her breasts accusingly in the defendant's face demanding that a full impression of his uppers and lowers be made forthwith to prove once and for all the true identalty of the child. Newfield wiped his fingers off on his overalls and applauded with gusto. What could have been more innocent? What more respectable? A clap or two for a pap or two and yet during this same warm and spontaneous tribute some small-minded, deceitful, fraud-ridden prudeling had snitched away his cucumbers, cramping his lifestyle into dribs and drablets. No sooner gone than recorded by that muteish magistrate and four-eyed scribe whose flashing pen dazzled the air like a glockenspiel. Making a spectacle of himself, he was. So cockeyed drunk with penmanship that he failed to realize he had puffed through his cigarette and was now smoking the holder. His judgeship working himself up to some terrible crescendo of judgment amidst dense fumes. Trembling all over, he rose in the doomroom and pronounced the awful cumulative effect of countless jurisprudential lapses and synapses, hereinafter called the verdict. Will it be chains or socks, cry the ankles? It was hard to tell, for the judge was a monotone with a wicked vibrato that shook his sentence to smithereenies. Just as he thought, thought Newfield, the man couldn't sing worth a damn. Speak up, your Honest, guilty or innocent? Outraged, his name taken in vain, the blasphemed judge opened wide his greatthroat and from the depths of his sacerdotal interior there came such a ringing and donging of churchbells as would wake the grand, the noble-hearted peacefully slumbering dead. Freedom, heyday! Heyday, freedom! Freedom, heyday!

Leaping out of bed, Newfield rushed to answer the summons. His thumping heart racing before him to announce his coming as he fingered his way cannily through the cold and darkened house. Into the living room and on with the light. God damn the glare of it. Stark naked I was and my frozen cock nowhere to be seen. Ah, there you are, you rascal! Shrunk up into the warm hairs for safekeeping. A man can't take too many shocks like that at any hour, but especially the wee. What time was it anyhow? Seizing the phone and keeping the voice down so as not to waken Alma.

"Hello," I said.

"Can't sleep, can you. Newfield?"

"What is this, a joke?"

"You must be worried about something. You must have something on your mind."

It was somebody else this time. The voice had more nose in it, like a woman's. Could it be that Peaoolee was in with them too?

"What do you want?"

"Now I'm glad you asked that. I'll tell you what we want, big shot. We want to see you trussed up like a plucked chicken at the bottom of the river slowly turning into soup."

"That all?"

"And we will yet, you motherfucking bastard. Mark my words, we will."

"OK. You know where I live," I said and hung up.

No sooner done than the ringing began all over again. Snatching the receiver off the hook and ignoring its gurgling pleas, I smothered it. On the couch under Alma's homemade tweed pillow. I've always been fond of that material, even when it was a dress.

Back to the bedroom to see if I had to sleep anymore and the Elgin said not necessarily. Unlike four or two, at three fifteen there was free choice. True there were forty-five fat ones remaining but consider the toss, the turn, the itch, the scratch, the gas pain and the ass pain, not to mention the fine tuning of blanket, sheet, and pillow to the Newfield scale. Hardly worth the bother I decided. And gladly, for the natural bent of all living stuff toward the horizontal had somehow left me standing out in the cold like a flagpole. Which is no cause, I repeat no cause for general wailing and gnashing of teeth, gums, and root canals. It's just that when you're an outsize man you give up some normal things. Like sleep and invisibility. But thank goodness the racket hadn't roused Alma. Softly percolating under the covers with only the top of her head showing. In the thin light from the hall her tangled gray hairs burning like metallic threads. She needs her rest, poor thing. I tiptoed about the room carefully gathering up clothes and was on my way out with an armful when the floorboard whispered crick. Bolt upright she came with her eyelashes beating and her startled face the color of dandruff.

"What is it, Orin?"

"Nothing. Just taking my things. Go back to sleep."

"Oh. Four o'clock already," she groaned, and quickly pulling the covers up over her head she raced back to sleep.

In the kitchen I lighted the oven and got dressed in front of its open door. A luxury, but at my age I was allowed one or two. After a restless night of uncertain dreams full of faulty information. But you can't be held responsible for all those vague, those dirty things that come into your dozing head unbidden and unwelcome. I'd be the last one to toss the first stone. Tough enough to cope with the waking hours of fluke and aberration. In which there was currently some talk of lynching me.

So far that's all it was, talk. It can't hurt but it does dampen the spirits. You may not believe it but buttoning on my overalls helped. The tug of the shoulder straps wonderfully soothing and then there's the secure feeling that comes with finding all the key parts safely tucked inside. Once dressed I set about making a cup of hot cocoa to brighten the vital organs. The rich, luscious milk stirred and watched over with the eye of a sentry as it whirlpooled in the pot. Is that a bubble I see on the horizon? Snatched away steaming from the flame at the first hint of trouble. Truly the cup that cheers and in tan my favorite color. Plus four slices of toast and a mason jar of Alma's blueberry jam. All spread gloriously before me on the dining room table. After last night I thought I'd never have to eat again and here I was back at the same old stand. The weaknesses of the flesh were simply amazing. Unlike the strong mind which could weld itself to an idea and hold on forever. *My* but this cocoa is good. A ray of sunshine in the black hour before dawn. Fuck the lot of them I say. I won't be budged.

When you come right down to it the whole business was sort of insane. Just another dab of jam in the upper right-hand corner will do nicely. I mean why did they have it in for *me?* Ah, that's much better. Let's forget about Carter who was nothing to any of them. I mean *really*. Sweet, but not too sweet. In fact perfect. Had I raped their daughters? Burned their barns? Picked their pockets? Dragged them into court on false and malicious charges to see them made fools of? Goddamnit, I didn't want to go anywhere near them, but they just couldn't leave me alone. Newfield the most sought-after man in town. The price of popularity. Only goes to show what I've always held concerning how everybody respects an honest man with high standards. It gives them someone to look up to. Hanging from the end of a rope.

But you mustn't get the idea that I was bitter or personally worried concerning what new injustices my fellow citizens might be working themselves up to. Dud firecrackers, the lot of them. All sputter and no bang. Somewhat queasy on an empty stomach, but a laughing matter when you've got a bellyful of blueberries. Gathered by me last summer on top of Balch Hill. Where they grow wild and sweet among the abandoned tombstones of the first Farnum cemetery. With its slim stone markers, knee-high and no wider than dominoes, which were always

176

being knocked over by lovers, weather, and deer, and propped back up again by old people. And me walking tight-lipped among the dead. Just whacking away at the bushes with an old pot until in fifteen minutes I had a ten-gallon milk can brimful of berries, not counting a few isolated stems and leaves. While these two city kids who had been up there all morning, humming and whistling and picking a pint one by one, watched speechless. And seeing me dump out a couple of dozen from the top in order to screw down the cover they packed up and left without a word. Lost a few more berries than necessary but it was a bargain. I've still got the look on their faces to show for it. Newfield never too busy to teach those people a lesson.

Blueberry jam, there's nothing beats it. Except maybe peach. Or the skin on a standing pot of cocoa. A succulent tissue of wrinkled nourishment. Which I skimmed off with a finger and as I licked up the vitamins from A to Z, Ben began barking. Not a yap or a bay or a growl but a shrill staccato alarm. Prowlers on the premises.

It had taken them longer than expected to get out here. Must have come the long route by way of the bottle. Under cover of darkness like cockroaches but that wasn't going to help them. I turned on the porch light and went outside. Fifteen watts may do for a refrigerator but they don't go very far on a moonless night. A few timid beams creeping out to the edge of the snow-crested grave of Alma's winter savory but no further. The driveway beyond shrouded in gloom with villains crouching in the shadows as thick as cornstalks. And the dog's barking like tracer bullets in the night. And not a gun in the house anywhere. What a relief! One less evil to worry about. Myself getting out of hand and killing somebody by mistake which I don't believe in. Just a knock and a dent to curb their trespasses will be sufficient. It's a wise workman who knows the proper tool for the proper job.

Standing alone out in the cold with a log in one hand and the sure knowledge of the presence of unclean eyes. "This is Newfield," I shouted. "Orin Newfield. I don't have all night. Who's first?"

"Expecting company, farmer? I'd say it's a queer hour for a party. But then you do things differently than most."

The damn cowards. Might have known they'd send out a woman first. "Who's that?"

"As if you didn't know. Quite the snob, aren't you? But you don't put your old friends off that easily."

"Shut up, Ben. Is that you, Miss Precosia?"

"You should have taken my advice, Newfield. I warned you something like this would happen."

"Step a little closer where I can see you."

It was her all right. Out of the shadows she came and planted herself at the end of the path as solid as a silo.

"Who's that you've got with you?"

"With me?" She looked around. "You're imagining things. There's no one here."

It sounded like the truth. Emptying the black of everything but cold air and one or two dead weeds. Chicken bastards! Running out on her at the first whiff of trouble. "Goddamnit, shut up, Ben!" I sent the log whistling in the direction of his barking.

"I like that," she said approvingly. "You've got a nice feeling for animals."

"That's *my* business. What are you doing out here this time of the morning anyway, Miss Precosia? Don't you sleep?"

"I'm a great walker. It keeps down the weight."

"Well go walk someplace else why don't you?"

"There's no reason to get nasty. I like this area. Besides, I saw your light."

"There are other lights."

"Let's put it this way, Newfield. You appeal to me. You have a nice smell of corruption about you."

"All right, that's enough. Get the hell out of here, you loony."

"You're abusing me, Newfield. I won't be abused."

"Just get out of here. Leave me alone."

"I couldn't bring myself to do that. You've been alone too much lately. Much too much."

"Not half enough to suit me."

"It's bad for the brains."

"That's your problem, not mine."

"No, I couldn't think of leaving you. It wouldn't be right. Why you're one of our very own. Look, you've even got our mark on you."

"Mark? What are you talking about?"

"Now don't tell me you've never noticed it. There. Above your eyebrow."

"That scar's from my old man."

"You see. It's in your blood. You're as evil as the next, Newfield. Why don't you join us?"

"Shut your face." I grabbed hold of a log and started toward her. Throw a little scare into the old witch. "I don't want anything to do with you. Nothing. Do you understand that? Now get the shit out of here before I lose my temper. You're a sick woman."

"What sort of holier-than-thou baloney is that? I shouldn't think any man who murdered his own father would stand on ceremony."

"That's not true. You know better than to believe those old stories, Miss Precosia. I never killed him."

"But I bet you thought about it, didn't you?"

179

"I think about a lot of things. You don't hold people responsible for their thoughts."

"Why not? They're part of you, aren't they? The most important part. The only thing that distinguishes men from cows. Frankly, I don't know what I'd do without mine. Oh yes, you're responsible for your thoughts, Newfield. Definitely."

She seemed so serious I almost laughed in her face.

"You *are*, Newfield," she insisted. "Just look what you've got in your hand there. Killed your father and now you're thinking that you'd like to start on me."

Tightening my grip on the log to make sure it didn't get away from me.

"Go ahead, you big dope. Try."

"I admit the thought did cross my mind," I said. Rearing back I hurled the log high into the morning sky. "But I changed it."

"Are you making fun of me, Newfield?"

"Go home, Miss Precosia," I said, weary of coping with her zigzag mind and turning back to the house for the milk pitcher. "I've got to go to work."

"Oh no, Newfield. You don't get rid of me that easily. I'm staying right here."

"Suit yourself."

I walked up the path and onto the porch, stomping the snow off my boots before going inside. Reaching for the door, I thought I'd just glance back to see if she was still there waiting for me at the end of the path. Then I thought not and went in the house and shut off the porch light. It's wrong to encourage people like that.

12

When I came out again she was gone. Lugging that heavy coat back to her sister. If not returned before daybreak there will be an additional charge of two cents per mile. Cash. Can't let the loonies get out of hand. I felt bad for the sane one though, cooped up with a night owl like that full of spells and enchantments. It was hard, but I suppose she likes it. Otherwise she could always move.

What's that? Off the side of my foot a something clinking down the frozen driveway. Feeling blindly along the ground like the bottom of a dark closet and oops! Jagged edges. What have we here? The neck of a broken bottle I'd say. I'd say the neck of a broken bottle deliberately planted there to sabotage traffic. Who's the wise guy? Over to the barn with it and a closer examination. Setting the milk pitcher down on a stool, I held the bottle up to the light for clues. Nice glass. Brown, with a hint of Indian summer. No respectable reason that I could see to break a perfectly useful item like this. Good for liquids, gases, or potting a geranium. And bear in mind no deposit, no return. Plainly a deliberate case of vandalism. The label said Budweiser. Dumping the evidence in the garbage, I went to work loading the mangers. Thinking it must be the nut. She didn't seem much like a drinking lady but those chins of hers don't grow on trees. Well you just go right ahead weaving your magic, Miss Precosia, that's swell with me. But the next time I find you spinning on my property I'm going to take that loom of yours apart piece by piece.

Putting her out of my mind, I gave it over to more important things. Like looking into Co-co's mopishness of the previous day after a night of clean lolling and dreamless moos. All gone. Up on her toes she was now ready to do herself proud. Eyes bright as jam and ears a-wriggling. Oh a lovely sight. Lucky for brother-in-law he hadn't done her any permanent damage. It didn't take a genius to see how relieved she was to have me back and so were they all. Cooperating beautifully. Hardly tiring me out even on short sleep. Working peacefully alone, I finally took care of everything and with no distractions from the help to sour my disposition. Other than thoughts of Alma, but she'd get over it.

After Dutcher had loaded up and gone, I left too, carrying a full pitcher. Back across the road to see if Alma had come to her senses. Seems only fair when you think about it, a sound night's rest should do no less for a wife than a cow. As you may have gathered, I'm a great believer in the healing powers of sleep. Particularly on a mild day in the mid-thirties with the sun going on and off and cloudbanks like loose bedding piled sky-high that you could sink into mindlessly and never hear the sound of words again or the crazy tramp of galoshes in the snow. I must be more tired than I think. I'll do the right thing by Alma though. Not a peep about yesterday no matter what. We'll make believe it never happened so as not to embarrass her and open wounds. I haven't been married thirty-two years for nothing.

There was something amiss with our mailbox. Gagging at the side of the road with its flap hanging down. Exposing Newfield's secrets to the world at large. Take care, postlady, that's a federal offense. I've had a little something to do with the law of late and I know my rights. I examined the interior to see if anything had been stolen. A single postcard inside where normally I might have expected to find at least a half dozen large advertisements and requests for donations. It was unnatural. This *is* Wednesday, isn't it? Perhaps she's decided to prune out the mail she feels unworthy of me. My how the ladies love to protect Newfield. Keep your filthy mitts off my second-class trash, Mrs. Otis, or I'll have your pouch. Ah well, it wasn't every day I received a postcard. And a slippery little devil at that. The milk in one hand, I clamped down on the fingers of the other glove with my teeth and pulled it off. Come here, you. Why it's even got a picture on it. Isn't that thoughtful. Probably paid for with welfare money. Now if I was to guess I'd say Indian Bend in the dappled glory of its autumn foliage. I turned over the card. *Indian Bend, its meadows once loved by the Abnaki tribe, situated one mile north of Farnum, Vt., on the Connecticut River in the dappled glory of its autumn foliage.* It figured. The line down the middle making for a tidy arrangement, the right side for the address—Orin Newfield, correct—and the left for the message. Only there wasn't any. Very subtle. Someone seems to have gone to a whole lot of trouble and expense to say nothing. Unless, of course, it was written in lemon juice and has to be held over a flame. I'll go that one better. I'll put it *in* the flame and flush the ashes down the toilet and see what the bubbles spell out. The dirty bastards. Trying to scare me off with a colorful picture of my final resting place. Postmarked yesterday from Brampton to throw me off the

183

track. The Farnum underground using the mails to defraud an honest citizen. Not Newfield they won't.

Fee-fie-fo-fum. Parked on my doorstep what is that I spy. A two-door Chevy in ministerial black fueled by the wafer of love. Peaselee's car. The Holy Ghost descending on me in a General Motors product. Outwardly I remained calm. But my heart suddenly shifting gears from pitter-patter to boom-boom-boom. And my stomach making indecent proposals to my asshole. Had Alma called him to spirit her away to join his angelic chorus of Carters? If so, it could only be a case of posthypnotic suggestion. I've heard about that sort of thing. Perfectly normal people breaking off in the middle of a sentence and going stiff as a board or taking their clothes off. I ran all the way.

Peaselee was on the couch in the living room, two coffee cups drained to the dregs in front of him. The useless scalloped ones she keeps in the breakfront with the flowers and handles that only a baby could get a finger through. Alma nowhere in sight.

"Orin, my boy," he said, getting up and taking my hand consolingly in his. "It's so good to see you again even under these unhappy circumstances."

"What circumstances? What are you talking about? Where's Alma?"

"Alma? Why she went inside to get us some more coffee. But that's not—"

I hurried into the kitchen to see for myself. You never knew about clergymen. Well today and weird tomorrow. Especially the high-strung old ones like Peaselee. They get sort of desperate with death staring down their tonsils. Worried about heaven and hearing voices and doing things they shouldn't. I believe it's too much abstract

184

thinking that does it. But Alma looked safe enough, standing over the stove watching the pot perk.

"Did you sleep well?" I asked her.

"I'm all right," she replied, staring at the pot.

"That's fine . . . fine." I put down the milk. Leaning closer to her, I whispered, "What's he want?"

"I don't know. He came to see you."

And I'm supposed to believe that. To see me. When you're the one he covets. To see me who has nothing for him but contempt and he knows it. Though it's true the man has no pride. Well . . . if you say so, Alma. The benefit of the doubt is yours. To see me then. My father, my confessor, come to wash away my sins and forgive me my handyman. For which I'm to be eternally grateful both now and in the box to come. Thanks for nothing, Peaselee. Without a doubt, these are peculiar times we live in. Men of the cloth going everywhere uninvited. Mad missionary zeal. On the other hand, it could be he's had his fill of Carter and wants to ship him back. Making this a laughing matter. I'm not averse to a small infrequent chuckle at the proper time. So I went back inside and asked him.

"What are you here for, Mr. Peaselee?"

"I'm sorry, Orin. I should have waited. I didn't mean to say anything to upset you as soon as you came in."

"You didn't. What is it you want?"

"There's no hurry. Sit down, sit down, my boy. We can talk about it over coffee."

I took out my Elgin and glanced at it. "All right," I said, sitting down opposite him and placing the watch before me on the table. "But I've got things to do, Reverend. So make it quick if you don't mind."

"You look tired, Orin. Have you gotten anyone to—a suitable replacement for—"

185

Such delicacy. Peaselee squirming, his thin neck rattling around within its clerical collar like a stick in a hoop. "That is, don't you have any help?"

"No." What's that disgusting smell he's brought into the house with him?

"But that's terrible! You can't do everything by your-self on a farm this size. It's too heavy a burden for one man. You need help."

"Good help is hard to come by nowadays." Camphor, that's what it is. Peaselee's soul already packed for the trip.

"You need assistance, Orin. Friends. Too much privacy only breeds grief and violence. I'd like to help, if you'll let me."

"That's nice of you, Reverend. How are you at handling a Chore-Boy milker?"

His blue hands shaking between his knees, Peaselee bent forward and said, "Come to church, my boy. I haven't turned my back on you and neither has God. He's there waiting to show you the way if you'll only reach out. All men need a point of reference beyond them-selves to steer by. Come to church, Orin."

"Not likely. But you can't say you didn't try, Mr. Peaselee. Was there anything else you wanted?"

"Yes I tried . . . I did try."

Alma came in and he struggled to get up a smile for her as she poured the coffee. And a cup for me. Naturally her husband gets the chipped one. Possibly signaling a new outbreak of rebellion. I've overlooked last night, Alma, but watch your step. There are limits.

Peaselee sighed and took his steaming cup. "Thank you, my dear." He peered longingly into it as if he had lost a sermon at the bottom. "It's so hard to know the right thing to say, to do. So hard."

"Not for me it isn't. But who could see straight with a hunk of God stuck in his eye?"

"Orin, please!"

"That's all right, Alma. I know Orin thinks I'm out of step with the times and that may be so. I don't seem to understand the world anymore. Somewhere back there after the war it took a turn that I wasn't able to negotiate. Today men like Orin are so sure of themselves. They think they can change everything. They seem to be seized by a frenzy to control their very existence. They have no patience to allow events to take care of themselves, to work themselves out. I don't understand it."

"You can't accept change, Reverend. That's your problem."

"Our church was built upon faith and change. But events are moving too fast, Orin. Much too fast. Now everything must be put in question, everything must be in a constant state of crisis. God help us, it won't do. Not change for change's sake alone. I have a feeling of being swept away in the current, of being dragged down and overcome by an irresistible force. I tell you these are frightening days. Without God's help I don't think I could bear them alone."

"These are *my* days, Mr. Peaselee. Only ones I'll ever have. They don't scare me a bit. I've never done for myself any way but alone."

"But what about your duty to God, my boy? You're forgetting Him. Are you afraid to admit your weakness? Is that it?"

"Don't make me laugh. Do you think I got this farm praying? Those parishioners of yours could stay on their knees until they had cancer of the caps and they still wouldn't own a place like this. As it is, most of them have been down there so long they don't have a pot to piss in.

187

All they've got is God and they have to check every Sunday with you because they're not even sure of that."

"Stop it, Orin," begged Alma, clenching and unclenching her hands. "You can't talk to the minister like that. You don't know what you're saying."

"I know damn well what I'm saying. He makes me sick with his duty to God. Look at my cows. They don't waste my time discussing their duty to God. They don't lie awake in the dark weeping for their sins. They just take care of their own business and so do I."

"You're a man, Orin. You're not a beast."

"That's so, Reverend." Getting up, I pocketed my watch. "But I'm not a damn fool either. Good-bye."

"Wait! I have something to tell you." Peaselee nearly upsetting his coffee cup in his eagerness to keep me from going. "Alma, please. Would you mind if I spoke to him privately?"

"Anything I can hear she can hear too. We don't have any secrets from one another, do we, Alma?"

"I'll go. I have to straighten up the kitchen anyway."

Since when.

"Well? What is it?"

Peaselee wiping his lips nervously with his handkerchief. "Yes, yes, I'll come right to the point, Orin. I'm worried about your safety."

"Is that all? Don't bother."

"For God's sake listen to me, will you, and stop being bullheaded."

I was so surprised I almost fell on my can.

"I'm sorry, Orin, but you've got to hear this. You know, I suppose, that he's staying at my house. Last night a group of men—I'd rather not mention their names—came to visit him and I couldn't help overhearing their conversation. The things they said, Orin! You can't imagine. I could hardly believe my ears. This evening they're planning to meet with others at the Senator's farm and I'm honestly afraid of what might be the result. They're not evil men, Orin, but they're so fond of him . . . and if they should start to drink. . . . Do you see what I mean?"

"I see." Scratching the itch out of my nose and wondering why this story. What's in it for you, Peaselee? "Well if you really think they're plotting to lynch me, why the hell don't you do something about it instead of sitting there and drinking my coffee?"

"That's why I've come, Orin. To warn you. But there's just so much I can do."

"You came to the wrong place. You should have gone straight to Tolliver."

"The police! But I couldn't do that. What if I've mistaken their intentions? I don't want to accuse anyone wrongfully. Surely you can understand that."

"Then what do you think I should do?" I asked innocently.

"Now you're being sensible, Orin. Oh that's very good. I've considered that. Yes, I've given that question some thought. Why don't you and Alma take a vacation? You've worked hard and you've earned it. Get away from Farnum for a little while and enjoy yourselves. At least until things quiet down here and people forget."

There it was. Another of Alma's employees hard at work. "I'm afraid there's something *you* don't understand, Reverend. I don't want any of them to forget. I want them to remember. I'm not going anywhere."

Peaselee stared down at his lap and shook his head sadly, the hairs in his ears trembling. "You're a complicated man, Orin Newfield. I don't think I like you."

"That doesn't surprise me a bit. You're all the same. Well you can keep your pie-in-the-sky-when-I-die religion. I'll work for mine here and now."

"Oh no, it's not that. It's not that you deny the existence of God." Glancing up with red-rimmed eyes, he pointed a drooping little finger at me. "It's that you think you're *Him*."

"I'm not without faults, Mr. Peaselee. Never said I was. But I'm working on them. Here's your coat."

He took it but didn't seem to have the strength to get it on. Fumbling with the sleeve and making faint whimpering noises at the back of his throat. I lost my patience and grabbed the coat away from him. "Here." Holding it up, I guided his hand into the armhole.

"I'm sorry, Orin. I shouldn't have said that. I did like you once . . . but you've changed so."

He made it sound so final I could have wept for the good old days of poverty and humiliation. "Sure I've changed. So what? Seems to me you're not as forgiving as you make out, Reverend."

"That's possible. That's certainly possible. I don't know anymore."

The old man taking it so hard I told him to forget it and handed him his hat. Holding an arm to help him out to his car and speed him on his way. The perfect host. Observed by a familiar face peering anxiously from behind the dining room window. At ease, Alma, for David and Goliath are at peace. But I wouldn't start packing for Madeira until further notice. The morning sun dazzling on the snow. Bad for the eyes but fine for the spirits. Peaselee's shadow grazing the ground like the rod of Moses. Merely a fairy tale—nothing doing. Another fraud of the Bible exposed. Opening the car door for him, I sneezed, rocking the Chevy back on its springs.

"God bless you," he said and got in.

I gave him a look.

"Do you have a cold?" he asked.

"I don't get colds."

"You're so lucky. I get them all the time. And the weather these past few days has been so changeable. Changeable weather is the worst sort for me."

I slammed the door. He rolled down the window in distress.

"I forgot to say good-bye to Alma."

"No. Don't get out. There she is."

He waved at the house. "Do me a favor, Orin. Promise me you'll be careful."

"Pull up to the end of the garage," I advised him, "and turn around there. It's easier than backing out."

My helpful hint for the day. Mind where you're driving now, you've got to spread the good word far and wide. Land in a drift and for my part you can stay there, freezing your gospel. You'd think he was turning a battleship. On your way, Peaselee.

It was then that I first noticed it but I waited until he had chugged out onto the road before going over. Parked in front of the log-filled half of the garage, the pickup truck sloping forward like a squatting cow. My new Ford on bended knees. Surely the bad influence of Peaselee knows no bounds. The two front Firestones flat and shredded, deep gash wounds in their innocent treads. It pained me to look at them. Shit! This time they had gone too far. A few pieces of broken glass littering the ground. I picked one up, rubbed the snow off on my sleeve, sniffed it, turned it over in my hands. Brown is for Budweiser. Sane or otherwise, Miss Precosia, some sonofabitch is going to pay for this.

But she couldn't have done it all by herself. Just look

how deep those cuts are. Though they do say that in their fits the mad ones are uncommonly strong and can do things no ordinary person would be capable of. But not *those* cuts. Maybe Ben wasn't barking at *her* at all. Maybe he never saw her. Maybe she Hold on, Newfield, you're running off at the mind. Which is bad for the liver and the small intestines or why else all this vexed farting. I'm sure there's a simple solution to the whole affair. Go to the Ellsworth house, knock on the door, confront Miss Precosia with the evidence, and smash her between the eyes. If she goes down your worries are over.

You can see how low I was. Even thinking of hitting women now. When it was a man who must have done it sure. But that's how waste always affects me. Unless, of course, it happens to be other people's which is out of my hands. If others wanted to throw away their money on strawberries out of season or threatening telephone calls that was one thing but these tires were *mine*. I didn't like it and I don't have to tell you I'm somebody who knows what he likes. My farm neat and my life neat and my goddamn tires just the way I've left them. It was remarkable how many things I'd found out of place recently. A distressing total. I intended to tidy some of them up that very evening.

"What's the matter with the truck?" asked Alma, who was waiting for me when I came in to wash up after changing the tires.

"Nothing much. A couple of flats. I must have run over some nails. Is there anything to eat?"

"Orin, you're not thinking of going to Russell's tonight, are you?"

Oh what big ears you have little Alma. "Funny you should ask. I understand from Peaselee there's to be some

192

kind of meeting there at which my name is likely to come up. I thought I'd look in on it."

"Please, daddy. Please don't go. Please, for my sake. It's no place for you. You'll only lose your temper. Will you do that for me?"

"Calm down." I took her gently by the shoulders. "You're letting your imagination run away with you."

Alma's eyes filled with tears. "All right," she said hopelessly. "If that's your decision." Turning away, she shuffled off toward the kitchen in her slippers. "I'll see if there's anything to eat."

Goddamnit, that's no way to take it. What the hell did she want from me? I don't want to be a hero, Alma, but I won't be less than a man. Even for you.

On my way and as usual the shades were raised all over Farnum. Everywhere people owning up in front of their lighted windows to show their neighbors they had nothing to fear. Petrified to arouse suspicions of normality behind the drapes. Grief and nose-picking hidden from view in back of the television set, fornication under the living room rug, arguments in the basement. The indecency of it. With real human beings reduced to living out of their back pockets in the interest of friendliness. I couldn't bear to look and drove quickly out of town.

Three quarters of a mile north on Five trying to remember where it was and as I turned left across the highway some south-bound tourist about a day's drive off begins blowing his horn and blinking his lights. Showing off his equipment to the peasants. Only way a nonstop jackass like that'd be happy would be if I drove all the way up to St. Johnsbury, turned at the light, and came back down on the right-hand side of the road. Fuck him.

193

This was it. A road even worse than the turnpike. So narrow Russell must use a shoehorn to get in and out. But romantic with potholes in the moonlight and patches of ice from the day's melt glistening like ax blades under the tires. I would have favored the good spare if there had been any room to dodge. And every bounce lowering my boiling point a few degrees. Until the road finally petered out in Russell's front yard with cars parked every which way. The scheming bastards tracked to their lair. Backing around, I put the truck in the middle of the road with its front end facing out. An ounce of prevention. Nobody was going to leave until I had my say. Walking in toward the house through knee-deep drifts and noticing the moon. How it bleached the roof and the ground and the snow fence and tinseled treetops. Shining out full-blast as if it would never have to go. It will though and without whining or any crap about change either. Even Peaselee could be expected to see that. Why is it I can never think of these good examples when it counts?

The one-story farmhouse was ablaze with light and through the living room windows I could see about a dozen of them. As usual sitting around on their fannies. Listening hard to Hatch and slyly eyeing the two bottles of whiskey set in the center of the room as a conversation piece. While Russell's missus hovered outside the circle slipping coasters under everything in sight to protect her valuables. Chunky antique pieces polished to a fare-thee-well and gleaming in the lamplight as if they were covered with oilcloth. A real housekeeper that one. But a dirty mind. Over the piano in plain view was a large picture of some naked guy squatting with his chin on his hand taking a crap. Thinking grand thoughts no doubt and so they called it art. She must have bought that the year they were away. The sort of filth Montpelier was famous for.

How Russell could allow her to keep such a thing in their living room was beyond me. I'll never understand people.

Suspiciously quiet inside. I wonder if they realize I can't hear a word. Speak up there, Hatch. Considering the number of big mouths assembled it was amazing. And the storm windows muffling the little noise there was. More like a town meeting than a lynch mob except I couldn't see anyone taking the minutes. So I appointed myself. Recording Hatch scowling at Russell and Russell nodding his apology. Afraid to lose a potential vote, the Senator shut his mouth. And the janitor opening and closing his like a goldfish around his cigar. Settling Newfield's hash with a single grim finger drawn quickly across his throat while LaBombard and Plunket and the rest shook their heads in agreement, patting one another on the back, and getting braver with every drink.

I move that this mob be adjourned forthwith. I second the motion. Besides my feet were getting cold standing out there and my nose seemed to have sprung a leak. Wiping it off on the sleeve of my mackinaw, I walked up to the door. If I didn't know better I'd say I was coming down with something. Which only made me more angry and the dinky brass knocker on the door topped it off. What the hell are you supposed to do with a toy like that? Fortunately I had my own along. Three well-placed bams to the midsection shook the hinges and brought down a light shower of flakes from the overhang. Anybody home?

"Just a minute. I'm coming, I'm coming. Don't break down the door," called Russell's wife in a high-pitched musical voice. Very gifted that way. They say she also screws around with the piano and organ. I really must remember that the next time I get to feeling depressed about Alma. The door opened and there she was squinting

195

out. Distinguished-looking like her husband. A braid of white hair coiled on top of her head, good skin, and clipped, clean fingernails which I admired very much as her hand shot up to her throat.

"Oh!" Falling back a step or two and catching her balance. Hiding her true feelings in girlish fluster—the politician's wife. "Yes? What is it you want?"

"Would you ask your husband and his friends to step out here a minute, missus?"

"There's nobody here right now. You'll have to see Mr. Russell some other time."

I glanced back over my shoulder just to make sure about the cars but naturally they were all still there.

"I don't know anything about those," she explained hurriedly, getting a little upset. "I'm all alone here. You'd better go."

Even *she* wanted to protect me. What is it about you Newfield that brings out the mother in them? Reaching out, I caught the door before she had a chance to close it on me and calmly stepped onto the threshold.

"Senator," I called. Slow and deliberate so there'd be no confusion in the message. "You and your friends have a visitor. Are you coming out or do I come in there to get you?"

That did it. Flushed out, the cowards spilling drunkenly over one another into the hallway until they saw who it was. Causing them to shut up and fix their jaws like bayonets. Mrs. Russell froze in her tracks and her eyes went white.

"You'd best stand to one side, missus," I said quietly, easing her out of harm's way.

"Take your hands off her. Who do you think you are? Get out of my house. You've got no—"

One furious glare from me and the Senator buttoned up. Careful, you old bastard. I've got a vote too, you know. Moving my eye slowly over the rest of them like a cage of twitching rabbits, enjoying their puny efforts to outgaze me Hatch frowned and removed his dead cigar from his lips as if he was about to say something. I laughed in his face. In all of their faces. The pious scum of the earth.

"I understand there's something you people object to about me. Well, here I am," I announced and watched them narrowly to see what they'd do. Nothing of course. Just stuck there like fence posts breaking wind. Why I was safer with them than home in bed—as long as there was a good light and they were standing in front of me.

"You have a hell of a lot to say over the telephone though, don't you? Great talkers just so long as there's plenty of running room. But when it comes to actually doing anything you've got nothing between your legs but raisins. The idea of *you* lynching me! The only thing you're up to is cutting a man's tires when he's not looking. Was that supposed to help Carter? Was that what you good Christians call an act of love? You turn my stomach. All right," I said scornfully, doubling up my fists where they could see them. "If you'd like to lynch me, go ahead and try."

Hatch's hand dove for his pocket. I came in on him fast just as he drew out a small box of matches. "You've made a mistake, mister," he said coolly, flicking the ash off his cigar with his pinky. "We don't even know you."

I couldn't laugh. It was too disgusting. Seeing a human being crawl that way. Hatch would deny his own mother to save his skin.

"The name is Newfield. Does that ring a bell, janitor?"

"No. I can't say that it does."

197

"Is that right? Look a little closer." I jammed my face down into his, feeling the sweat of his flesh. "*Orin* Newfield. Now do you remember?"

He pulled away. "I never saw you before in my life," he said.

"Me neither," echoed Plunket who was standing at his elbow. "Shit, this is a private party. You must be nuts barging in here."

"Do you know this individual, Senator?" asked Hatch.

Russell looked me straight in the eye. He shook his head. "No," he said. "I don't know this man. He's a complete stranger to me."

And the rest of them looking on with a single blank expression on their faces. My hands began to twitch. It was some sort of a trick. The kind that school kids play on the fat ones with glasses whose names are Four-eyes or Porky. How was I supposed to remember what they called him with them staring at me? He must have had a real name. There was a birthmark, I'm sure of it. On the side of his neck to witness the pain. That everybody wanted to see and touch. Or was it a burn? Trying to shake me up and jumble my thoughts. The prickless cowards, what did they want from me?

"You know damn well who I am," I thundered, with the blood pumping in my ears. "Orin Newfield, that's who. What the hell are you trying to pull?"

Relaxed and grinning at Russell, Hatch put his cigar back between his teeth and lighted up. "As far as we're concerned," he said, puffing the words out of his mouth contentedly, "Orin Newfield is dead."

Plunket and LaBombard caught him as he fell. A string of blood trickling from the corner of his mouth. Hubbell snatching up the cigar from the floor and running around stamping out hot ashes. Everyone yelling and swearing and shaking their fists as they surged forward while Hatch struggled to hold them back, pleading with them through split lips not to do anything foolish. But it was Mrs. Russell who really interested me. Standing in the corner with her hands to her cheeks she bobbed up and down, shrieking and striking the same wild note again and again like a pile driver. Undoubtedly Russell was a spineless bastard but I couldn't help feeling just a little sorry for him. It must be a real cross to be married to a woman with such gifts.

Slamming the door behind me, I went for the truck. Trudging along through the snow in the moonlight while the noise in the background grew fainter. Unscrambling my mind and thinking, all right then I'm dead. It could be worse. One less crime to blame on Orin Newfield.

13

"*You* know who I am, don't you? Come on, give us a kiss. Can't you see I'm back safe and sound?"

Ursula nuzzling up to my cheek. Swiping away at it with her tongue. Hooo! It felt like the damp sole of a cleated hiking boot scraping across my morning stubble. A warm, friendly, slobbering salute to remind me who I was despite dismal rumors to the contrary. And for her a few grateful strokes on her white muzzle to show it's mutual. Now that's enough of that. Affectionate rascal. Ursula was generally inclined that way and the same, more or less, could be said of the entire herd. Of course we mustn't forget they're only dumb animals, right, Peaselee? Just a barnful of beastly love. But every little bit helped on this icy first morning of my death when the blood squeezed through the heart like Vaseline.

Newfield milked them and grained them and fed them their silage and the sound of their munching muting his rage. Keeping his temper under lock and key as if it was the door to the boobyhatch. Temporarily forgetting injustice and thinking only the good thoughts. Of his farm and the work that he loved and his wife who had stuck by him through fat and lean in spite of the cunning whispers of evil advisers. Oh he was a lucky man, this Newfield. Dealing exclusively with black and white animals. Especially when you stop to consider the conspiracy of gray loose in the world. Subversion and helpfulness running rampant. Not that he'd escaped untouched as you've doubtless noticed. But he refused to take them lying down. Thou shalt not allow the shits to step all over you, sayeth the cowkeeper. And acted accordingly. Did Hatch and his gang seriously imagine that they could cancel a man of his dimensions out of the Farnum history books by wishful thinking? A bizarre notion. It won't square with the facts. For the janitor's sake let us hope that the nose is the gateway to wisdom. But Newfield had no illusions. If more than one blow was required, so be it. He was nothing if not persistent. And sooner or later Hatch would come to understand that finally there is no mistaking the firm, irresistible tap-tap-tap of reality.

The freezing rain that had been falling since before dawn was over now. Behind the milk house the giant Norwegian spruce packaged in ice, its limbs hanging low. Icicles as long as elephant tusks dangling from the eaves of the barn. When loosened by a little sun they were capable of splitting a man's skull open. Dangerous conditions. The ground so slick I had to shuffle, avoiding big steps. Driven by a sudden curiosity to see how the handyman's house had fared since my last inspection.

Unlocking the door, I went in. Dusty but everywhere I looked it was as if they had never been. Fine . . . fine. Except for the Carter smell. It still clung to the walls like cobwebs even though Alma had aired the place out from top to bottom. What the hell must I do to get rid of that bastard? His aroma congesting my lungs with poisonous memories. Of evil returned for good. The plague of self-pity which kills even the strongest. Clear the air, Newfield. Another handyman in here would help but there was no one to leave the herd with at the moment. I made plans then and there to go looking somewhere out of town for a new one just as soon as Ben apologized. Meanwhile I turned on the tap in the kitchen to make sure that the pipes hadn't frozen. The water splashing cold and peppy into the sink. Lovely, but that's enough. The finest plumbing in the state of Vermont for free and still he spilled my milk. Uh oh, there I go again. Careful. But truly it was hard to understand that sort of ingratitude. Made me sorry that I had ever come. I was about to leave but above the sink in the corner between the window and the wall cabinet was something. A spider capering on his web, dime-size with fidgety legs. Stop that dancing, goddamnit! I put my thumb down on his black back and squashed him up against the cabinet. No more than a tiny smudge was all that was left. Saving him from a fate worse than death to judge by the popular report. Alone he would certainly have been miserable in this deserted place. At least with me here he had had some company.

The air on the outside smelled one hundred percent better and I helped myself to several lungfuls. As I went slipping and sliding back to the barn and twisting my bad knee in the process. Sonofabitch! Still on my feet though. With the pain shooting up my leg and out my asshole in an agony of mutilated farts. Which reminded me of my old man. A few well-chosen words of thanks to him for the inheritance. Achilles had his heel and Newfield's got his knee. I snapped it back into place, easing the suffering. Now suffering's a great character builder if you happen to be of a religious turn of mind but otherwise it just hurts. I tried to ignore it. Chipping away at the ice with the blade of my shovel and then, with a pail of salt in hand, sprinkling the driveway from the road to the milk house.

But the knee got worse, stiffening in the cold, the hinge locking in place, and after a while I was dragging my leg behind me like a dead tree trunk. Somewhere in one of my drawers there was an unused elastic support garter that Alma had once given me as a present. At first I couldn't dope the thing out and when she had carefully explained what it was the HO-HO-HO's rocked the house and brought tears to my eyes. But nobody had to know. To think I had fallen to that.

As I feared, Alma was on sentry duty at the dining room table when I came in. There was no getting around her.

"Morning," I grunted casual, and walking as naturally as I could, made my way past her into the hall. Avoiding her sympathy at all costs. But it was the strangest thing. Not even a how-are-you? When I figured she'd be fairly busting with questions about what went on at Russell's last night. By Jesus, could it be? Another new leaf turned and perhaps this time entirely for the better. Even in pain I was hopeful despite the disappointments of the past. Optimism such as yours, Newfield, is a curse. But there was strong evidence in the bedroom where I found all of her drawers emptied out. The contents neatly sorted into two piles on the bed. Not a clear-cut separation of white and colored, I admit. There's no reason to lie to yourself about these things just to raise false hopes. But ladies' garments have always been a mystery to me. It's possible that here we have some other perfectly sound principle of selection. And in the basement I could hear the washing machine in action again for the first time since I had killed the rat. Thumping and sloshing and it wasn't even spring. Alma, you went down there all by yourself. Oh it sounds promising, it sounds awfully promising.

The goddamn garter, where the hell was it? At the back of my top drawer folded inside a pair of torn socks that I hadn't been able to bring myself to throw out. Which was lucky because after the way I had carried on I'd sooner have done without than call her in to help find it. I've got my pride, you know. It was a funny-looking thing and no mistake. But a nice shade of tan. And look at that stretch! I sat down on the edge of the bed and rolled up the leg of my overalls. Thirty-three stitches ringing the cap and forming a round pleat. I've never ceased to admire the sewing. Beautiful workmanship. Not my field but I know a good job when I see one. The frozen knee still rusty and tender to the touch, though it wasn't too painful. And with the garter on I could even bend it. Quickly pulling down my overalls to avoid embarrassment and it suddenly came to me what Alma was up to. The last day of the calendar. A final spruce-up washing away the dirt of the past. A clean slate for the New Year. I could sense change, new resolutions, the air positively bristling with renovation. It certainly would be welcome, but this time I intended to go slow and avoid pitfalls.

"Careful if you go out later," I told her. Standing by the dining room window and passing the time of day with my hat on. While the knee thawed out underneath and no one the wiser. "It's slippery."

Alma kept on polishing. In her old blue bathrobe pinned closed at the neck. Newspapers spread before her on the table. Polishing her shoes as if they were going to be entered in some Four-H competition. What an improvement.

"They take a nice shine," I said admiring them.

For the first time then she seemed to take notice of me. Glancing up and fixing her eyes on my knee. But how could she know? Goddamnit, was she laughing at me?

"What's the matter with *you?*" I demanded.

"I'm leaving, Orin."

"You're what?"

"You don't need me."

"Oh shit, let's not start that again. I thought we were through with that."

"You've *never needed me.*"

"Who the hell says I have to *need* you? I love you, isn't that enough?"

"No, not for me. I see now that it isn't."

"We're married, Alma. Thirty-two years. This is no time for making new discoveries."

"It's settled, I'm going away."

"All right. You're going away."

"I mean it."

"Fine. Go ahead. What'll you live on? How are you going to support yourself? There's not a damn thing you can do that anybody in his right mind would pay for. I mean *nothing.* Even on your back you couldn't make two cents. Have you thought of that?"

"I swear to God . . ." Rising and fumbling with the shoes and catching them up. "I swear to God, Orin, this is the end."

And off she goes. Should I wave good-bye? Moving out of range of my foul mouth. Running away from the dirty little details of reality but the ringing of the telephone put a stop to that. Stapling her to the dining room floor. She turned to me helplessly as if she was about to say something. Her face dissolving in tears. Of repentance, perhaps? I have a forgiving nature.

"You know," I said, stopping on my way to the phone to lay a soothing hand on her shoulder, "you've got it ass backward. It's not *my* needing you but *your* needing me. You think you don't, but look how wrong you are."

She shook me off, thrashing about like a bird with a broken wing.

"All right, I'll get it. Stop crying. There's nothing to be afraid of."

This would be the last one. My patience with these people was gone. I had given them the kid-glove treatment far too long. These sneaky, chicken-shit, back-stabbing, cock-sucking, ball-busting blowhards of the universe. Snarling and shouting and cursing even before the receiver reached my mouth. Blasting their ears with thunder and lightning. Letting them know where to get off. I held up finally and listened. There was nothing left on the line but silence. That should do it, I thought, and was about to slam down the receiver when this pleading voice came on at the other end.

"Just a minute. Please. Hold on. This is Augie, Mr. Newfield. Augie Dutcher."

"What the hell are *you* doing there?"

"*Gee*, that was really something. I mean wow! I'd give my left nut to be able to swear like that. Who did you think it was, Mr. Newfield?"

"You should have been here an hour ago, Dutcher. What do you want?"

"Oh yeah. Well, I've had a little accident with the truck. It's nothing serious but I wonder if you could come down here and help me out. I'm stuck."

"Where are you?"

"Pay phone in the hotel. Why do you ask?"

"For crissake, Dutcher, what's the matter with you? I mean the truck. Where's the truck?"

"Oh. That's in a ditch. You know the hill into town. I'm not fooling, it's like glass today—the worst shape I've ever seen it in. I thought sure I could make it up to the top. Very nearly did, too. But the whole rig just suddenly got away from me. Damndest thing you ever saw. Slid off the road as if it was wearing ice skates. I guess I'm

207

lucky at that it didn't jacknife on me. No harm done though and if you could bring along your tractor and yank me out I'd be much obliged. Could you do that? It'll only take a few minutes. Are you there, Mr. Newfield? Mr. Newfield?"

"I'm here. Listen to me, Dutcher. Around the corner from where you are on Wheelock and South there's a Texaco station. Go in there. They've got a tow truck. It'll have you out before I could even get started."

"I tried them, Mr. Newfield. You won't believe what happened. The first thing the guy there said when I came in was you testified for Mr. Newfield, didn't you? I said sure but what's that got to do with towing my truck. He said plenty and told me to get the hell out. Isn't that something, Mr. Newfield? Get the hell out, he said, and I never even saw the guy before in my life."

"Wait for me by the truck, Dutcher. I'll be there as soon as I can," I promised him and hung up.

One fine day, LaBombard. When this has all blown over and there's no reason to bear a grudge anymore I'm going to drive up whistling to one of those bright, streamlined, high-octane pumps of yours. And drop a match.

"I've got to go into town," I told Alma. "Dutcher's had an accident."

She looked at me as if she couldn't believe it had been him on the phone and didn't know what to make of it. Where had they gone, those wild-eyed midnight assassins of the moon? Her colorful imagination let down by a neutral shade. It *was* Dutcher, Alma. Would I lie to you? Only when necessary. Shrugging my shoulders and buttoning my mackinaw.

"Good-bye," she said as I went out the door.

Was that a hint of forever I heard in her voice? Empty drawers where there used to be a wife. A sealed coffin and the flat thump of the falling clods. Newfield buried inside along with her old bathrobe. And his missus tripping away in tan shoes to dine and dance in the stews and fleshpots of Rutland and Brattleboro. Is that what I deserve, Alma, after all my years of devoted service? Not even a gold-plated pen and pencil set or an engraved pin. So upsetting I almost slipped on the ice again walking toward the tractor shed. Staining the lining of my hat with the sweat of injustices known and suspected.

Enough, enough of this pointless brooding, Newfield. You know you can't trust what she says anymore. She's not going anywhere. Consider her elaborate preparations, the washing, the polishing, the sorting of clothes. Does that sound to you like someone about to leave? Can't you see she's only stalling? Is there a law against running away in a dirty outfit? It's like suicide, either they do it or they don't. I believe you must be getting silly in your old age. Tormenting yourself when you really don't have a thing to worry about. That's so, I don't have a thing to worry about, I told myself. But I was worrying all the same.

Riding grimly into town high up on my tractor. The damp hair at my temples turned cardboard in the cold. Looking down at the icebound world through dull, stiff-lidded eyes. Until a doe broke from cover in front of me like a bandit, leaping the road in a single bound, skidding on the ice, righting herself easily, and disappearing into the thick pines on the other side without a branch left quivering to tell the tale. The grace of the thing. Choking me up with amazement, phlegm. I hawked up a glob, sending it spinning, and turned around in my seat to check the result. A pus-yellow quarter stained the ice. Bad news but not unexpected. Men being such miserable animals. Even their spit isn't at home in the world. And mine less so than average. Blowing my nose as I rumbled darkly past the courthouse where an icicle hung from the tip of Jacob Farnum's bronze beak like frozen snot. I sympathized. My own feeling so uncomfortably red and sore. Thinking then this must be it, I've finally caught it. Death always coming as a surprise. Choking up with a few sniffles, some fever, an ache, a pain, and before you know it the cuticles gone blue as sapphires and the slow, weird cackle rattling down and out. First the germs and then the worms. Here lies Newfield packed away for all eternity with a lousy headache. But it's not too late, my boy, it's never too late. Remember, there are no atheists in foxholes. Let us pray. O Lord, whatever I have and no matter how painful, please God, let it be contagious.

At the crest of the hill I pulled up and looked the situation over. Going down head-first was out. It would be too risky to turn on that stuff given the incline. Dutcher halfway down. Marooned on the hood of his truck and waving both hands wildly as if he thought I didn't see him. The dunce. Backing around at the top I eased the tractor down, keeping the right wheels on the shoulder to get whatever traction there was. Descending slow and steady. Inching my way. Just a little bit more now. No problem when you know how.

"All right, Dutcher," I said, pulling up the emergency brake. "Tie us together and let's get out of here."

"Shit! My aching shit! Shit on it!" Falling all over himself on the ice as he got his rope and hooked us up.

"Make that good and tight. I wouldn't want to lose you."

"Oh shit!" And down he went again. "You ought to say something to your selectmen, Mr. Newfield. You really ought to. It's a damn shame what they get away with in this town. Just look at those sandboxes over there. There's not a grain of sand in any of them. I bet they could be sued for something like that. Boy would I love to sue them. Make enough to retire and go live in Miami Beach all year round with the palm trees. Doesn't that sound great? I bet they *could* be sued."

"Come on, Dutcher. I'm a busy man. Get in and make sure you're not in gear."

I started up. The rope came taut and the tractor paused for a second, getting the feel of the load behind. Then slowly dragging it out. We crawled toward the top with me swiveled around in my seat keeping an eye on the rope all the way up. It held though.

"Thanks a million for coming out to get me," said Dutcher after he had untied us. "I hope you didn't mind."

"You better go ahead," I told him. "Don't wait for me. If you finish loading before I get there just leave the receipt in the milk house."

"Will do, Mr. Newfield," he snapped, with a click of the heels. Jumping back into the cab of his truck as if it was a cockpit. Revving his engine and giving thumbs up to the ground crew. Am I dreaming? Pulling around the tractor, he blew his horn good-bye. Right through my head. He was really full of play was Dutcher. People like that should be stuffed and hung up in maternity wards as warnings of what's in store for the little buggers. It ain't funny.

Turning up my collar I started home. Past the silent agony of Peaselee's stained glass. It's living flesh nailed, speared, baked senseless in the sun. Oh that's hopeful, that's very hopeful. No house should be without one. Past the green-shuttered library with its 1789 tacked out front to the clapboards—the oldest building in town. The shades drawn on the second floor where the schoolteacher lived. As if the sight of me would cancel her contract. Turn her to stone. The crafty old whore, she knows which side her bread is buttered on. Next mothers will be yanking their

211

children in off the street, rolling up welcome mats, bolting their doors. It wouldn't surprise me. Farnum giving New-field the cold shoulder and the cold, empty street. If nothing else they knew how to look after their dead. I never did care for crowds

At the corner of Park I stopped the tractor and wiped my nose in anticipation. A mystery about to be unraveled. Down the block Miss Ellsworth was just coming out of her house. Amanda—the daylight sister. Waddling on the ice like a penguin. Through the crooked gate in the broken picket fence with a shopping bag folded under her arm. Bent forward and watching her feet as she came. If you don't mind, Miss Ellsworth, I have a few questions to ask you. Some queer things I'd like to get straightened out. Now then, have you noticed anyone missing from your house recently after dark? Night before last, for example? Wearing that coat you've got on and a World War I aviator's helmet? With a bottle of beer in her hand? And which brand does your sister favor and what the hell is it that she wants from me? It would never do. She'd think I was as nuts as her sister. But on short notice it couldn't be helped.

"Morning, Miss Ellsworth."

Her head shot up, only her eyes visible under the khaki scarf that covered her face like an Arab.

"Oh," she said, blinking nervously.

"If you don't mind, I have a few questions—"

But that was all I had a chance to get out. She was already rushing away, scurrying across the icy street as fast as she could go.

Her, too! I laughed myself into a coughing fit watching her scramble. So undignified for a good, sweet, charitable old lady. Careful, Miss Ellsworth, you're going to bust a hip that way. We'll talk about this some other time in private. I understand. You've got to live here with these people for the rest of your life, right? Dangerous to be seen out in the open consorting with the enemy, right? Mum's the word, right? She fled across the empty parking lot into Dan's supermarket. As I drove slowly by, I roared at the store, "Just keep her away from me, you old bitch. Do you hear me? Keep her away or I won't be responsible."

I was almost home when I met Dutcher on the turnpike, loaded and heading back for the highway. That was fast. I didn't really think he'd be finished before I got there. Half the cans left behind for tomorrow if I know him. Hurrying to meet some lady friend at a roadside diner where he could eat a hamburger, play the jukebox, and get his new fur collar stroked all at the same time. While my milk sat around on the outside evaporating. I waved him down and asked him how come so speedy?

"Your brother-in-law is there, Mr. Newfield. He pitched in and helped me. Just like that without my asking or anything. It was damn nice of him and particularly with me so far behind schedule and tonight being what it is. He's a real gentleman if you know what I mean. I left your receipt in the milk house like you told me. Bye now. See you day after tomorrow."

"What's wrong with tomorrow?"

"You forgotten? That's New Year's Day."

"Oh . . . yeah."

"Happy New Year, Mr. Newfield."

So Ben has come to apologize, admit his mistake, renew his option on my tractor. Worming himself back into my good graces. About time.

"And don't do anything I wouldn't do," he shouted as he went. "Yahooo!" Blowing his horn as if it was midnight. I took out the Elgin. Only nine nineteen in the A.M.

I drove back and put the tractor away in the shed. Climbing down and giving my ass a good rub to get the circulation going. Noting Ben's station wagon parked in front of the barn. With him inside running over his excuses to make sure he knew what he was going to say. Staying away from the house as per instructions so as not to start off on the wrong foot. The meddler suddenly all tiptoes and polish. You're learning, brother-in-law. Keep it up. I let him cool his heels a bit longer while I went to the milk house. Glad to see the cans were all gone there and my receipt tacked to the back of the door. Everything seemed to be in order. After sweeping out the snow they had tracked in, I folded the receipt and added it to my money clip. As good as gold. Thinking maybe I'd try St. Johnsbury for a handyman and save a little by going back with Dutcher one morning. Then I thought of sitting for an hour with Dutcher and changed my mind. Some things it's better to pay for.

Ben didn't hear me at first when I came in. He was down at the other end working the barn cleaner. Coming up behind him, I cleared my throat loudly to open the tubes and let him know that the boss was back. He just went right on pretending he didn't know I was there. Cute in a way. Trying with all his might to make a good impression. Hard at it as if the place was his. Laying it on pretty thick, I'd say. I tapped him on the shoulder and he turned around. Shut off the machine. Looked at me strangely.

"There's no need," I told him. "Who asked you to do that?"

"What do you want?" he inquired.

"You better begin again. That's not my idea of an apology."

"Apologize? I don't get you. For what?"

214

"Oh that's funny. That's very funny. I'm in stitches."

"I don't know what you're after but I wish you'd get out of here. I'm busy."

He turned on the machine and went furiously back to work like a demon. Reaching over his shoulder I shut it off. "I'm not much for the humorous."

"Look, I'm trying not to be nasty but this is private property. Posted no trespassing. Can't you read the signs? Now just get off it. I don't intend to waste any more time on you. I've got work to do. That is if you don't mind," he said and angrily switched the machine back on.

"What the hell are you trying to pull?" I shouted, and grabbing him by the arm, spun him around.

Well I'll be damned! I'll be damned, drawn, and quartered. I ask you, did you ever see eyes like that before? Something unnatural going on there without a doubt. As if they had lost their color and were trying to hide for shame in the corners. He was actually serious! Having heard I was dead he really believed it and was taking possession even before the reading of the will. Stealing early to avoid red tape. Poor Ben. I let him go. It would be mean to keep him back from his work any longer. I can't understand it, he always seemed so easygoing. They're the first to go, Newfield, the very first. Burying their longing in other people's competitive sports. Pushed to the brink by reports of spectacular touchdowns that will never be theirs. Wanting somethings for nothings and quick. Poor poor Ben, but I had to laugh. For you know how lately I've been a trifle uneasy about myself, and here he's the one who's gone and done it. Just look at him suck up that shit, will you. The man's a whirlwind. Clean out of his mind. I've got to run and tell Alma about this right away.

Not quite so slippery now where I had salted and I

picked the good spots hurrying back. Thinking practically. Of where we'd have to send him and whether it was going to cost me anything. The medical bloodsuckers looming large on the horizon shoulder to shoulder, palms out. And me knowing the exact state of his finances, Tottering. Under those circumstances, Mr. Newfield, and all things considered and with the patient's best interests foremost in our mind, we, that is my colleagues and I, advise you to shoot him. Don't you fret, Ben. They can't do that to a senior citizen who has faithfully served his country. There are Veterans Hospitals for people like you. Why there's even one in White River Junction. That's not so far away. A stone's throw. Listen hard and you can almost hear your own cows mooing. Of course you'd qualify, you served in Los Angeles, didn't you? Best care in the world and they probably won't even charge you a penny. You lucky stiff. Beautiful nurses tripping about in tight white uniforms with peek-a-boo buttonholes. There ain't nothing too good for an old soldier. Rose gardens with benches and picnic tables under the elms. I think the best way would be for me to ask Alma if sometime she'd like to go down to White River Junction for an outing. Break it to her gently. Stress the positive. She always did love picnics.

The storm door was stuck. Frozen into its frame or warped maybe by the recent sudden shifts in temperature. I gave it a good yank but only succeeded in rattling the glass. The door was locked. Which surprised me, though it shouldn't have. Alma being as anxious as she was of late about the threats to her husband's life and limbs. Taking unusual precautions. I suppose that's wise with all of these cranks and fanatics on the loose. I knocked. Nothing. And then I heard her footsteps coming hesitantly toward the door. Is it friend or foe? A friend, Alma, a friend. Let down the drawbridge, unbar the gates. Hurry up will you, I have news.

The inside door swung open.

"What is it?" she asked expectantly.

I jiggled the knob of the storm door impatiently. "Come on, open up. I've got something important to talk to you about."

"It's locked," she explained.

"I know that, damnit." I shook the door. "Open it."

"I can't."

I looked at her framed behind the glass. Hair neatly combed, black dress, shined shoes. Wearing her wedding band which she never did unless she was going out. Eyes already traveling, a long way off, strangers. If she's done anything to Alma I'll kill her.

"Open up!" I shouted.

"Go away." She started to close the inside door. "You go away and stop bothering me."

I watched it shoot forward. Hairier than most with the knuckles white and bulging. My fist smashing into the glass as indifferently as if it was a lilac bush. Jagged pieces splattering all over the inside, tinkling on the dining room floor, falling at her feet. Reaching in I unlocked the door and grabbed her before she could get away. Catching up her left hand.

"No," I said, gazing at the familiar burn scar at the base of her thumb and stroking it gently. "Not *you* too. Not *you* too, Alma."

"Leave me alone," she cried, pulling her hand away.

Was this happening to Newfield? Had he come to the wrong house? The wrong wife? There were the newspapers still spread on the table. The can of polish still with its cover off. Neutral, right? Who else would know that? Goddamnit, I think this *must* be me. Please Alma, look

217

again. Isn't there something in this face, something you recognize after thirty-two years of lying nose to nose in the same bed together? Oh sweet piss and corruption! Then whose shriveled skin have I gotten into by mistake?

"All right, you've had fair warning. Haven't you caused enough trouble? Come on now. Just get out of here." In the doorway stood her brother, a frightened expression on his kisser. He was holding a shotgun at my back. Small wonder he was nervous.

"Alma," I said, pitching my voice low because it was none of his damn business. "Do you mean it? Do you really mean it?"

She refused to answer. To look at me. Glancing casually at the growing puddle of blood at my feet as if it was a barrette in a five-and-dime store that she didn't especially care for and was about to move on to see what they had in the way of hairbrushes. Stop! Wait a minute, Alma. Come back here. I think that may be *my* blood. The back of my hand gashed wide open from knuckle to wrist and I never felt a thing. What do you know about that! Far too many distractions in this life. Can't you see I'm bleeding, Alma? No help? Not even a cookie to ease the pain? She stood there motionless, saying nothing, offering nothing. A kiss-off without a kiss. Newfield looking around more lonely than Christ. Where were his loyal disciples? No Peter to take his part? And what had become of his faithful wife, the short one of the charitable oven and the warm impulse? Her brother anxiously watching, ready to throw down his gun and run at the first sign of resistance. The fool, doesn't he realize that only a madman would resort to violence? There'll be no violence here. No violence. I've got to think this over. He fell back as I brushed the barrel of his gun out of my way.

Enjoying the crunch of the glass underfoot walking out the door.

"I don't know who you are, mister, but stay away from my sister. Do you understand? Stay away from her."

Somebody was whistling. It was me. I don't like whistling and stopped. Blowing my nose and the blood sliding under my cuff down to the elbow. Tickling my crazy bone. Sound the alarm, doctors, nurses, sutures, ether, Mercurochrome. All I had was a snotty rag. Improvise. Wrapping the handkerchief around my hand, I pulled the knot tight with my teeth, stemming the tide. I believe you could tie a knot in just about anything, Orin. A regular Houdini. Dumped into the water bound, gagged, chained, padlocked, and sealed in a canvas bag and still he lived to tell the tale. If *he* could do it, why not you? Shuffling along the turnpike planning my escape in the confusion. For instance I may have made a mistake. Perhaps . . . like at the trial . . . Alma meant well. Denying my existence in order to save me from worse. Believing they couldn't harm a man who wasn't there. Oh Alma, how am I supposed to know the right and wrong of it? Why do you do these things? Have I misjudged you?

Out of the corner of my eye I saw Ben. Scampering up and trotting along beside me, sniffing the ground and wagging his tail. At least I knew where he stood. "What do you think?" I asked him. "Is she to be trusted? I can't tell anymore. Though I don't feel any different. And till now I always imagined madness fell on you like a tiger breaking your back in a blink. One day nothing and the next there's Harry Truman in bed with your wife or poisoning the water supply. Maybe it doesn't happen that way at all. You know I never realized it when I turned forty, and fifty was no different. Perhaps it's more like that. With everything looking just about the same.

219

Only making less sense. Tell me honestly, does this mean anything to you?" I asked him, but there was nobody there. He had gone. Fled. Deserting me like the rest. Oh you're hard, Ben. A hard dog. No sympathy for the warped tears of cripples. Ah well, who could blame him?

"What's the matter, Mr. Newfield? Anything wrong?"

Who's that? Someone was stirring. Don't tell me there was still one righteous voice left in Farnum not afraid to admit the truth. Wait. I've seen that beard before.

"Do you know me, old man?"

"Where's your truck, Mr. Newfield?"

"My truck? What about my truck?"

"Did you have an accident?"

"I was born. Isn't that enough? Now quit stalling. What's your name?"

"You're making fun, Mr. Newfield. It's Ethan Spooner. Come on, you know me."

"Oh, it's you, Spooner. Good man. I should have thanked you. I always pay my debts. That lawyer gave you a hard time, didn't he? The bastard."

"It wasn't so bad. I'm glad if it helped you. But I only said what I saw."

"A dangerous practice, Spooner. Very dangerous. You're out of fashion. That sort of thing can kill you. Are you married?"

"You know I'm a widower, Mr. Newfield. More than fifteen years now, God rest her soul."

"It's just as well. They're all ass and tits and promise, Spooner. Running naked through the sunshine of your mind. Snares for the unwary. You can't imagine what goes on in those heads of theirs. The treachery, the deception. Believe me you're well out of it if you are. Living or dying they'll break your heart."

"That's a thought. Care to step inside the bus and

220

warm up a bit before going home, Mr. Newfield? You look a little cold."

"They'll tear it right out of you. Like a coupon. Yes they will."

"That's a real bloody handkerchief you got there. Come on. I think there's a clean one inside I can give you. It's all right. Come on. I could use a little rest myself. The ankles begin to ache when I stand too long. How did you hurt your hand?"

"My hand? Oh . . . that."

In New York. What was it he had said? Reaching for a little girl's ball under a parked car on Second Avenue when it suddenly started up, crunching the bones. Don't get me wrong, sir, this isn't charity. I'm a worker. It's only that I can't do the job anymore with the fingers bandaged up this way. I can see you understand. So could you kindly help out a good Samaritan down on his luck for the moment with a little change? A half dollar would be wonderful. How about a quarter? A thin dime? Fuck off, I told him. O thank you, sir. Thank you very much, sir, he said and whipping the handkerchief off his hand waved goodbye. It was healed. A medical marvel. It might be catching. I peeked under mine to see if anything had happened. Maybe Alma was still waiting for me at home, the glass intact, my hand perfect. No. Still there. And bleeding a little more now for having broken the clot.

"Right this way, Mr. Newfield. Don't be shy. There's nobody home. My boys are all gone."

"Yes . . . you have sons, don't you?"

"Watch your step."

"Run away, have they?"

"It's nice and warm in here, I've got a gas heater. Look out for your head. Have a seat, Mr. Newfield. I'll see if I can locate that hanky for you."

221

"Ungrateful sons of bitches. No better than wives."

"Here we are. Let me sit down first. Ah, that's better. Now let's see the hand. My, that's quite a cut you have. Looks to me as if you may need some stitches in that. Does it hurt?"

"They're all alike. They should be throttled in their cradles before they become dangerous. A stitch in time, Spooner. Ha, ha! I'm afraid you missed the boat. It's too late now."

"The boys will be back. This is their home. It's only temporary. There, how does that feel? Too tight?"

"Don't be too sure."

"No, they'll be back. Wayne's only spending the holidays down in Windsor visiting with the state. They pulled him in day before yesterday for driving without a license. How the shit did they expect him to have a license when they had taken it away from him? It's not fair the way they pick on that boy. They won't give him a chance. When I heard about Wayne I was glad that Elrod had left town for a while. He's gone to Boston to find something. There just aren't any opportunities for a smart kid like him around this place."

"Could I have a drink of water, Spooner?"

"Sure thing. That's some cough you've got."

"A tickle. Just a tickle."

"Maybe you'd like something stronger. What do you say to a bottle of beer instead? It's good for what ails you. Besides it's practically New Year's Eve."

"That'll do. Anything."

Above the windshield the sign read KEEP YOUR SEAT UNTIL THE BUS HAS COME TO A COMPLETE STOP. It had. About eight years ago. The old man got up with the help of his cane. Pushing his belly down the aisle before him like a wheelbarrow. In the rear all of the seats had been torn out and replaced with mattresses. Climbing over them he opened the emergency door and pulled a couple of bottles in out of the air. A windowbox I suppose. With no electric bills to worry about and nothing to defrost. Spooner had the right idea.

"Would you hold these a second?" he asked, handing me the two bottles. "I'll get something to put them on."

He dragged over an orange crate and set it up between us in the aisle. I put the bottles down and he opened them.

"Well," he said, handing me mine and raising his own to his lips, "there's nothing like getting an early start on a fresh year. I've had more than my share of this one. Happy New Year, Mr. Newfield. I hope it's a better one for both of us."

That seemed safe enough to drink to. I figured it couldn't be any worse. But what's this? I didn't remember that beer tasted so good. And how it went down smooth like egg whites. Taking the edge off my cough and the fuzz off my eyeballs. Though discouraging how little they give you in one of these bottles.

"Don't be glum, Mr. Newfield. There's no call to feel bad. You're a lucky man. I mean you just won your trial and all. And you've certainly got a wonderful farm."

"Damn right."

"I'd say it's the finest farm anywhere around these parts."

"You're goddamn right."

"Why that herd of yours is about the best there is. I've never seen better. You don't come across milk veins like those every day."

"You've got a sharp eye, Spooner. You know your cows."

"That-a-way, Mr. Newfield. You're feeling a little better now, ain't you? How would you like another beer?"

"I think I'd like that, Spooner. By Jesus, I think I'd like that a whole lot."

So stretching myself out on the seat and hanging my legs over the seat in front I had one more. And then another to keep it company and maybe five or six after that, but I lost count. As Spooner droned on about the old times when there were still sunnies and napoleons in the river that you could actually eat and the only way to get from Farnum to Stratford once the winter set in was by horse-drawn sleigh with a liberal supply of whiskey on board to keep off the chill.

"And the best part was coming into Stratford. Oh that was rich! I'd be standing up red-faced and howling at Ulysses S. and cracking my whip in the air for all I was worth and causing quite a stir. Stoned out of my head I was. And the old ladies on the street crying, 'Look out!' and scared out of their wits. I tell you, Mr. Newfield, you couldn't beat that for pure satisfaction."

He went on like this nonstop. Happy to have somebody new to talk to. I didn't mind as long as I didn't have to listen, and he kept his voice low so as not to interfere with my thinking. A pleasant sound that made it seem real cozy inside. While the windows of the bus grew dark and the old year ran out.

"Would it be all right with you if I stayed here tonight, Spooner?" I asked him quietly, staring out at the blackness.

He broke off in the middle of the story he was telling as if there was someone banging at the door.

"Did you say something, Mr. Newfield?"

"Could you put me up for the night?"

I could hear him getting up and fumbling in his pockets. He struck a match and, lighting the kerosene lamp that hung from the roof of the bus, he trimmed the wick

224

to cut down on the smoke. It took my eyes a few seconds to get used to things. When they did I could see he was worried.

"You're certainly welcome to stay, Mr. Newfield, but won't Mrs. Newfield be anxious about you?"

"No," was what I told him. No, I don't think so. She's gone visiting. She won't be back for a long time."

"Well then be my guest," he said, plainly relieved that everything was in order. He clapped me on the shoulder, his beer-soaked whiskers tickling my ear. "It's good to have some company. By God, it's a real New Year's Eve. Have another beer, Orin. Do you mind if I call you Orin?"

"Suit yourself, Spooner. I don't give a damn."

"That-a-way, Orin. Did I ever tell you of the time they hired me and my brother, Will, God rest his soul, to paint the stables behind the old Farnum House and the scaffolding broke? You see, Orin, Will was a great one for natural joints and wooden pegs, not caring much for nails, and when . . ."

I knew it was there if I just kept on. All afternoon I had been working my way toward it. Like some summit that can't be seen until you break out above the tree line. And with the last beer it finally came into focus. A solution so logical it amazed me that I hadn't stumbled on it before. The trail led straight to Hatch. There's your ringleader, Orin, now you've got him. It's not the first time he and his mob have used that brother-in-law of yours. Probably telling Alma all sorts of lies. Poor thing, she didn't know what she was doing. And I hadn't been too much better either. When they tried to scare me off I laughed in their faces. Then they buried me and I laughed some more. And now it was the farm over my dead body. Proving once again that there's no winking at evil. But I'm not going to lose my temper, Hatch. Oh no, I'm not going to do that. I have something else in mind for you and your friends. After all, murderers can't be allowed to roam free, now can they?

"Spooner," I said, "do you have any paper?"

". . . but you know, Or, Will was like that. Falling meant nothing to him. He wasn't one of your complaining Carters, whining every time he busted a little something. All told I believe his left arm alone must have been reset at least seven times. Surprised the hell out of the whole family when he finally died in bed of the mumps. It must have been an especially bad case. Did you say paper, Or?"

"Yes. Do you have any?"

"Last month's *Valley Gazette* if that'll do. I'm not a regular subscriber."

"Writing paper is what I want. And a pen if you've got one."

The old man looked somewhat shamefaced. "I'm sorry, Or," he apologized. "Elrod took our pen with him to Boston. He's the writer in the family."

"Never mind. Just get me some paper. Hurry." Emptying my pockets with the left hand and throwing things down on the seat beside me. Finally fishing out the pencil. I gnawed away at the end, sharpening the point, and spat out the splinters.

"Can you use this?" he asked eagerly, showing me a couple of large paper bags.

"They'll do." Sweeping the empty bottles onto the floor, I tore one of the bags into two sheets and set them down on top of the crate. Smoothing out the wrinkles.

"What's up, Or?" he asked, catching some of my excitement.

I looked at him.

"Sure, Or. Sure."

"And stop calling me Or, goddamnit!"

It was difficult getting a good grip on the pencil with the bandaged hand but once under control the rest was easy because I knew exactly what I had to say.

Dear Sir   (I began)

A lynching has taken place in Farnum Vt. that you may not have heard about because it is a fairly small town so I am taking this opportunity to bring it to your notice. The name of the victim was Orin W. Newfield. (To the best of my knowledge the W did not stand for anything in particular but I suppose you will need all such details for your investigation.) Mr. Newfield was the owner of one of the largest and most prosperous dairy farms in these parts and he was respected by all who knew him. When you come down here to look into this matter I am certain that the facts will bear out what I am saying. His murder therefore may come as a complete surprise to you. As far as I can tell the motive was simply grand larceny but I will leave that for you to decide and have no intention of telling you how to run your business which I suppose you can handle or you wouldn't be where you are.

It happened this way. Early on the morning of the first of January Newfield left his farmhouse and walked across the road to his barn carrying a small pitcher in which he usually brought back milk to the house after finishing his chores. He had been out there working for around an hour when his brother-in-law (Ben Barlet by name) came in with a group of men—maybe six or seven all together. Their ringleader, Virgil Hatch, was looking mean and swinging a coil of hemp rope in his hand. All of them had been drinking and some like Wesley Plunket and LaBombard who runs the Texaco in town were pretty well loaded and threatened to do him up because they said they did not care for the way he treated his handyman but that I am sure was only an excuse. Newfield told them that he was not going to be scared off that easily and to get out which as you can well imagine only made them angrier and while he tried to reason with them Hatch picked up the milk pitcher and clouted him from behind. Newfield toppled over like a gravestone. When they saw what had happened all of them were pretty sure he was dead and grew panicky and began pointing fingers at one another and arguing about how best to dispose of the body. It was Hatch who decided on the river since it was still not quite frozen solid. They bound up the farmer's ankles and tied his hands behind his knees and roped the ankles and hands together. Then they dragged him out to one of their cars, drove down to the Brampton Bridge and dropped him in before daybreak with no one the wiser. It was almost a perfect crime if not for me.

Reading over what I had down and so far I liked it. Dwelling on the particulars like someone with a mortal disease who falls in love with his symptoms. The rope, ah now *there* was a nice touch. And tied just right. A fascinating experience. It's not everyone who gets a chance to look in on his own corpse.

"Don't touch that!" I warned him.

"But it's your money clip, Orin."

"I can see that. Don't touch it."

"I was only going to pick it up from the floor and give it back to you."

"Leave it there. Leave it right where it is. If it's on the floor then that's where I want it. Do I make myself clear?"

"Sure, Orin. I only thought to help."

"Watch your step, Spooner. Just watch your step. I've got my eye on you."

Now where was I. Ironing out the second sheet with the side of my hand, I settled down and went on with the letter.

And do not expect to find any evidence of a struggle because as I have said there was none and you will only be disappointed. I am sorry I have no more clues to give you but that is the way it is. Believe me you will not get much cooperation hereabouts. They will deny everything but do not let that discourage you. Naturally once you dredge out Mr. Newfield's body your worries are over. It looks now with the ice in the river like this will have to wait on spring and you had best do it early before he gets too far downstream and you lose him altogether below the Wilder dam. Say the middle of March if the winter is not too hard. Meanwhile my advice to you (and you can take it or leave it just as you please) is to arrest Hatch immediately before he escapes and lock him up as he is one slippery and deceiptful item.

You are probably wondering how it is I am acquainted with all of these details of the crime which does not surprise me. I am not at liberty to say. But my conscience was bothering me and I thought somebody should know the real story of what happened to Mr. Newfield early on the morning of the 1st of January when he went out to his barn and you would not likely get it from anybody else. Excuse me if I do not sign my name because in spite of everything I still live here in Farnum and hope to for many years to come.

Yours truly.

Folding the letter I put it into the second bag and addressed it to the Attorney General, State of Vermont, Montpelier.

"Now I don't suppose you have any glue?"

"Glue, Orin?"

"Skip it. Let me have some flour."

Spooner produced a half-filled two-pound bag of Gold Medal and I poured a little white mound into the palm of my hand and spit into it. Stirring it up with my finger into a gray paste and sealing the envelope. Wiping off my hands and stowing the letter carefully away like a bomb in my mackinaw pocket and thinking that should do the job. I was laughing. I was laughing so hard that I could see I was upsetting the old man, which there was no reason to do. His face gone almost as white as his beard. Pulling nervously on the ends of it and trying hard not to look at me. So I decided to stop laughing and started to cough again which seemed to do him a world of good. Spooner rushing off and coming back with more beer. I downed mine in one long gulp and tossed the bottle onto the floor.

"It's hot in here."

"That's Elrod's doing," he explained, pleased that I had noticed. "He's real handy that boy. Got the idea that we were losing too much heat so he stuffed these rags in the window frames and corked up the spots that had rusted out underneath with clay. Isn't that something though? Only fifteen years old when he first did that but already you can see the way his mind was working. I think you may have misjudged him, Orin."

I got up. The legs a little cramped and wobbly from sitting all afternoon.

"Have you ever thought about giving the boy another chance?" he asked hopefully.

So much for hospitality. One way or the other there's always a bill that they try to stick you with. "I need some fresh air," I announced and went outside.

Stepping down from the bus and feeling it swaying for the first time. Moving under me as if it was alive and going someplace. Rolling through the night just like they say. With me on top, holding my own against something more my size despite the spinning and the dizziness and the treetops flying past my head. Looking up at the cold white lines streaking the sky like chalky fingers on a blackboard. I could hardly believe it. A sign at last. It was wonderful. I couldn't stand still, running and jumping and leaping up and down in front of the bus taunting Him and daring Him to knock me down, to sweep me off the face of the earth. Exposing Him for what He is, a maker of Hatches.

"All show, aren't you?" I yelled. "But this time I'm not winking. Do you hear, I'm not winking. I've had enough of your goddamn waste. I've just done for your handymen and it's your turn next. And don't think you can weasel out of it either. Not on your life. I've got your number. They'll be no second chance this time. You've had it!"

"Northern lights," said Spooner, nodding his head in approval. He sat in the doorway with a pipe in his mouth looking up.

I stopped in the middle of the deserted road to catch my breath, heart swelling and booming out so loud I could

231

hear it in the stillness. While sucking in the cold, black, pine-scented night and thinking there is a sonofabitch force loose in the universe. There is a force eating away at us, chomping on our days and dreams and swallowing them up alive. And the damn fools call *that* God. They can have him. Who betrayed his only begotten son and would do no less for a stranger you can be sure. I've had about all I'm going to stand from that one. A mother whose dearest wish was that she might die quietly and not cause anybody any trouble. A father who didn't even want to bring his son to the hospital after mangling the boy's leg with a cultivator because he didn't believe that anything he might have done could be so important or justify the attention of others. A wife who promised him everything and gave him only stillborn lumps so that she could save her mothering for a blockhead of a brother and hold out the possibility of someday a farm too.

"But understand, Spooner, it's not revenge. No, not revenge but justice I'm after. And I'll have it, too!"

Spooner sat framed in the lighted doorway, his eyes shining out like two bright windows set in a vine-covered wall. He was singing. An old love song and tapping his cane on the frozen ground in time to the music. Making a whistling sound through the gap in his front teeth as he sang. A big tear rolled down his cheek and got swallowed up in his beard. Drunk I judged. Hadn't heard a word I said.

"I'm going to bed," I told him.

Singing and tapping he didn't even look up as I stepped over him and climbed back into the bus. He seemed to have forgotten all about me. That's an old man for you! I didn't suppose he meant anything personal by it. So much to forget at that age, they can't be expected to remember everything.

14

Dark. With Alma restless and tossing and making these sad little birdlike wheezes of alarm. Struggling against the nightmare guns and knives of Farnum, and all because of me. I'm sorry, Alma. Forgive me. I didn't mean to bring you into this. No matter what I do somehow everything gets turned into a joint account. Reaching over to comfort her and discovering that she had put on a few pounds in the night. My hand resting uneasily on top of Mount Spooner who groaned softly and fell silent. All at once I was feeling terrible with everything aching. My hand, my knee, my head, my heart, and the air sour with the stink of stale beer turning my stomach. I had to get out of there quick before I did something I'd be ashamed of to the old man's floor. Ruin his housekeeping. Snatching up my folded mackinaw from the mattress where it had served as a pillow, I groped my way quietly toward the front and tried hard not to step on any empty bottles. No reason to wake the host. Bye, Spooner, and thanks. A good party. Don't think I'm not grateful.

But the party was over now. The lights blown out of the sky and not even a star left like a forgotten paper hat to mark the occasion. Only six feet four inches of Newfield shivering in the dark. Though the cold morning air did wonders for the queasy stomach. Still I couldn't stop shivering. Buttoning up the neck of my coat and pulling my earflaps down. Plunging into the new day all a-tremble, haunted by the ghosts of yesterday's griefs. Maybe I'm running a fever. I stepped onto the road and looked back in the direction of the farm as if I expected to see the herd out-of-doors and glowing in the black. Phosphorescent with health. Take good care of them while I'm gone, Alma. Don't leave the plugs on Co-co too long. Scratch Nicole's ears if she gives you any trouble. Remember Consuelo has six. Good luck. Turning around, I struck out for town with the letter safely tucked away in my pocket.

Everything had seemed all settled before I went to sleep but I could see now that there was something missing. One small detail overlooked. The realization coming more as an annoyance than a surprise. As you know, I like things tidy and it put me out to think I could be so careless. More like Carter than Newfield. For what would happen when the Law arrived from Montpelier wearing black suits in black cars with official license plates and started ringing bells and asking questions. Nosy Italians at the door, pale city faces under black fedoras. No one would tell them a damn thing. I warned them about that. So they'll expect no better and bring their subpoenas and their lie detector machine and set it up downstairs in the clerk's office at the courthouse. And Hatch's friends will file in calmly and calmly sit down and lie till their tongues are black and blue to save him. I'll never figure out that man's appeal. Then the Law will huddle together to study the results, evaluating and comparing notes and getting excited and finally deciding that they can't tell for sure one way or the other. Because what they don't know is Farnum and how all of the witnesses would have made one stop before arriving at the courthouse. Dropping by the back door of Putnam's where the old fox who didn't care to have his daughter molested would have slipped them each a couple of small white pills, tranquilizers, with which to best the machine. And so nothing would be decided, definite, in spite of the letter.

When Barnett would appear. Having read about their investigation in the *Gazette* and come across the river to meddle and get his picture in the paper, cufflinks flashing. Revealing the missing man's travel plans and how Newfield intended to leave on the first of the year, the very day he dropped out of sight, aboard the *Independence* and how he was probably at that very moment fine and dandy in Madeira. A grand little spot for a vacation. The Pearl of the Atlantic! Saying no, I didn't make the reservations for him myself personally because I suppose he didn't want to publicize the fact that he was going it alone. You know how it is with a married man, he would tell them, winking slyly, and they would thank him for the information and even when they had checked out the ship's passenger list and found no Newfield aboard but only a Dr. Newburger from Little Rock who specialized in children's teeth they still couldn't be certain that the letter was not a hoax.

So of course there'd be questions for Alma, too. While she sat grieving in her rocker by the living room window and telling them of the phone calls and how something awful must have happened. For if Orin was alive he would have sent her a card. You see, it was her birthday and he always sent her a card on her birthday no matter what. I never sent her a card in my life but that wouldn't make any difference under the circumstances. With Missus

Russell and Missus LaBombard and the rest of her new friends hanging around to console her with no news is good news. But for her the not knowing would be what hurt the most. And it would be worse in the spring when they dragged the river and found only some old tires, a baby carriage, a bicycle chain, and one torn rubber size 6½. Just half the size of the man they were looking for.

Leaving everything up in the air, in doubt, and the Law not knowing finally what to make of it. Unable to charge Hatch with the crime because uncertain whether one had actually been committed. And the janitor free. And the janitor laughing up his shifty sleeve at the sudden and remarkable disappearance of Orin Newfield. It was disgusting.

Oh yes, they would have their theories all right. That he had been frightened off by his neighbors for instance. But the farmer was a rich man with an iron will who had lived all his life in Farnum. Not the sort to just up and run because of a few threats. That maybe he had skipped out with another woman. For there had been rumors. About a Mrs. Bromhower and about the real father of her brat. But the widow was still there. Hadn't seen him since last Christmas Day in town when he had offered her a ride home. Always a gentleman, Mr. Newfield was. Or that, as the letter said, he had been done in by vigilantes. But if so, where was the body? It could hardly have been spirited away. A man that size just doesn't vanish one morning without leaving a trace. The final piece in the puzzle seemed to be missing. A mere detail and yet without it nothing would be conclusive. Such, I'm ashamed to say, was the flimsy, toothless, wishy-washy letter I had written. Raising more questions than it answered. And only a few short hours ago it had seemed as foolproof as Sing Sing. Ah Newfield, you poor drunken dummy! Can't you see what's needed is some muscle, backbone, some solid evidence that can't be sidestepped or ignored, internal organs with fingerprints to set the record straight? Just remember I'm new at this sort of game. But I was learning.

A dog barked on a distant farm. That was about all I had for company at that hour except for the crunching of footsteps. Which for a minute I thought might be Miss Precosia coming back from her evening romp after not finding me at home. Only they turned out to be my own. Farnum's lone off-beat tramper. The exercise helping to take off the chill. All the way into town and limping down Main Street where my neighbors had thoughtfully left a few nightlights burning. Silver bookmarks to say they'd be back bye and bye. Take your time, citizens, I can bear it.

The Farnum House green and white shingle creaking softly in the wind. EST. 1797. Restaurant and Bar. An Authentic New England Inn. Original rusty hinges. They charge extra for that. Moving along past the Magic Dollar which for the first time in human memory was dark, with all of its goodies pulled in and locked up. The management afraid to trust the innocent bypasser. Another of your insults, Hubbell? I'll mark that.

It was then that I started to become uneasy about the post office. Maybe that was closed, too. More conspiracy. I peered in anxiously beneath the sign on the fancy glass door. There was a single lighted bulb inside above the clock revealing everything. The place was deserted. Nobody at the two writing tables. Their ballpoints chained and lifeless. Nobody on line in front of Stamps or Registered. The windows barred and shut. Against the wall a red, white, and blue machine bulging with unattainable stamps. I don't give a hoot what time it is, Mrs. Otis. Goddamnit, open up! What about box holders who are early risers? Washington will hear of this, postlady. You've had your last warning.

Straightening up and kneading the kink out of the small of my back, I took in the sign pasted behind the glass. Wishing me a Happy New Year. This holiday do pressing me no end. Halfheartedly I tried the door and it opened. Came out as smooth as a Vaselined thermometer. "Unlocked," I noted, stalking in.

My boots clumping noisily on the hard linoleum floor. Streaking the tiles with slush. Good! From now on that's what happens to anyone who gets in my way, Otis. The stamp machine was prepared to serve up two kinds, the regular purple threes and the red air-mail sixes for those rushing to throw away their money. For three cents I could afford to be patient. I took out my letter and placed it carefully on top of the machine. But going through my overall pockets I couldn't find any change at all. Not a cent in one of them. And my money clip missing. And my watch gone. Great balls of bullshit, I've been fleeced! Picked cleaner than a drumstick. Then suddenly chuckling remembering last night and Spooner and the look on his face when I yelled at him. They'll be safe enough with him I should imagine. Guard them with your life, old man.

But I needed a dime right now, this minute. I tried the coin return just in case. You never know. Come on, New-field, stop wasting time. You're good with machines. Think of something. No, I couldn't do that. Standing there in plain view where anyone coming down Main Street could look in the window and see what was going on. And the stamps almost within my grasp. It was infuriating. It was . . . Goddamnit!

The toe of my boot catching the machine and lifting it several inches off the ground. By chance you might say. It banged down, rattled around drunkenly, settled back into place, its innards jingling. And out of the slot slid a three-cent stamp. Ah Fortune, you minx, I thought you'd forgotten all about me. Glancing out the window just to make sure, but not a soul in sight. How gratifying. But what's this? Something had gone wrong. I didn't order any air mails. Watching in amazement as the machine proceeded to gag up stamps one after the other from both slots until finally it belched to a halt with two long tongues hanging out, one purple, one red. If I didn't know better I'd say the damn thing was trying to make a mockery out of me. Everywhere waste and inefficiency like a plague. Was there to be no end of it, no getting away from it in this world? But no matter how I nudged and jiggled and prodded the stamps, I couldn't stuff a one back in to save myself. So tearing them all out, I slapped a single three-center on my letter and posted it. Out of Town. The rest I rolled up and dropped down the chute marked Local. One stamp coming my way might pass for luck but anything more smacked of greediness. Made no sense to undermine the righteousness of my cause so late in the game. When the letter was already in the hopper doing its stuff with no return address and so now there was no turning back. It was up to me.

On my way out checking the pictures on the wall and recognizing many of Farnum's leading citizens among them. Soon there'd be a new one hanging up there—Hatch, full-face and profile. I could hardly wait. Wanted for suspicion of murder: one pompous ass, ex-janitor, and evil influence. Shrimp-size with a cigar. Exercise extreme caution. Believed armed and dangerous. Shoot to kill and best wishes. The thought of it cheering me up a dash.

The clock read four forty-seven but it couldn't be relied on for accuracy any more than a dead rooster. Mailmistress Otis no doubt moving the hands around willy-nilly to suit her convenience. Late starts and early quitting times the order of the day. A bureaucrat to her fingertips that one. And me caught without my Elgin unable to make the necessary adjustment. Newfield unsprung in time. Seconds, minutes, hours slipping and sliding by in a dizzying jumble with no visible record which was which. I don't mind telling you it gave me an eerie feeling. Free but anxious. With a number of errands to run yet before daybreak, whenever that was. I had to hurry.

Coming out the door I stopped cold and pulled back into the shadows. Diagonally across the street in front of Beezee's Lunch with its Closed, Sorry We Missed You on the door was a car, motor running, lights on. A small, grayish, foreign model, whitewalls and that sort of thing. It didn't belong to anybody around here as far as I knew. Nothing to worry my head over. I went about my business, crossing Main toward Putnam's and was caught briefly in the car's headlights. The driver called to me but I kept on walking. Not so fast as to suggest I had anything to hide but not so slow as to seem idle either. Past the drugstore in the direction of Park and the Ellsworth house. He began blowing his horn. A snooty tenor bleeping like New Year's Eve was still on. Shrill enough to wake the town and bring the volunteer fire brigade running. I had no choice. Shut up, I'm coming.

The car sported a New York license plate and the young couple inside matched it to a T. The woman rolling down her window as I came up on the passenger side. A good-looking foreign girl with dark corkscrew curls in a red turtleneck sweater somewhat rumpled. Wearing a chain around her neck from which hung a single pearl in a gold cage nestling between her tits. A mighty handsome piece I'd say. Wonder if she'd mind if I examined it close up? And her dumb-looking husband in a black turtleneck with one of those short college-boy haircuts. Big ears, big nose, and sad droopy eyebrows. They were Jews all right. I'd seen a lot of them when I was down there in the city. We can do nicely without that kind up here, thank you. He spoke with this funny accent but I guess you'd have to call it American. Surprised me a little.

"Say, could you help me? This place is called Farnum, isn't it?"

"That's what the sign says."

"I *told* you," he said snottily to his wife. She let it pass. Poor little thing, she looked tuckered out. "But why can't I find it on the map?" he asked me, placing his map on the wife's lap and shining a flashlight on it.

"It's small." I leaned helpfully through the window into the warmth to study it at close quarters but didn't seem to make much of an impression on her. Too beery I imagine. She practically jumped out of her seat, turning to the back to fiddle with a blanket. There was a kid in a knit hat under it. Suppose I'll have to be a bit more particular about my hygiene in the future. No telling who you might meet.

"If that's all, I've got to be getting on."

"Well can't you *show* me first?"

"Not on that one. That's New Hampshire. You're in Vermont here. Where is it you want to go, mister?"

"Oh, hell! I must have crossed back over the river by mistake. I'm looking for Hanover, New Hampshire. You know, Dartmouth College."

"I've heard of it." I should have figured. Only they didn't have a ski rack up on top, which fooled me. "Just keep going straight ahead through town. About a half mile out you'll see a fork in the road. Take the left and you'll be on the Old Turnpike. Follow that straight through and it'll lead you right to the Hanover bridge."

"But isn't that way west? Won't it take me further away from the river?"

"Southwest. The turnpike swings around. It's a short-cut."

"I see. Say, thanks a lot. That helps."

His missus smiled at me and rolled up her window. It was a nice smile. Wonder how long it'll last? Not an inch beyond the dead end at the Bromhower place I should imagine. A shame. But it was a nice smile anyway.

There was a light on at the back of the Ellsworth house when I got there. Which already told me something encouraging. I walked around to the rear and stood well back in the shadows watching. Sure enough it was Miss Precosia sitting at the kitchen table. In a tent of a plaid dress, her silvery hair cut straight across just below the ears as if it had been chopped off with an ax. She leaned forward, giving all her attention to the music propped up in front of her. Blowing softly into a wooden tube. Playing something that sounded like a sickly green Blue Danube. Her sister must be a grade-A sleeper I thought. Miss Precosia's big cheeks were puffed out and looking bright pink as if she'd just come back from a long, long walk. Marvelous for the figure, she said. But as far as I could see not one lousy bottle of Budweiser in sight to clinch the case against her. And the music continuing, rising and falling in gusts, sweeping the notes helplessly along. So, Newfield, you've come at last. Changed your mind, have you? I thought so. I'm never wrong about these things. But what's the matter with you? I mean you're looking smaller, grayer, and those eyes of yours could pass for two bloody eggcups. Anything wrong? Devil take me, I didn't see that! Why it looks like a bandaged udder with five little nipples sticking out. I'm afraid you've got a bad abscess there, my friend. Poor

Newfield, does it hurt? I shouldn't wonder. I could never play with a hand like that. And I'm sure you're aware that music has been my whole life. Oh didn't you know I'd dropped the violin? Much too uncertain an instrument. Totally undependable. I play the recorder now. Ah there's an instrument you can count on. Look, all I have to do is plug up one of these little holes and it's done. Naturally there *are* a few problems. Sharps and flats, for example, are produced by covering only half a hole, but with my size finger I've had to give them up. I've always found them an unreliable group of notes anyway. Yes, I suppose it does eliminate some of the fine shading but it clears things up wonderfully. Besides you couldn't tell the difference. Listen. And the endless Blue Danube rolling on. Miss Precosia covering every inch of that damn river until I came to know every twist and turn. But my patience finally ran out and I was about to go, none the wiser. When edging closer to the window for one last look I spied her shoes under the table. High wrinkled black ones with the laces loose and dangling. The sort of shoes you'd expect to end in ice-skating blades, only these had soles. Oh fine soles, wonderful soles, water-stained, snow-flecked, damp soles. Surrounded by scattered drops of water pimpling the wooden floor.

There it was. Of course she goes out nights. Haunting the back roads mindlessly in search of somebody to talk to. And wandered across Mink Brook only by chance. And made those mad Newfield visits mouthing nonsense. There was nothing to worry about after all. Why I was as sane as Solomon. That's a relief. Proving, you see, that nothing ever turns out quite the way you think. I had wanted love and had gotten pity, I had wanted justice and had gotten charity, I wanted sons and she gave me miscarriages. But now it would be different, for now I knew exactly how everything was going to turn out. I had willed it. There would be no more teams, no committees, no helpers this time. No assistants to meddle and botch. This time it would be all Newfield and only Newfield. New-field alone, but that should be enough. More than enough I'd say.

Miss Precosia was right. My hand was a bit blue and puffy around the edges of the handkerchief and it did hurt. But I made an effort not to think of it while tugging at the front door of the school. Locked, as I expected. I tiptoed around to the side of the brick building and tried the windows. No luck there so I moved to the back. Al-ready it was lightening up in the east over Brampton, the sky the color of cement. Push on, Newfield, hurry. It's getting late. Aha! Very careless, janitor. I knew I could depend on you. No reason to break anything if it can be avoided. I was easing the frame up high enough for me to slip through and had one foot in, thinking so far so good, when suddenly a dog went off, barking like a burglar alarm. At first it flashed through my head that he was waiting for me on the inside but then I saw him behind me. One of those small naggy yelpers. Beagle by name. And this one a particularly cranky sonofabitch dancing furiously around. Must have something to do with Hatch. I gave him a good hard steady look and he got the mes-sage. Just sort of dried up. Dropping his tail between his legs, he went skittering off. Smart dog. Knew how to get along with people. An animal like that will live to be a thousand.

Climbing in and looking the place over. A huge silver boiler took up most of the room with the only light pro-vided by a tiny red bulb over a glass-covered gauge and thermostat. Tinting everything bloody. Peaselee's Hollywood nightmare of the end. There were garbage cans against the wall, a couple of bags of something piled nearby, and on a rack some rope, a hose, and a coil of metal conduit. In the corner a small rolltop desk. It sure as hell wasn't the principal's office. I'd say I struck it right first crack. My eyes kept wandering back to the boiler. All it would take would be to disconnect the safety cut-off valve, turn up the thermostat high as it could go and get out of the way quick to watch the fireworks. The walls blowing out, the bricks flying, the steam shooting sky-high like a geyser, scalding everyone in sight. It was just a thought. But I didn't have any more time for jokes. I took what I came for and left.

No, I won't call it stealing. Never stole anything in my life. I'd say it was more in the nature of an adjustment. Restitution for taxes paid to educate other people's brats. About time I got something back. Hold on a minute there, Newfield, not so fast. We're going to get to the bottom of this. Find out the real owner. Now then, is this your rope, Virg? And him nodding his head yes, gentlemen, I believe that's mine. But how did it—Exactly. That's just what we'd like to find out from you. And him choking on why and sputtering why and the color draining out of his cheeks why you don't think that I—'Fraid so, Virg. Care to tell us about it? And them patiently waiting out his ex-cuses in silence while watching his eyes until he began blinking to hold back the tears and his lips turned white as ash. Bye, Hatch, sorry I can't stay to hear the rest.

It was going to be a fine morning, a wonderful day. The sun already up, the sky blue as a pigeon's egg. And the air luminous and smelling like fresh laundry. On both sides of the river the hills standing out from the earth so sharp you'd think someone had drawn a line around them. Above me the silver girders loomed up blue in the early morning sunlight. Crystals of frost diamonding the surface

245

of the metal. No wind to speak of now. The trees, pine cones, everything dead still as if holding their breath on the brink of the new day. I hadn't felt so satisfied in years. Scraping off some hay chaff from the barn that had stuck to the side of my boots. One more clue in case they run short. We wouldn't want that. Then climbing into the crotch of a V formed by the steel girders and squirming around. A little cramped but cozy. Humming as I tied the knots. Which is no mean trick behind the back with the fingers of one hand stiff and puffy. But if you want to get something done right you've got to do it yourself. Get in there, goddamnit! In there, you hairy tickling sonofabitch! Calm down, Newfield, or you'll ruin everything. Fuck you. Ah, there you go. Sweating over loops and hitches and pulling the knots tight as I could. Let's see them try getting those out. Well, Newfield, I had my doubts there for a while but you've really done it. I owe you an apology. It's amazing. Why I've never seen anything like it! A rat trap in which to catch the evil of the world. Congratulations!

I could hear the sound of a car coming in the distance. Well anyway, that I think is everything, or almost. What do you know! The little foreign one just coming back at the crest of the Farnum hill, sunlight twinkling on its windshield. Took him long enough. They won't ever get to Hanover at that rate. As I crawled to the edge, one of the knees of my overalls caught on something jagged and ripped. What a time for an accident! Damnit, and a perfectly good pair, too. Maybe you'll be able to do something with it when you get them back, Alma. Don't cry, and remember not a word about me to any of them. You can tell a cow anything but good-bye. Looking down at the smoke rising from the small patch of water that was still left like a warm keyhole in the ice. Ought to be good for a cold, I should imagine. Oh yes, definitely, it was going to be a perfect day. With a lot still to be accomplished. One side, Alma, I'm on my way. Look out below. Here comes Newfield.